THE LAST CALL

Dr. Rajeev Madhavan Menon

PG PUBLICATION

Delhi - 110089 (India)

Edition : 2024
ISBN : 978-93-6210-313-0

Price : 650/-

The Last Call
Dr. Rajeev Madhavan Menon

Cover Page & Book Layout
Jyoti Singh

Published by
PRAKHAR GOONJ PUBLICATIONS
Reg. Office: H-3/2 Sector-18 Rohini, Delhi-110089
Office : A-4/57 Sector-18 Rohini, Delhi-110089
Email : prakhargoonj@gmail.com
info@prakhargoonjpublications.com
Ph. 7982710571, 7838505899, 011-42635077
Web : prakhargoonjpublications.com

THE LAST CALL

"Life only becomes peaceful if there is no crime involved in it"

A book on concerns related to certain communities that highlight people being directly involved in crimes and it shows how they make it their life when they are oppressed.

The work is set to give a fair view of how much crime can force a detective and prove their presence is worthy of it.

DEDICATION

The work is dedicated to all those readers who have a deep interest in spy thrillers, action pact narratives, or know community relations in India where they can connect the case and explain how it folded with the actual past.

It is also inspired by certain actions that had their huge complicated outcomes in the past and hence gives a pure note to the way things were made popular as inspection and detection became a core way to settle it or they may have never been closed.

Lastly, it is a work that is based on a social background so it is also dedicated to all those who suffer at the hands of higher ranks and give a fair view they should not misuse their position in society.

Book description

This book revolves around the activities of the culprits done by people to gain pride, power, lust, and all sorts of crimes they do to achieve their wishes in their quest to find their Goal for which they want to gain by using force.

The book moves around certain places with each chapter dwelling on a separate story that speaks the volume by which the crime is first committed and the skill by which it is cracked open to possibly be solved by the intelligence who has to do a deeper search and investigation to make it possible.

Mainly the work focuses on the criminal background of people in various places, how they become professional in their field, and the way the higher order can make things work in their way to set things into accord by closing the cases as the criminal becomes the ultimate victim by it.

The work goes further in connection to the countries of the Subcontinent where the intelligence teams have to do raids, and take permits and most of the highly classified villains use such places as their secret bases. It hints at the problems connected to the areas of these countries as it gives a cultural touch to the way all stories are created and how they can make an effect.

It is a final testimony shown in each chapter that no matter how strong and political the mastermind may be, the final hand that shall fall onto it belongs to the police and it shall make it clasp tight behind the bars. It is they who must be feared being an authority before they wish to cross the boundary and commit any such crime or they shall go to the place where they began it all and their ends being definite.

CONTENTS

1
The Gauhati Conspiracy

It was a dark night, few voices could be heard from a cafe where most of the men were joking about a nasty cut. The mood was an absolute joy as Adheer had just won a football match for the team and all of the people were over the moon about it. Yeah yeah, we knew you would score the last Goal, one of the people said, drumming hard due to the sharing part of the celebration. Now we need to get out of here before they come or it will be a total mess, there was a noise from behind them as adhere said this and a glass had been broken that hinted the purpose of the other side.

He pushed the sports sleeves, stood tall, and let others go away from behind to protect them. Fond of us are you? A hooded man said, trying to knock the footballer out with a glare. I don't have a taste for grudges, but if you want to, then I can get the chance. There was a sound of knuckle on the knuckle and the fight had become serious so the cafe owner told them to get out as it can cause heavy damage to the place and he was in no mood to spend extra for what these players do at night.

Gauhati looked very peaceful between the mountains with its perfect place in the middle with the way it welcomes people to this fold. The clouds slowly rose and turned away as shopkeepers could be seen stocking their carts alongside the main market side. The voices and shouts of people who were selling nuts, beetroot, and other items that can be seen very clearly. Adheer was one of the strikers in the local club team and the fights amongst footballers are well known where he has to face certain challenges as opponents or knock them down in a fight later.

Football is somehow very closely connected in this culture, but children or youth can also be seen playing cricket, hockey or even throwing hands with punches to boost their physique. Few young boys could be seen lifting dumbles, others using their hands in martial arts and the culture had grown well in recent times making India proud of their role. However, there is a dark side to Gauhati in its secret inner corners as it is the crimes that reside in it where onslaught, slashes, or even murder has become habitual within communities with more news coming with deaths being fresh.

Inside the valley where the upper village people describe it to be best, a case had happened a few days ago. One of the residents who calls himself to be from Bangladesh and had been settled here for the last 10 years had been stabbed by someone without a hint in the air. All they knew was the fact that the immigrant had some sort of argument from an outdoor person who had denied him the right to travel or get permits from other states as a touring agent and next they knew that the Bangla had been dead with no race of who had killed him.

It is not of much importance as using blades or knives is somewhat known here. It was rumoured that Bangladeshis used unmatched heavy coins to turn them into blades so they could do the most damage. The practice may be somewhat banned, but the use of weapons is still in practice among them. Many people use sharp knives, heavy blades, or even professional slashing objects to kill people with their hands. Slaying a human has become more than known practice here with borders close by and dead bodies transferred at heavy prices to count for the riches.

Call the agent he will know what may have happened here, one of the Bangla community members had said in the local language as it won't be prudent to speak things out in the lingual speech that is known to others. In Gauhati, people speak Assamese, and Bodo, and people of Bangladesh who had migrated mainly speak Bengali as their natural strength for their speaking comfort. I don't have enough money left to try the offer and call him, honestly, a Bengali lady said with fear in her voice and she had some worry to say this too.

He doesn't have that much taste for ladies, you know. We will be safe, the detective they had called last time to investigate had a huge fondness for physical pleasure that made them feel uncomfortable taking help from anyone later. However, at the end of such circumstances, they did get someone who was of great help and closed the case down to let them recover fast. I feel he can be called you know, the lady replied after a pause and it was time to find what made this stab so popular so it was going to be headline the next day on the news.

A news reporter was sitting in her office with a smoke pipe to please as a few cameramen retreated from the scene the next morning. She looked at people approaching and started to talk with delight on her face. Did you get the spice for the matter? We need to show it in the right order, she said to the person in front and he nodded. Lots of clues. Even the agents may be tracking them, we got them first, he said, showing him some photographs and the leader felt pleased to find things in the right direction to make a further case.

Back at the scene, a person had come to talk with people and he showed his card to enter as the Bangla lady offered him a chair and a hot glass of water to sit in. My name is Sushant. I helped to solve the last case that happened here. It looks more tough this time, he said. The man was strongly built being 6 feet in height, he wore a black cloak with spectacle in his eyes. The man had a thin moustache and a fondness for beverages as he liked to fill in his thirst. He used to have a liking for spy novels but dropped them as he grew up as he was a man of real instincts rather than ideals to follow.

Simply, the agent is known to work hard when it comes to cases and only charges people if he can crack down on the case as he comes from an elite landowner family and has no lack of money to cover out his desires. Let me see the doorknob, Ah yes, blood marks as I thought, he said, thanking the people who let him in. Please do not allow any stranger to open it as I ask a few police members to come and check in for it, they nodded and the detective tried to take a close look at the place to find more clues on the murder.

The travel agent was missing from the city and may have simply gone to Mizoram from the border line but it is not sure he killed the Bangla. We need help to solve this messy case, Sushant said looking into the broken mirror and the dead body. The clues are scattered and I can call Dushal, the inspector to help with the post-mortem if you like, he said, asking to be permitted to do that. He may not be from our family, but he is our community member, so you know the process sir, the eldest member of the Bangla group said with others seated around and the detective agreed quietly to them.

This city is known to have secret agents who work with the sole purpose of killing those who had come from the cross border as they feel the outsiders had been traitors who just came to capture land, agrarian places, or community settlements and convert them into their place to live and own it. We may not be able to find everyone, but so much we kill is more pleasing as a better way to repel things out, they could be heard talking when the last case had surfaced but for now the detective had to first confirm whether they had any hand in it or not.

The streets looked as busy as ever but there were hushes when people went past the Bangla area as they felt this may be the place of the suspect. Don't cross the road, it may be risky to walk alone there dear, A woman could be heard taking their children away as an outsider offered some treats to them. The place was well known for football players to party with her but now after the murder, they even don't prefer to visit the empty nights as they fear coming into the group after the murder becomes famous in the news.

We may show you the slash on his front cheek, Look at this, the news reporter was highlighting the person who was showing the case. Funny they get to the bodies before we do, a policeman could be commenting as he was watching the evening news. As per the recent reports, the body has not been tested thoroughly and till then if the murderer is from Mizoram, he may be gone outside for good, the reporter said with a smile as the policeman closed the TV, lifted his spoon, and started to eat his favourite biryani forgetting all about the case.

Back in the Bangla colony, Sushant had summoned Rasheed, a Bangla-born but well-settled inspector in Assam for now. He has been known to handle a lot of cases with his skill and wishes to join the recent murder. I may need to check it with my sharp eye If you allow me, the inspector said as the colony was busy with their daily routine work and hardly had to consider anything to do with the man who died recently. Sushant let him be on the spot, opened the closed door, and showed him the exact place of the murder himself.

The man was upside down. His face crunched with scars sticking to this wall and he was like in a state of fit the detective told him in an official tone. What about his lower body? Was he in the form of a limp or was it a cross-section on the floor? Rasheed asked as the detective showed by acting on the body of a dead man and the policeman understood that it was done from behind as he had just tried to open the door and he was stabbed without even a word from the murderer making it a clear case of death.

I have asked the informers for a trace. The person from Mizoram is called Xatang as I can call it. He is known to trick people before and may be involved, the inspector said, taking out a photograph to show. If you have any links in Mizoram or close by, this can be helpful you know, he said handing a photo which the detective felt to have seen somewhere. This is the man on the hit list for the robbery last year in Tripura, won't he? Now he is seen here. This is interesting if you ask me, they both exchanged a smile in an empty room looking over the photograph for a reference and the detective had kept it in his pocket.

Hello, Rasheed speaking. What's new on the person now? He asked, receiving the call as it came. What now? One more murder, could it be done similarly? Where then? He raised his eyebrows with surprise looking at the detective who agreed to come with him easily. They locked the room in the same condition and had come out to figure out the problem. This place is almost filled with blood stains, nothing else if you consider my words, he looked disgusted by the prospect of it and how much he may have to run so he can trace them and punish the actual criminals at large.

Go in with your camera, Rasheed told Sushant who simply stepped in trying not to disturb the wreck. The case was more severe than the previous one but ironically it was one more Bangla man who had been killed. Rasheed came in after a clear hint to come and checked for the Identity but could only get a border pass and this time the person had been permitted to travel across by officials. One more death, what else can we get from the man? Rasheed asked as the detective asked him to look in closely. He showed him the crunching marks, wounds of the same kind on the body and this was going to double their problems as they had been late once more.

Media has once again reached before the post-mortem could take place to find the main cause or severity of the slash. One more dead, why do they target only Bengali people? A news reporter, a male this time asked openly as many people watched him bring news. The person was a well-known trader and had been permitted, so why kill him now? It is the irony of our area you no, he said as the local policeman who was also watching it had closed the TV and had no hope that they were going to reach the culprits sooner as they were more sharp than their skills.

Ah yes, Devang. Put the file here the other inspector said as the assistant brought him some news. Xatang is off to Bhutan sir. We have traced him The inspector felt disgusted but knew the travel agent was cunning enough to flee away from their grip. He started to read the official file of the records and he was able to notice that the trader may have been involved with the crimes as the name had appeared in connection to the travel agent.

Dushal speaking sir, he called Rasheed to give some crucial update. May I ask you to go to room no. 35 of the hospital ward in the local hospital sir? The senior agreed from the other side as he spoke. There you will find a female person called Aparajita whose brother plays football in the local club, the senior obliged, waiting for more. They create slashing weapons as I can deduce and sell them to Xatang. I would like you to confirm if my suspicion is true checking the file of crimes you had sent to me, the phone disconnected and Rasheed was on to his jeep again trying to fend off the concern before it became outspoken.

Mis Aparajita, I am happy to see you have been walking now, a nurse said, wearing official white robes and offering her a letter from someone. This had been sent by your brother, to be honest, the nurse said, asking her to stay for some moments. Adheer had gotten wind of the trap and had sent him a written message so she could leave the place from the opposite room. I had been tipped to take you from the secret room if you please? The nurse said smiling as they both turned away towards the inner passage without waiting for anyone.

Hi, Sushant speaking, a person said, giving a call to Rasheed as he entered the hospital in a rush to catch the offender on guard. Do not enter from the main gate. Go to the outer corridor that leads to the passage to the inner portion of the surgery room, the detective said, proving handy once more. The nurse was helping Aparajita to come out from the secret door as the inspector stood with a smile there You both are under arrest for conspiracy, he said without a wind of how he got the news and the expression on both female faces was no bigger than a shock.

It doesn't matter to me. My plan had already worked, the weaker female said, coming with him quietly into his jeep and going away. What plan was missed? To hand over blades to crush the opposition by yourself? He smiled looking at her from the driving seat as she smirked. I won't be telling you that easily, would I? She said as the vehicle started they both were taken to custody. With details from the inner group, it came to the reality that the nurse was involved in crimes to send false medicines to Bangla villages so certain people could die and they were all linked together.

Sir, the bad news is that the nurse had managed to send false gas to a village and we can't trace the victims, Dushal said, calling again as Somebody else had started to plan a more dangerous plot in public. Sushant had to be on the scheme of things or it may become late before they act.'Sir. We have caught a person who was selling gas balloons in Dharamgarh, You think it can be the case after all? Devang replied as Dushal asked about the progress and they needed to collect all clues together for a better result.

A sound of blas came very loudly as the policemen ran away in search of the crime scene. There were almost 100 people dead before they could reach and they had somehow managed to pin a person onto the floor. I am just a small planner, the main fight shall come to your city soon. You make a note of it, he said, trying to shoot himself but

Rasheed had been cunning enough to remove bullets from his gun and clear the plot. Now come with me. We shall determine how or where you can do it more, he said, taking the man by his gun as the whole area circulated in a mess of rubble and massive holes in it.

Sir, This is Kaveri speaking, a female inspector said in the phone call to Rasheed with some information on the medical case looming soon. We have found out the plot by Aparajita and her nurses. We can soon catch more before they succeed in it, she said as the senior felt bit calm and said Good, get them soon, The phone disconnected and he was still checking for bodies to count destroyed brutally by the blast as he felt sad for those who had died but couldn't do much for them being late on the place.

What kind of emotion is this? Can't even feel for the dead and simply claim to be puppets of a strange bloke, Devang said watching the area being cleared as police dogs ran to find more damages happened in the place which were not openly visible. Check for all the recognized faces or people dead if you can, the senior said and Anirvan had come to the spot as a bomb specialist to track whether there was anything still left. The fear hadn't gone and there was some strange sound like a beep as he traced it from his device.

I am fine with it. This comes daily to me honestly, Anirvan said, taking out a defusing device and cutting off the wire before the bomb finally started to load. 30 seconds, 15 seconds, 5 seconds, Here we go, he said flicking a button and the other bomb was simply diffuse as Sushant came panting with his breath out of control due to running a mile. He hadn't got a vehicle and had to manage on a local rickshaw which had made him arrive late and he had a word of apology to Dushal who waved it showing him the place was badly damaged from all angles.

The frontiers. I know they may be involved for sure, the detective said without much explaining to do so as they were known for political murders. What did you say? Is it sure? Anirvan had stopped and tracked but he didn't need to do either. There were 5 bombs still to dismiss if he hadn't defused the first one as they were all connected to it and the core was being removed, no one was going to blast anymore so they were all safe as the team started to go away from the chaos with thoughts on how to counter the fear of the frontier.

If your guess is certainly correct, then the agent may be a trick to lure us or let the trail go to the other side, Dushal said as Sushant sat in the busy station talking over it. They were active when I tried to find the trap last time, maybe they hired shooters to distract and let the bombing take place, the detective said with some sort of humour in his eyes. The juniors at the police station agreed with the senior inspector but they don't have much clue to prove it for now as the night might come to them, there will be some relief.

The evening was more pleasing for them compared to what they saw during the blast. Kaveri and Jwala had been able to catch a few nurses and they were now starting to speak. We were under Mithali, the main leader, one of them said with a few tears in her eyes. She threatened us that our families would be dead if we didn't distribute wrong medicine to people who don't belong to our community, she said with no choice but to confess. Kaveri punished those who were not speaking and they also admitted to sending fake parcels with toxins and poisons instead of medicines that not only killed Bangla immigrants but also resulted in the death of a few locals who were trying to stop them from doing it.

She used to be the head doctor in the main hospital, sir, Jwala said with fierce eyes that prove her name to be spot on. Before she joined the frontier she used to be famous for her public service but one day Bangla immigrant kidnapped her son and they sent her his dead body wrapped in a suit, it made Rasheed feel disgusted but the crimes happening now can't change the course of what had happened in past or any solution to it. Find if there is any missing report from the past about her son with any criminal connection he ordered and 3 hours later he sat alone in the night even this late in the police station willing to solve this.

He was trying to match the criminal booked for charges of murder for the son's death and if you remove the beard from the current trader they had found dead, the photograph matches almost. Only the anger in the eyes has changed to fear in them if you look more closely. This man had been the main culprit and I may have to fix the case by trying to close his file, he felt angry as he slammed both photographs onto the desk, lifting a jug of water and helping himself to some calm. Let's get cracking, then, at the brink of the dawn. I will have them, he said as he left the place with purpose.

It was dark as Rasheed passed the woods, knocked on a rich house in the close cover of trees and someone answered. Yes, what can I do for you? A young lad had come out with no fear but true politeness. I need the jacket of the last body of one who takes care of them. Did you get me? He said with a rasp in his voice. The lad didn't flinch as he went in and called someone of old age. Yes Mr. Suit you are here, what can I do for you sir? He said in a calm voice as he asked to come in, he had closed the gate behind the inspector offering a seat for true comfort and allowed him to talk.

Where is Xatang? I may like to ask one last time, the inspector said not willing to sit but had finally decided to do it My eldest son is not here if truth be told sir, the old man said with a strange pain. He had left me years ago as you know sir. I promise you to update the police if he comes here, the man said looking towards the younger lad strangely. Show your hand to me, dude. Where did this new clothing come for you then? Rasheed had stood up before they could react as he felt movement from behind and he lunged straight forward. There was a sound of gunfire, a strange smoke into the air and Rasheed had pinned xatang onto the floor by his strength.

Surrender now or face the price, the inspector said as the police horn sounded forcing the father and the younger brother from doing anything silly. Now don't be so brave to be sent to the prison too, Rasheed said, dragging the touring agent by the shoulder and forcing him to follow his stroll as he talked. Come in, We have a lot of questions burning in our throat, the police inspector said the main traitor had been caught to find out about the entire mission now and they may soon catch Mithali.

The word to look for a secret mission started to spread around the police team as they went in to check for hospitals and came empty handed. No clue, she is not doing any further practice, few of them said not left blank as they did bring some medicines to test and they proved to be toxins. We do have the evidence before we catch the person. Test the finger prints and match them from past records. She must have shared her data in the past when she may have served as doctor, the team did agree and they wanted to catch the lady badly before she did further damage or it could become severe.

A call rings loudly and Sushant answers it. I may need your help in the afternoon, was the voice of Jwala, the female police inspector and the detective agreed. He took his black cloak, put on his spectacles and started to read a newspaper headline that talks of the intruder being apprehended by police last night. Very good, the agent is with us, but someone is still spreading the news, wondered why the inspector squad may need his help right now the main agent is in the pocket and being investigated.

There were a few strange scenes going on in the jail inside. Aparajita was certainly in a mood as she felt the police may have fallen for her trap. You search me around Assam and Tripura as I plan to escape from here, she thought to herself as kaveri interrogated other remaining nurses and one by one they told their stories, force applied to do the work and Aparajita smiled seeing them all go against her simply. No word of her sir, the female inspector said as the nurses refused to tell the exact location of Mithali and they were left to be in a prisoner's condition inside the jail struggling to live a proper life.

Send the documents for trial, we shall see what can be done, Rasheed shouted as the junior inspector was preparing to do formalities. The main villan has tried to turn away and she had jumped on to one of the supporting nurse to use her torture trick. Before anyone could realise Aparajita had her knife out and she had taken it close to her throat with a threat to police. Out of my way or I shall kill her, you understand? She shouted as the nurse under her grip told the police that Mithali is also called by the name by which they have brought her but the victim was released by Kaveri punching the imposter and Mithali fell onto the floor.

There was a strange sound of a icegun from behind and Jwala had hit the tormentor and she fell onto the floor again stunned by speed but not dead as they needed to find the list of crimes as a confession. You all are guilty as you didn't accept that Mithali was amongst us from such a long time as we were interrogating you, Sushant said as it was who he had tipped them to create such a condition where Mithali may try to do an ambush. They had searched for the last few days and there was no clue and his hint proved true once more as Rasheed clapped him on the back.

Good job, let us see what she has to say now, Mithali or Aparajita as she was called by her nurses was awake now to talk. I may ask you to tell me what happened on the night of the football match, the head inspector asked without any introduction as she was handed a cold coffee to sip inside the jail. I planned the riot. It was my brother they had to target and i used him as a bait to force them from behind, she said speaking as she has no clue left now. My girls were ready as they pinned most of the rivals from behind and soon they were dead. We deported the bodies to Rangpur in Bangladesh, she said with a smirk like she has done some huge honour.

Tell me the morning of the day when a man was found dead inside his own room in a Bengali colony, the inspector persuaded her to be totally honest. I was involved again. He was my own junior. A volunteer who used to exchange medicines for toxins. He had denied doing it anymore, she said with a sad face. I had no choice but to simply kill him before he may expose and I ask Xatang the touring assassin to do me a favour, she said, smiling further with some pain in her eyes.

The plaster bomb, toxic gas, people on the floor. Is this all planned or it's just an instinct? The inspector asked as the old doctor started to shy away. I did it for Ulun,you know he surely is? He somehow escaped from the gender case last time, the inspector was reminded of Ulun, a political leader and frontier member. He offered huge money and one night of date with him, she smirked showing the monetary transaction in her phone which had been handed to her to show the testimony to police.

Kaveri and Jwala was in outrage as they couldn't believe the level to which this doctor had gone in her vengeance. You put nurses into threat, force their families to support you and even use tribals to fulfil your mission, what kind of behaviour is this? One of the female inspectors asked as she shook her head with no guilt or sadness for her actual crimes in heart. She sat there as she may be reporting the head of the hospital about the tricks done in a backdrop and she felt simply fond of doing such tricks in her own city.

What shall we do with you now? Send you to jail or leave you alone? Rasheed said looking disgusted as Sushant found a way to settle it. Let's set a trap for Ulun. He has been missing from longtime when it comes to being on the other side of bars, they all agreed and told Mithali to call Ulun as she is looking to have one more date with him being urgent. Hello dear. I shall be more than glad to have you with me again honestly, the frontier member said as she gave a call but he asked not to bring police with her to his secret base which she didn't hesitate to say no.

You have been the best to deal with such stages. I presume you do the honours Sushant, Rasheed said to the detective with pride, handing a document on past crimes of Ulun and how he had survived in most cases. Leave it to the doctor, she would insist the frontier brain does not have security as it could cause issues of privacy, won't it? The detective said, looking at her with pure hatred but she agreed calmly. A police vehicle was sent if any problems emerge and Dushal had been asked to stay in backdrop 100 metres away watching the movement closely to which he agreed too

Half an hour later Sushant stood in a warm place where Mithali was simply looking inside the cabinet from where Ulun came out. He hasn't been seen out for a moment but then he was seen wearing the official white dress, a person with beard and eyes like a lion and he came out shaking hands with Mithali as Sushant simply caught him from behind suddenly to surprise him. What's this? Cheating at my own place with freedom? Ulun said with no security in his place. You have dismissed them so they won't see us dating sir, Mithali said in her sing-song voice and Sushant had him simply handcuffed before he could certainly say a word.

Sir, We have a perfect seat for you. Not at the political place but at the bars, Dushal said as he had a past grudge with the member who tried to take his job away in a false case. It's a mess planned by all. I shall see to it that you all are taken out, Sushant came holding him and they had taken him to the police in their vehicle as Mithali was also asked to come with them or she may try to plan another plot. Sorry for this but we can only decrease the number of years in jail for you, Devang said as she was also handcuffed and both of the villains were easily taken off.

I may not ask you tough questions sir, Rasheed said, asking the politician to accompany him towards the main room. Your custody may prove more painful to us than those who had faced your wrath sir, he said sneering as the politician may soon try to forge links and might call who follow him to get him released. Your crimes are published before you are taken here sir, Sushant said handing him a press release as he stared in it with disgust. Once I'm out here, I will see what I can do against you, he growled looking at the policemen who had started to smile. They showed him an order and the politician's expression changed with it getting worried.

Dushal, are you ready? Rasheed said with no more politeness against the corrupt person. In very rare cases we get the permission to thwart your political schemes sir, There was pure disgust in the head cop's voice. He dragged In by the shoulder into the outer side of the station so other dressed men could also see him. He handed Dushal the order who was ready to go for the strike and with a pleasing smile to close down all crimes, the inspector had shot him without any mercy. It was surely strange as he shouted to help or will see you later' like words but he had met his end falling onto the floor.

The case may be closed for now, Sushant said as the dead body was taken over from the place and Dushal covered it with a torn cloth so it can be sent for the process of the dead in Indian customs and be cremated. I am thankful for your services Mate. Here is your honourable mention, Rasheede said once again shaking hands with the detective gladly. Take the procedure sir. Her case should go to court as it is described in the order, Jwala said feeling glad that the case had somehow come to the close after the corrupt man had been punished for crimes.

2
The Guard of the Dock

It was a warm day, so hot that people were out of sweat as they passed through a fish market in Kolkata. It has been somehow tough to swallow the heat, to fight it out and most of them were looking for refreshing by chilled milk or soft drinks so they can keep themselves warm. A sound of a horn takes place close to the port as a ship arrives and people who were at the dock run away in sweat to help the captain and people in the inner yard.

A man could be seen with a round cap and his hair in a muddy colour as he asked the other to cover the area. Pack up now. The deal is done for today, he said looking pleased with himself. He paid a few currency notes to the members who were in the crew as sailors and it was somehow brought to his attention that they should stay here till the next day as it is not good to go back into the waters tonight.

Kee bolchi? Ami karun drives with a sailboat , one of the members said, showing him his skills as he knew how to lift the lifeboat and make it connected to the hull. Yes, it's not easy to be inside the waters. The waves may be high the man said again as other crew members nodded not with calmness but with some sort of disgust.

Karmokar as they call him is connected to this port as he is the security guard for the port area. They say he is not what most of the people know about him as he is known for taking bribes, sending lifeboats packing and it may be foolish to go to the sea if he had been denied. He is known to kill but has never been arrested honestly, the other crew members told one who had shown the wish to go into the sea and he also felt dull knowing it as he had seen the guard pay some money to the crew recently on not to go inside.

There was a sound in the lower area, a man could be heard shouting and the crew couldn't recognize whether it was the guard or someone else. All they could hear was the push of a boat to go inside the waters and a sound like a thump like someone had been thrown inside the waters by force. I would get more money for this, a man could be heard speaking who the crew can't hear clearly due to gurgles. Inside the waters, a boat was bobbing with karmokar and a young lad was in a very severe battle. My father won't leave you safe. Mark my words, will you? The lad was speaking as their voices were still brimmed with water splashing inside.

There was some movement in the fish market however as few cries could be heard louder. A man by the name of Devenandu has been witnessed crying and says his son has been lost. What's all this mess? I wonder if you know the price to make the racket here? A subordinate who works with karmokar asked him as the man kept shouting about his son being lost. Please help me find my son. He is not here, all I can trace is that Karmokar took him to help with some boats, he said, still loudly crying and finally being wounded by the subordinate that stopped the shouts.

It has been a similar kind of mood in the market as every week or so the security guard may come who shows that he has been willing to take a son or family person to help with new ships coming. There is a lot of money, Ami promise korochi, he would say asking one of them to lead and the locals may fall in his trap seeing the riches. He would simply take his price from the ship owners and may either throw the member away into the sea or would simply plan to finish the life once the task was done favouring him bigger money by crime.

It is not going to work like it does. I am from a higher rank here, Devnandu said, fuming at the way the subordinate had hit him. The man had also wounded the subordinate due to which people had to come trying to ask both of them to stop fighting. This will not bring your son back. Try to think of it being calm, the locals had said and Devnandu let go of the subordinate stopping it. He decided to call someone, a smart agent who could help him and it was finally time for a detective to check for what happens to people living here.

Back at the sea, Shubnendu had managed to get out of Karmokar's grip as he tried to finish him. The young lad turned his hand, knocked him over and the guard toppled into the boat as the lad jumped clearly into another one appearing from the back shore suddenly. I was looking to get a grip on you. I shall tell the boss you do the crime to be paid, Someone had come as he may be from the crew with hardly any hint of the arrival. Now the battle started to rage between the crew member and Karmokar as Shubhnendu paddled away to the other dock in search of help to protect himself.

Let's make a deal, I can't fight you. I admit to you, the guard said, offering the crew member some money. In response, the member took out a smaller harpoon, hit the guard and he was more wounded than ever. The security member had gone with his boat not interested in killing the dealer and his paddle was too out of sight in the night. The security guard had nothing to offer to anyone as he was drenched wet, his notes had got wet and it was an absolute joke on him.

Hello, this is Kartik, a man of around 5/9 feet said entering into a fish shop as Devnandu cleared the mess allowing him to come inside. The man looked pale but had sharp eyes even to see inside any trick. He was not older but maybe around 24 wearing blue jeans and a t-shirt that had Polo written as a brand. He looked for the area to check in, was offered Mishti Doi and he had settled in to talk. Tell me now, how can I help you sir? He said looking into the shop owner's face with curiosity.

This is my son shubhendu. Yesterday the security guard of the port took him by my permission to look for some sailboats, but he is missing from this place now, the owner says handing a photo of his son and giving other details like how the son is capable of swimming, catch fishes and even fight out intruders if he had to face them. Sir, any doubts about the port guard as I had heard a lot of things about him, Devnandu obliged, saying that a subordinate had come to stop spreading news of his son's absence and the detective obliged, looking for more crucial inputs as they discussed the case for clues.

He is not known to be polite as I can deduce from the past, the detective said checking for some outdoor photos of the son who may be seen submerged but well able to protect him from fish in the visuals. Your son is a good fighter honestly. We will find him soon, the detective said with confidence after seeing it all. Shall we take help from the police or not in this case? It's up to you if you may need, the shop owner agreed and felt calm as the detective had promised to figure things out and he had left as the son's mother could be heard crying.

I will get them soon. My revenge shall be over, the father fumed looking into the outer corner as a few fish baskets were exchanged at cheaper rates and he didn't complain. Being popular is not an important factor anymore as his powder to chant the food has somehow come to a close. He needed to find his son somehow so he could bring the riches back in the form of minerals from the deep sea. Their trade won't suffer any losses but there shall be a low in the numbers so he wanted Shubhendu back and safe. I will be able to fix the whole mess if He comes back, he whispered, ignoring his wife in the room upstairs and having gone outside to make a bigger deal to have certain amounts.

Back at the main Bazar station, a police inspector was seated in his comfortable chair enjoying his mood. He had a dashing look with his glass on and he had been reading stories of people not found alive once they were taken to the shore by the security guard. What's the point of being on guard if you can't protect them? He said with a few fingers on his pointed beard. Sir, I want to have an appointment with you, a call came as it was Kartik the detective on the other side and Chakravarti the inspector obliged standing up as it was the right time for him to come in for a talk.

What brings you here you good fellow? The head inspector welcomed him, telling his juniors to bring a cup of iced tea with the detective waving as thanks. I have got a case of the famous shop owner Devnandu, he said, making the inspector feel sad and surprised looking at him directly. Son's out of place again, is he? He had been missing for quite a time now, the detective felt a bit surprised as he said this. Devnandu had not told the detective about the criminal nature of his son who had a taste for women and he vanished whenever he had to fulfil his desires. Ah well, It may be critical this time as he was taken by the port's guard, the inspector stood up suddenly as he said this with a strange connection to the cases rising in numbers.

I am updated, however, to be honest with you, the inspector said, taking out a report from his file and putting this on the desk to elaborate further. Shubnendu has been sighted at the other dock close to the port, injured but alive, he said reading this through. The detective watched the image and a lifeboat can be seen in the backdrop. That belongs to the industrialists who invest in steel corporations, doesn't it? The inspector agreed, explaining that he has also been undercover and has reached the right time to protect the land by smart analyses.

Now Kartik, I give you the real task, if you probably wish to have some adventure outdoors, the inspector looked sharply as he called Vignesh to come to his office room who did follow the word. This is the real image of his son. The one you got has been edited before it has been printed to trick you, the inspector said as the junior handed him one more black file. The inspector said that Devnandu has been involved in some sort of illegal activity but what it may be is not known to anyone as he uses his son to be the focus point hiding his crimes behind the worst mess.

YOU may be the best to find what has been going but it may be risky when you swim under the waters, Can you do it mate? He smiled making his work tougher due to conditional advantage. The spy assured that he would be on board to crack this as the inspector assured that the son would be dropped home safely. We will catch Karmokar soon too. Don't worry. I have a plan for him too, Vignesh said, coming back to the room with a plate of Rasgulla as they spoke about the case. There was some laughter and the detective had gone finally as the junior fixed the evidence back against the stronger parties involved.

You always look for the bigger picture, sir, hope we will succeed, a lady inspector called Yamini said, offering him one more glass of tea. It's not what I may look at. The thing is I am not able to find what he may be up to right now, he always had a grudge against Devnandu from the past when he had somehow survived the blame of illegal mineral traffic and the inspector had never forgotten it. We hope there will be no more political parties making fun of us again, Vignesh said and the inspector had still been relaxed as he only gets angry when people try to trick him from behind.

A light was coming from a torch as the young lad looked calm outside from his place being a dock. He looked for a moment and then found another person of his age was coming to him. Come, we have orders from officials to take you back home, the person said and as Shubnendu watched him wear the official dress he smiled looking back Yes, I have been here for 2 days now. Thanks for the help, he did get fresh food the earlier morning as a lady of late 30s had offered him and the lad had made good friends with her, not being much personal this time as he wanted to go home.

Please fill this in just for the record, the other person said and the missing son obliged by filling in his details but not mentioning the number he used at home for tracking. He referred to the other number and the security person had called for the person to drop him home safely in a sailboat. It is not going to be easy however as Karmokar has also recovered from last night's showdown as he sees a ship off and he has some hunger in his eyes as new boats emerge and the man is waiting to give a decent fight.

There was a sound like a cell being thrown into a pipe, an opening of a few loading pipes, and the boat in which Shubhendu had been received started to fire. Stay in the boat. The guard will trace the opponents the one who had been paddling told the son as more fires could be heard. One of them passed very close to the paddler but his life jacket had saved him. I am alright, it's been a kind of daily practice now, he said opening a box in front of him and triggering a device that sent sparks into the sky and the firing from the other side stopped due to the effects the gunpowder had made into their skin.

This place is not safe, I Will accompany you, for the safety measures, the paddler said, taking his short knife and pistol to be safely pouched in his pocket and being ready to strike if required. Thanks for helping me, I am grateful for it, the son said looking towards his father's shop but a few more men had come holding fish knives and trying to lunge. This was Shubnendu's area so he knew how to play with those who didn't like him as he wished to be part of some action too. I will see who tried to trick my family into submission last night, he said loudly, looking very fierce and lunged to punish them.

He lifted three of the opponent's men on the floor with strength, disarmed them and the other went away as they did fear him somehow due to that power. He had been against them except the port guards as he didn't consider them worthy of fighting but what happened that night had made him think for the future. I am glad to see you off sir, the paddler shook hands and went as Devnandu came in front disguised as a salesman and the son simply cracked a joke on him being missing from 1 year in the city knowing who he was as he hugged the son.

The subordinate had seen the son fighting with the allotted men and he went to the port telling Karmokar about his being back. He did survive, surely bigger parties may be involved with him, the Guard said missing out on a big fish with true riches I could have got a huge sum if He had been kidnapped. I had no intention to murder him you see, the subordinate chuckled as one more boat came and this time Karmokar let it go simply without stopping it and had no wish on asking for the tariff from the owners as the boat went away from sight.

Kartik was walking through a small cluster of homes as he felt his eyes looking for something. A pistol toy was thrown outside and He couldn't figure out why it may have been there. either it's a trap or it wants someone to grab it, he said looking for his options and he decided to follow the movement. He stayed on at the place for 10 minutes and then a beautiful girl who may be around the age of 21 came out trying to tell her brother's son to be off from playing with the toy. He knew what may happen in a few days so Kartik decided to act as a refuge who needed safety and she felt it perfect to let him stay in an empty home next door.

The place belongs to my brother. He is a rich owner, the girl said laughing as he asked how much to pay. You first get familiar with our service and then pay when you may leave, she said sending a fresh meal cooked, and the spy felt obliged as e had not fed himself properly being on the trail against Devnandu secretly. He looked for some clues and felt a familiar photo on the wall which was hanging there and he finally recognized it to be Devnandu's son in person.

We are cousins in relation you see, she said, shying away not to have a gaze at the photograph as he looked frightening even this close. What kind of person is he for you and the family? The spy asked as he was handed the key. She didn't want to talk with him about her cousin and simply asked him to get settled in the next home as details can be shared later to him. He keeps missing everyone but we know where he goes, she whispered as the spy walked off taking it as information for the future.

He called Chakravarti about landing on an exact place he wanted him to be mostly in such a case. How did you find the relatives of that so-called mastermind fellow? The inspector felt happy to see the progress. I am going to find it more if luck stays with us, he simply said talking on the phone as laughter could be heard from the backdrop in the station. The spy disconnected the phone, told himself to be brave, and lifted a pillow to give himself comfort and felt sleepy after having a nice meal.

It was almost night when Kartik woke with something disturbing his head like a strange kind of pain. He looked for the lights and turned them on trying to find more activity. To his surprise, a figure came to his vision with a knife to hurt him or with a plan to directly kill him. If you have found my portrait, why not I shall find you too my friend? It was Shubhnendu and Kartik knew he couldn't call the police this far to help him. It may look like a trap to him as he fell asleep after the meal and he realised what may have happened to him after eating as there would be something mixed in it.

Are you ready to join the dead bodies we throw at the port friend? The son laughed, looking at him straight for the first time with a sneering face. Your father is the main culprit then? Kartik asked with a dry throat as the son came a bit closer. I must confess it is not him but I who do the honours, he said with a movement but Kartik was fast and he punched him in the face as the son fell with a horrific sound that shook the smaller place. Kartik was smiling as he had finally called Chakravarti to come to the spot at night and handle the matter as this may be their best chance.

The girl came running from her home shouting for help from the police. This man is responsible. He has hurt my cousin if you can see by his face. Please help me to protect, the police looked from Kartik with a phone in hand to Shubhendu fallen onto the floor, and examined the person wounded by the physical strike. I can find a knife in his hand clasped tightly sir, surely, he was on the attack, Vignesh said, looking him up and down. Good, Let me take Shubhendu for a treatment of my kind, the head policeman said, looking at the girl with some interest and thinking of sending her to jail.

Vignesh checked for a drawer that had not been cleared off and he could find a huge amount of money in it. You didn't clear it to celebrate last night and left it there as recovery. I am happy to get more evidence, he collected the money to be presented at court later and told Chakravarti to handle the other evidence. He turned over a strange box and found out few illegal medicines and acid for turf which was similar to that had fallen onto the floor and all of the police guards felt disgusted to see what they may find further as the head cop rounded on the female figure too.

You are also under arrest miss Ishita We knew of your plans to mix slow poison in people's meals before your cousin killed them and they were thrown in the sea for personal pleasure, the senior said as Yamini came in suddenly taking the honours to capture her and ask to come with her quietly. Who are you? I have been tricked by my smartness this time, Ishita asked Kartik who smiled and didn't say much as the head cop told him to follow on with his vehicle too and the detective felt pleased to do it.

The police station had a lot of noise that evening but Devnandu is not informed of the arrest or he may have sent goons to attack them. He will find out soon what happened to his son as he is busy counting his money with heavy sales happening this whole day. The game is not over Kartik. Devnandu is busy out there transferring more into his account and we have to catch him, Chakravarti whispered before the son could demand his phone and connect back home to update him on the current state.

The detective nodded with handshakes all around and he had simply gone to find what else may be hidden as crime in the backdrop of a fish market close to the sea. I will surely be disgusted if this may be my home, he said walking past the place and he could sense the mood of being in much more confidence than previous nights. Kartik stopped for a moment to gaze at the lights close to the port, he had no wish to go there and he had gone out of sight with no interest in the place.

As questioning kept happening back in the jail with harsh treatment to those who had been brought, things were coming to reality. We poisoned and murdered the relative of the steel company owner, the son confessed as he was severely hit with force by Vignesh. You wait for my father to know what you have been doing, the son was repeating first but when he was forced to the knee, he had started to accept his crimes. It was much easier for Yamini to force Ishita to confess, accepting that her brother had been provided the homes by Devnandi to bring people as a trap and they would poison them after which they were killed by Shubhendu either by knives or using a shotgun.

The gun of a victim or an offender? Chakravarti said, quoting the son's own words which he had said when he was found last time. I feel that you are pathetic with stooping so low as far as I could think, the head cop said, sending Arun and Kaushal back to the place where they had caught them at night. After one hour of hard search, the gun was located and Chakravarti told them to send it for ballistic report to prove its strike and match it with Shubhendu fingerprints so they can make a very strong case this time with no loopholes.

Devnandu has been wondering why his son didn't return from the shoreline this late. He called a few officials but they were not picking up his call as a secret message had been sent not to receive him on the phone. The senior inspector had played well this time using certain links as they were after a shark and could be cut in pieces if they didn't play smart in the water. He asked Yamini to prepare a charge sheet as he asked more questions and Shubnendu confessed to the acid flow in last year's drain crisis, accepted the murder of a schoolboy and his list of crimes kept looming high.

Things were folding faster now as Vignesh arrived in the port in the form of a sailor, offered a boat to Karmokar, and lured him to follow him. The security guard tried his best but didn't have enough strength to match the police and after 50 minutes of paddling, Vignesh had forced him to push towards a shoreline where few guards had been waiting. The end of the bet If you ask me, the police officer said, throwing the guard into the water first and then dragging him on to the surface. The men on his side caught Karmokar and took him for questioning by force so they could get more information on the crimes committed by the gang.

We already have the boss or his son if you ask me, Vignesh told the security guard who was slapped hard by Dharmesh, the junior inspector, and fell onto the floor. We have enough evidence to show that you accepted and offered bribes to keep ships of rich people, do you confess? One more slap and the guard tumbled back in pain. He started to tell about a conspiracy, one that involved him, Shubnnendu, and Devnanddu, and finally, the police were on the right side of it as he told them why they killed and threw people in the waters and the plot connected.

It was evening and Devnandu could be seen fuming after he had found that his son had been simply taken into police custody. I will send them all to hell if you ask me,' he said, talking to his wife for the first time in days. I have told you not to mess with authorities. You have done it many times, she said feeling sad for her son being taken but with less pain about the problem as she knew there was no chance to repel the forces you have a grudge with.

It is our son they have taken, you hear me? Devnandu shouted as she sat with a calm face. Yes a son has been taken who was involved in murder, trap, and financial robbery, she replied as she had hardly cared for the person who was missing. The son had declared totally committed to the father so she didn't have much to do with them. Now she walked back upstairs as she doesn't live here much and had only come 1 week prior from her mother's home to see the conditions out.

Back at the station, an official had come with bail papers for Shubnendu in the hope that they would be accepted. Sir, We have them in the trap, Dharmesh said as he punched the man who had come with the papers to request the bail. Chakravarti came out looking for the man and he recognised the knife seller who was one of the main involved in the whole case. Bring him in. I need to interrogate him too, the senior inspector said and Dharmesh dragged him by the shoulder as he cowered with fright.

Hello Mr. Saha, what brings you here? The bail of your master or the threat of Devnandu as a puppet? Chakravarti asked, telling him to sit on the next chair. I come with a warning that this jail will be burnt if you don't release him honestly, the man said with no fear as he was prepared. In response, the senior inspector took out a file and showed him the countless names listed in it. all booked for charges including minerals, sand supplies, robbery, and even murder. Soon they will be here unless they kill themselves as you goons like to do, he laughed as there was some noise of people in the jeeps at the backdrop which was taking them to the station with their voices loud.

Leave him to me, sir, I want some old scores to settle, Dharmesh said, coming forward as he hit him with a kick harshly. The junior inspector was given the honours as he took the knife seller to the next compartment and started to punish him. Now tell me, how many knives a day? 20, 50 or 100? He said as he recalled a past incident where a neighbour's son was killed by the same knife and he wasn't able to protect them. The seller began to tell his pain, the way he started as rich, and how he got habitual to it as more secrets came to reality as he opened up.

One last question, where is Jagan? I will ask this straight, is he dead or under your capture? Dharmesh asked as Chakravarti came to find out how it all may have happened. They have told a false story that the steel company's son has died. That has been the main trick where the dead bodies were used to form a pack and keep insulting the company owner. I have no idea. He may not be dead, you know, the seller said and Dharmesh kicked him again using his police stick to give harsh punishment and he finally spoke.

He is in the port, locked as a captive, Vignesh went in and brought the security person from the port. Together the policemen started to put them into harsh core torture and finally, the port official spoke in pain. I have kept him safe under Devnandu's orders so he can get money regularly from the company owner, the guard told the exact location and Dharmesh felt a bit calm after it was told as he called the owner to come to the police station as they have some leads.

Shubnendu has been acting to fit after he had been taken with severe punishment in jail. Yamini had prepared the chargesheet and people who had been brought in the jeep were now telling about the crimes. Few of them talked about taking chains of people who come in ships. One of them showed a mark of argument as he joined the gang late. The subordinates were under the grip and all they wanted now was Devnandu who may only come if he finds out that Jagan has also been rescued.

The steel company owner arrived in half an hour with some hope in his eyes. Sir, We have captured these men. They confessed to the crime the senior inspector said, looking at him straight. The owner was surprised to see Devnandu's men in the cell and felt a bit worried. Don't worry, we have worked it out well this time it will all be safe. Let's go to the place now and get your son, he said, asking Vignesh to come with him. Dharmesh is here with Kaushal to take care of the place. Would you not? Both of the junior inspectors agreed and the senior person led the owner to follow him as they went past the people who had committed the crimes.

As soon as the senior had left, a kind of panic started to rise in the criminals as they started to fight. Dharmesh knew this kind of problem was coming so he simply fired gas from his device and they all went to sleep. He told Kaushal to keep all of them under sleep or they may create mayhem. Devnandu's son and his cousin were treated with the same plan and he was out of feeling now as he simply fell back into the cushions inside the jail. The junior inspector felt calm as the case was in the grip After years. They had to lose a lot to see this happening, but somehow there will be calm in the port.

Devnandu was waiting to act as the senior inspector arrived. He softly hid himself on the opposite side of the cell where Jagan was kept and started to whisper strange noises. It was somehow going out to be against him as the owner took out his son first and the inspector lunged. Before the political criminal realised what may have come. He had been thrown on the floor and Chakravarti launched punches after punches making him feel terrible on the floor in pain. The son called for his father, finally opened his eyes and they met as the police inspector grabbed hold of Devnandu and forced him to come with them.

You will take me to court. I will fix my case again, he rasped, seated with the inspector in the front seat as Jagan felt happy coming out of his misery. NO more mercy. I have told my juniors what to do honestly, the inspector said as the culprit cowered with fear finally. The vehicle had stopped in a place and to Devnandu's surprise he could see one more bigger vehicle already standing there Chakravarti had planned it well as he had told to make the gang asleep with devices when he may be absent from the place so things remain quiet.

He called Vignesh and Dharmesh to come out and force all of the caught persons to wake. In their strained posture and tiredness, Devnandu was surprised to see that they started to fight as he was also thrown amidst them by a senior person with glee. It was fitting for the case as he had started this game to throw people and be killed so finally in a brutal scuffle of men in the crowd Devnandu and his son died closing the case once and for all as Karmokar and Ishhita were murdered by the mob.

Jagan sat with his father as he was helped to walk slowly after taking him home by car. The father helped him to get fresh after thanking the police for help as his sad mother finally woke up seeing the son home and felt joyous. They all were finally pleased to see that their son had been brought safely and he would come out of his torture and fatigue as soon as the case was finally fixed with the help of a legal process as the culprits were officially recognized by the court explaining the violence to be favourable with such an end.

3
The Candle Maker's Web of Lies

The sun was setting in a beautiful city as people were packing back to go from a picnic spot after some fun together. The place is well known to welcome people with hotels and resorts surrounded by lights as people get back. They were happy to get one of the best experiences and had paid the guide who felt grateful for the way they had been treated and the voice of the groups could be heard in tents as they trudged back from their tours.

A boy of around 15 came running off as he could be seen holding some money. You had paid us extra sir, he said giving a note back to a rich family owner who turned it back I know I have, just take it as a goodwill message, he said packing the tents and leaving the place now as the boy smiled going back with a word of thanks and feeling elated for it. The place had seen such gestures on many occasions, but not all the time they had been done without purpose as visitors wished to expand their foothold here.

Trivandrum looks beautiful in its marine backdrop with people selling coconut water, and coconut oil and putting their favourite south Indian dishes on, asking the visitor to have a few local tastes. Many people are selling things as they could be seen carrying candle boxes, fresh cakes baked in the oven, or trying to celebrate amongst neighbours. The mood can't be more effective than it looks but the place has some secrets to hold too.

Mandy a Christian from the origin, was looking for some boxes where a secret was hidden as he counted for the notes received in exchange. Send this to the port. No word to anyone or you shall be dead before it comes, he rasped in his voice as vannakkam could be heard in the background with more people asking for some food treats in the nearby bakery with laughter. The man who had been asked turned around, started his bike, and went before anyone could find Mandy on the streets as he had vanished too.

Kartavya speaking sir, a voice came from inside the bakery as the owner called in the local police. I have seen the Christian vanish with orders for some boxes. What do you say? He asked in his calm tone with nothing usual sir, as a customer was trying to hear and he had given the rich curd drink for which he is famous. There you go, I may not charge much for it and the usual taste is enough, the owner said, disconnecting the call finally with some suspicion from the customer who had asked for the order as he was talking.

Back at the port, someone had come lighting his torch as it was dark. Mandi came from behind with no hint to the one whom he had sent with boxes. He crouched low and waited for a smaller ship to come closer. As he heard the horn and the hul falling, he expected crew members to come and his wish was going to come true today. He watched with patience as his man proved loyal, handed the boxes with money for exchange, and being happy the boss had gone away hoping to get some more gold soon to sell out

Here you go, sir. We shall not return to our place tonight. If you ask me honestly, it may be risky, the assistant said, looking at Mandy with some glee. Why not? You think I can't trick the police or you fear my status? The assistant shook his head thinking it was just a tip and the boss thought it was the same. He agreed to get a quarter outside the port's area and they went away feeling true grace as a cameraman ran away from behind who had recorded their activity and they would soon be in huge trouble to do that.

Kartavya had summoned the police as he couldn't find the big boxes outside that used to stay in the close corner of the Christian's candle shop. He had a big smile as the police reported positively informing on how well the raid went for them. We did find some gold falsely left behind to test whether it was pure or not, Ganeshan the police inspector said as he took off. I will keep an eye on him if he returns, the bakery owner said as the police went away with a smile hoping for more updates to come soon as they may be able to track the people involved.

The next morning the whole of Kerala was in shock as Mandy had been exposed by the person on the port. Gold missing, a trader in search. We may presume the government must do something to clear the shop or they will be hoping to give a statement later, a female media person said showing the clip as Mandy's mouth was open in disgust and surprise not expecting this. Who tricked me from behind? He thought in anger as the assistant was on the floor asleep after drinking the last night badly and laughing a lot.

The candle maker was in fits of anger as He was not sure about it and wanted his revenge to fix the course of the process. It can wait for now as he may have to run from here or it may be the end for him with police coming who can track and capture him to expose all the secrets he hides. I need to leave the pla, He whispered, taking out certain money from his expensive clothes so he can plan the departure. Where should I go? Ah yes, Out of the state, he thought counting the notes and he stood up with an eye on the man on the floor.

The christian stood up quietly, changed into an old robe he had prepared to run if police caught him, and went in a glimpse of sunlight as the place looked beautiful in its fiery backdrop. Sir, I have seen Mandy change clothes and run from here after getting money last night, a call rings in the bakery shop that is closer to Mandy's candle shop. The local bakery owner from the port tips Kartavya and he smiles, hoping this to come somehow.

Alright, I expected him to do this. We will find him soon, the owner said with a broader smile and a pastry in his hand to share. He took his phone and decided to send a message to the police on the take off by the smuggler with a hint that he may cross over to the state. As Ganeshan was now ready with his team, he doesn't want any mess this time as it is required to catch him at all costs to find the reality. The tip was going to prove handy somehow and the team started to make plans.

Sarvan, you go to the port to search. Mahesh you go to the candle shop and Pranay, you come with me to check, Ganeshan asked people to spread as they wanted mandy badly. The gold mine and its illegal send-off to abroad was not a new case and the chief inspector wanted to close it down by some way or another. I mean to find out why it has been happening so quickly, he said, alerting the bakery owner to be on watch if anyone comes. People did come to the candle shop but Mandy had planned it well, allotting a robot to do exchanges as it handed them the selected packages and received money directly through UPI.

They needed to be very specific if they had to search the rooms inside as the Christian had fled off to Chitmangalore and made it tough to find him in Kerala. Alert the boat owners of the local state. I need to take their help too Ganeshan said, ordering the missing person's report, talking to Viman in Karnataka who was chief of boat authorities. We will catch him on guard sir. Don't worry. I also want to close this case out, he said, ensuring the police and the search were in the total swing as the robot had gone back to its place in the evening so Mahesh entered the rooms to search inside.

Kartavya saw a man in strange clothes coming to the candle shop at night. He had been one to whom he had offered a curd drink and he texted Mahesh. Without a noise, the junior inspector turned, lunged from behind, and pinned the person down. Where's the gold friend? I have you this time, the inspector said, recognizing the person who had robbed 3 gold chains two months prior and had been missing for a long time as police desperately wanted him to close the case.

Let's have some questions that can settle my patience, I am very curious to know it, Mahesh said in an official voice to him. The person put his best energy to let the grip get off but the person was stronger. He felt pleased. Dragging him off and throwing him onto the bed arranged to have candle packages in the past as he turned upside down due to the force and they were finally going to face each other for a word and find more.

I am just a supporting person. I don't know who owns the gold that is sent to the ships, the man said as Mahesh started to record their talk for future evidence and custody. How long have you been working with Mandy's friend? He said ignoring the excuse and the man said it's been 4 years now. He came in touch as a candle maker himself and they used to put golden lining on the package to attract customers so they could tell them about the gold and how to claim it.

Your plan may have worked but it's not personal just to get riches or is it honestly? Mahesh further asked but the person denied for a while trying to hide a few things that can be seen from his eyes that must be revealed. Finally, after a few hard hits that shook the whole place with candles broken, the man accepted that it was a bigger plan with a few stronger people directly involved who asked them to export gold illegally and they would look for their safety while they carry the process.

Sarvan was on to the port with his boat bobbing above the sea. He waited for some time and then saw an official boat coming to rest above the water. This is what he was looking for as he lunged before the person could step out. What's this, who are you? I demand to know, now, the man said in a strong official voice. He may have been connected to a higher status but Sarvan was under the orders and he threw him onto the muddy ground before he could ask anything to let his clothes get dirty due to the fall.

You will pay for this, I bet, the man said in pain as Sarvan tied him with ropes and started to search. Ah well, son of a minister. How much gold have you sold my friend? The junior inspector said, looking straight at him with disgust. That's not your matter to consider, hand them over, the son growled, still tied in ropes and trying to get them off as Sarvan found a few documents, a visa, and something that could help the team which he put in his pocket with a smile.

Now we can fight it out, the inspector said, releasing the son and starting to hit him with punches. For a moment the son felt stronger to fend off, but once Sarvan started to use his kick boxing, the opponent had no answer and soon he was simply thrown to the ground. You know what? I can shoot you now, what if you are a minister's son? They have caused a lot of trouble to my family, it would be perfect revenge, but I need answers first, he said forcing him to sit on his knees and respond to his arguments as they spoke.

The son revealed a bigger plan: how they used to offer gold to foreigners and have heavy benefits from it. Usually, it was done to gain riches so they could get money to be used in elections to get a clear win and become stronger to rule again. A political rift, Your dad is involved in this too I suppose? The son simply replied how his father used to be a small rank official in the department that looks after industry but he gradually started to rise and now Sarvan found out the way by which suddenly he had been sworn in as minister one evening with no one to challenge him.

Who commands the ships dear? The inspector asked, recording it word to word as he spoke. Hans, a friend of my dad from South Africa, he said this time with pure honesty. Where can we get him now? What does he do? The son said that Hans can be found in the Swiss embassy where he works as an undercover medicine operator helping with the progress of the Indian mission on secret medical aid. The inspector felt it may be tough to get a hand on Hans directly but he thought about what he should do with the son. I am leaving you for now but If I catch you once more in the sea, that's the end for you, the son agreed and Sarvan sent the voice recording to his boss.

Ganeshan was pleased by both juniors but the search was still not complete. Atharv had joined in as a secret spy in their team to help with the search for Christians and the mystery was becoming deep with a lack of evidence. They can't find Hans for now and till when they can do it, they can't prove all men to be together. We will set a trap sir, I know we can get him too, Sarvan said, coming back to the place with handshakes all around and they agreed to use it.

Mandy was feeling better as he was seated in a hotel but his assistant had been caught who had been left behind by him. Ganeshan had sent Mahesh to find more clues and the man had been handcuffed as he started to show much fatigue and the junior inspector had brought him simply. You deported the gold on his order, is it true? The inspector asked as he took him back in his police vehicle. The assistant agreed but he said that his brother had been kidnapped on the order of Hans due to which he had to do this.

You have been part of the crime, I can ask to decrease the number of your imprisonment only, he said, not believing the story. Sarvan took the word sent to him by Mahesh and he had sent Atharva to check whether the goldsmith was true or not. It took the spy some hours but when he returned, the fact proved true and the brother had been recovered safely inside Mandy's house after a search operation done on the tip of the spy that proved handy for them and it felt better.

Back at the bakery shop, Kartavya was arguing with someone as he sold out all of his cookies today. I am not here to buy anything from you. I demand to know the trail of the gold mines, the man said, looking fiercely like a Christian and the owner didn't reply at first to him. He sent a message from his device to Ganeshan asking for a photograph of

Hans and had a glance at it. If you keep out the glasses that look heavy into the eyes, the man looks similar and Kartavya smiled at him being his chance to taunt him.

I am going to Senegal this week. A pure ceremony to attend, will that please you sir? The outsider smirked and moved to hit the owner but he turned away. Not so angrily sir Hans. You were known to fight with the lions in the past in Africa, a voice said from behind and they let the operator go this time or he may have made the whole place a complete mess. He is worried about the gold, at least we are on the right trail now, Sarvan said as he saw the man vanishing from a soft tunnel close to the candle shop.

A call comes to Ganeshan from a secret person in Karnataka and his ears stand up hearing the news. He has seen Mandy in a hotel, resting with a beer in his hands and offering gold to the hotel staff who refused to accept it having no interest. Ganeshan had a plan and he told the secret person to become a goldsmith and go to a person telling him he had lots of money. Ganeshan sent an image that he told him to use as a hologram and the secret person agreed to set the bait as they needed to catch the candle shop owner.

You think he will fall for it, sir? Vikrama the IT head asked as he shared a few details of online transactions in Mandy's account last evening besides the cash he owns. Ganeshan felt a bit calm as he saw one of the more familiar details and he recognized who may have been the main culprit. I am going to meet an IPS officer today, what should I offer him? Pure gold for sure? Ganeshan asked the It head to check the details of the official member and he obliged by sharing the past details of the last 2 weeks where the money kept coming fast in his account.

A door opens and Mandy looks up to see someone coming to him without ringing the bell. Hello sir, it's top secret. I want to exchange gold with you instead of money, the person said, wearing rich clothes and offering him some money. You are late, I don't own the gold, instead I do have cash If you like and you can be in my gang, the Christian said, lifting a candle package to mark their secret meeting. The person agreed and together they stepped out as the resident made a check out from the hotel walking away easily with a smile.

It happened so quickly as they reached the bus stop to run away. Atharv came knocking the candle shop owner down with some strength as he took the VIP pass out from his pocket. After abuses between the new arrival and the man fallen, the outsider who had been helping him revealed himself to be from Karnataka police and he had handcuffed the gold smuggler before he could say anything to them. Together Atharva and the police person took him to an official jeep and via border after taking permission, they took him back to Kerala inside the capitol so Ganeshan could finally get to know why Mandy had been so hopeful to send gold abroad and his crimes.

The candle shop maker was asked to sit in the main room of the police station. Ganeshan lit the place with a candle as he saw and offered the man a few cookies from the bakery. Let's start, shall we? Why did you run off to Karnataka? I presume you had more plans to settle there and get rich, he said looking at him calmly before taking the option of violence as the last choice. The shopkeeper said he had a connection to expand his business abroad by getting more riches that also included gold as he sold a huge portion for candle makers and their actual families to become rich.

Who is Leonard then? Ganeshan asked without much argument as he knew it may be tough to get more about the IPS officer from this man. I have no idea who he may be? The Christian said clearly with no fear in his eyes. Where I can find Manohar Katju then sir, this may be known. I am sure Mandy shook his head but this time Ganeshan had used violence as he dragged him down from the seat and he was on the floor asking for help and mercy by the grace of lord.

You destroy so many families and ask for mercy, do you? He hit the man right close to his cheekbone and the victim felt his one of teeth broken with a lot of pain. I can do you a favour if you explain the reasons or I wish to send you in style, you get me? Ganeshan said with his fist raised and hitting Mandy on the forehead now as he was still on the ground. There was no commotion from the other side and no voices as this was a police station and the junior stayed calm to witness the main leader in action trying to find the truth out from the smuggler.

One last time Mr. Candlemaker, who is Leonart and why is he important to the Swiss embassy? The person looked with true fear as he was taken by surprise by the names. He had expected the police to know less but here he is facing severe concerns. Leonard is in Sri Lanka, waiting for orders of the new instalment of Gold he finally said, accepting his crimes and the way he was involved by scattering gold.

A phone rang and Mahesh was on the other side. We have found the location of Katju sir. He is hiding in a gold mine, shall we crack it? The chief looked pleased to hear and has sent an online document as a permit to arrest an IPS officer being in league to send gold illegally from the state. I shall not bother you much, the only thing that degrades me is the way you have burnt so many hands instead of lighting them with your candles, he said, remarking on his profession and the trickery he did behind it making things come back to normal to proceed.

I can be useful. I have some more information on Hans and what he may do next, the candle maker said, trying to get a few years off being behind the jail. I am not interested in the offer, I have already made up my mind, Ganeshan said as he called for Atharva and handed him a letter to visit the Swiss embassy and he can now wait for the plan to come true. Mandy was taken behind bars and had been thrown into custody till the further process of legal statute arrived at the station.

Katju was brought to the place for inquiry without much force. I am a senior and you must behave calmly with me, he said looking into Ganeshan's eyes who was still not recovered from his argument and punishment of Mandy. The junior cop shook his head and showed him an order on to his desk. You are not a senior anymore, I already have a letter of your removal from the ministry where you work sir, he said laughing loudly.. It felt like a joke to Manohar but the junior had prepared things on the right course so there may be no loophole left.

You let me treat him well sir, if truth be told. He hurt my cousin badly while on duty charging a false case, Pranay said, coming to figure out the course of the process and how it may go. You are the most junior and you will trick me for the mess that has spread here already? He said firstly with glee but then changing the emotion on his face as he saw Mandi being locked behind with true evidence and he may have no chance to escape.

Sir, how many checks have been sent to your bank account in the last 2 weeks if you let us know? Pranay started to ask, reaching for the statement on the desk to confirm. This is my account, It shall be my choice to see how much or may not, he stopped as Pranay lifted a hand to hit and connected close to his prominent eyes. You are no more a public servant, We have the right to punish you, Sarvan said, knocking him down as he cried with pain and insult at his position openly done here at this station which he had opened with an official request a few years ago.

Your efforts are of no use. Leonard may have gone from India before you caught him and with no strong evidence, you won't be able to punish me as we speak of my crimes, he said, falling on the ground but his attitude still in a clear vision of what was coming next. We have your man already. My agency has worked this well to cover sir, Ganeshan said as one more call came and Atharv could be heard panting with some heavy box taken into captivity in his hands alongside Leonard caught at the port trying to run away back to Colombo as a naval agent.

Now sir, what is the plan? I may ask you to clear it, Ganeshan asked Pranay to get some rest with a glass of coffee as the chief started to interrogate his superior from the past. You opened this place, made us honoured but now what shall happen to your renowned name sir? He said, slamming him on his knees as this time he felt miserable. I shall see you all in the court and you will pay a heavy price for it, he smirked even in pain as Ganeshan gesture that they had already paid the price for the actual gold lost and there was not much left to ponder.

Another call comes to Ganeshan, this time from a politician who was also involved and he demands to release Katju urgently. Sir is not here, Once he comes, we shall send him to your home surely, Pranay said, receiving the call as the politician abused and asked the leader to mind his language. We are coming to your home sir, get your security ready, Sarvan said taunting him and things have crossed waters now as most of the people involved may be tracked easily except Hans.

The irony is that they don't have enough time left to catch or make a trap for the politician in the process as so many inner folds have made it more messy. The other inspectors did feel for their chief who may get hands on the senior officials but may not be able to simply catch him. I am rest assured that one day he will also be in our grip, Sarvan said to Pranay who felt miserable but still proud of the way they had held on the course as bigger players had been under capture somehow except the Indian politician.

The medical agent was walking in his room, thinking

hard about it. Should I go back to Africa or remain hidden, he thought as a few messages kept popping up on his phone and he dismissed them. I need to figure out how to leave from here as Katju may have been caught by now and I must be on their list, his sharp mind started to run for the plan as a few people kept coming with the wish to seek his special testing on sciences but he had told his assistant to tell that he can't be disturbed and she let them go away with refusing for the appointment on chemical testing.

I need to see whether your vehicle is fit to be used for travel sir, shall I?|, the assistant said with polite interest and he obliged not taking his eye off his phone as more messages continued to come demanding him to hide out and he was still in deep thought. The assistant had been tipped off by the police officials and she did have a role to play as she slowly walked outside, crossed the lane, and opened the garage where she did some tinkering to the vehicle's upper bonnet and returned handing Hans his keys with a smile.

Ganeshan has told Kartavya to come with him with a special taste for special moments. We are going to catch Hans, he is one of the most fierce Africans. It may not be easy, the chief said as the bakery owner laughed at being in trouble all the time. Have seen you catch Rudolf last summer in a friendly fight, Hans is nothing compared to him, they chuckled as Manohar and Mandy had been sent for further custody of 7 days so they could progress with their task on hand with a serious intruder on the run for life.

You are right, I may be able to fight him off, even if he is more strongly built the chief said as he drove with the owner alongside him. They do find how to crack jokes even in the toughest of situations and the men had been talking about nature, how to cross borders, and seal on rules with illegal traffic on high recently or why these things pop again so often.

I was offered to come to an African country with a free visa in exchange for mixing my bakery products with heavy rates but I declined too, the owner said laughing and he knew the friend would not raise his eyebrows in suspicion for the joke as the bakery owner was a kind of true nationalist. They do give chances to most of the people. It's up to us whether we take them or decline them with a slap on their face, Ganeshan laughed as their place to catch the missing man was coming closer and he continued to drive.

The British squad has been sent a tip on someone with illegal activity in the Red Sea in the late hours. People from the Visa squad have been told not to offer any permit for foreign requests and the medical staff of all the hospitals had been alerted on high alert. Hans had planned the trick where he may disguise himself as a lost policeman and the group may get him to go over. As the evening progressed, the marked man started to go away, simply traced at the final exit and Ganeshan reached there in quick speed to arrest him.

The news was showing a man in front as Hans had played well for publicity. A different face by his name was shown as he did have high regard in the Swiss embassy and he didn't want to lose his status even if he was sent to jail. He sent a false update of his leaving to Africa due to certain medical issues and the embassy had accepted it last night. The papers were filled with headlines on the involvement of IPS officer Manohar and how much he had to offer foreigners by his pocket. Mandy was taken into scrutiny and his role was more highlighted.

People were talking of their own cops or officials involved in crimes everywhere with disgust. There was less news on the African as the police chief reached to arrest him but he knew how to handle such types of blokes. A secret spy had tipped him that He may pretend to be an Indian missing from the police squad, may show fake licence of a gun and they must deal with it. Ganeshan knew it as he had handled such types of plots in the past so he is ready to fix the whole case by himself and close it.

We are looking for a missing person from our group, have you certainly seen him lately? He said, looking towards Hans with disgust arriving at the place. You are not an Indian sir, so how could you pretend to be a policeman? The chief said, asking him to come out or he would make the car explode right now. For a moment the missing man thought it might be a trick but then a light popped inside the car as he realised the assistant of his clinic had tricked him, who had asked to check his bonnet before his last trip.

He jumped out just in time as the vehicle exploded and there was a fearful look on his face but he was not going to give up that easily. There was the sound of knuckles as Hans hit Ganeshan and other policemen converged to cover the fight. The bakery owner hit him badly on the face taking his revenge at last and with 15 men on to 1, justice had somehow prevailed for them due to the fact that the true person behind the gold conspiracy was in their grip now and they took him back to the station.

I am not going to ask you hard questions sir, Ganeshan said forcing him to sit as he was not looking happy on being tricked. I am not going to answer any of them if you please, he said in his English tone as Ganeshan took out a file of past crimes committed by him under the pen name of Stuart Clibber both in Sri Lanka and India to which he agreed without much a word and wanted to say more but the chief stopped him gesturing to only speak when he is asked to do so.

Three men were killed in a drain opened at your entrance, what's the reason for that? The African wanted to make snide remarks but he took out a chemical instead. To test whether this works well or not. It's a treatment for wounds related to ankles. He laughed at throwing it so the chief could catch it. The same goes for the wound on the eyes of my assistant, the scars of the local children, and other crimes. I did them all for fun, he showed no regret for his crimes talking them over.

The charge sheet was prepared with the names of Mandy, Manohar, Leonard, and Hans with their crimes committed both in India with links to the foreign communities so they could be punished by law for charges related to theft, robbery, drug scam, illegal documents false trial, and countless number of murder with decree to the law reasoning the scope of their crimes as affirmed in the judicial consent for which official documents were sent to proceed it and close the case.

A word has been sent to naval staff to search for missing people who had been used by the Africans for medical purposes and if possible, they may try to find traces of the gold. Ganeshan had no hope of finding gold as his state had been taken to be on the fourth front of it by them. There was no news on the financial crisis but the officer knew that soon there would be a condition where the state would fall below and only his seniors and superiors may be responsible for it.

There had been a certain lacking portion in the process to wrap up as they hadn't been able to arrest or capture the politician. He had led the whole concern being one of the main suspects and he is still at bay with more damage coming to the state which no one can affirm with him. No wonder there may be one more cunning and mad person like Hans who can get help from our corrupt politicians and cause more mayhem to become part of headlines in the future.

The African was sent behind bars as his visa was taken, his robes were changed, he was told to stay quiet behind them or he may never be able to go back to Africa and the whole team looked delighted to finally close the case down. I am honoured to be part of it sir and see it close, the bakery owner said finally being released from his spies duties as Atharv came in to see all gone well and he added more to the charge sheet with more details on confiscated gold and how it was planned to be sent without any tariff that made Ganesan finally broke into a smile feeling comfortable with the result being on their side.

4
Smoke, Secrets and Dreams

It was a peaceful evening with a lot of voices and echoes of joy in the background. a city of this calibre looks perfect to show its culture when it gets at night and make its presence felt. Mumbai was filled with noises of people coming in large numbers outdoors. You can see people either on carts on the Mumbai local train or somewhat wishing to go back from their work. Get the doors closed, they will soon be here, a Pub owner said as people started to gather in the backdoor and voices started to go loud from inside with music as the core part of it.

A man of around 30 showed a ticket, he was permitted and he crept quietly with a bag on to his shoulder going in. For 15 seconds the CCTv that would capture the man's face had gone blank as something had touched it and the person had gone inside with his bag hidden from others. This way sir, your seat is allowed, a lady said, handing him a napkin with a plate as he sat down to get his meals with music and sound in the backdrop as he was willing to be part of something fishy.

Do you have something special for festive moments? He asked at the counter after taking his meals and they told him of a drink handed only for the night with crackers. The man felt pleased with her and asked to add in as he paid extra from his card which had someone else's name on it. The man must be a highly efficient killer or criminal so he just sat there trying to munch his food as the music kept booming louder inside.

His moment to celebrate was just coming soon as it turned into a dark night with lights all around for some festive mood to arrange a party. With shades from the smoke billowing from a few smoker's pipes, the man could think of what it may look like in a few minutes if he were to go for the ultimate kill. They didn't have mercy for my brother, so why should I? He thought and decided to make his plans come to action as he simply took out a device to activate the fear he had hidden in the bag and it was launched without anyone's notice.

There was a sound like a horn from the bag, it started to show time and the person stood up before the lady who was helping him could call the man back. It was just a kind of warning as the horn sounded and in the next 5 minutes, everything changed. A Blast from the secret bag, people were running and everything was in smoke as a few of the people who were bouncers fell onto the floor without much of a hint of what may have happened to them as one of the bouncer's boyfriends came to see her lying on the floor dead.

No safety. Not a chance to be safe in the city of lights, he started to cry as the fire raged around the place and he somehow took her dead body with him into the inner circuit with the help of people who had come out safely from the blast. Calm down, we ensure the person shall not be left running away, the security guards said but he told them not to touch his hands as he felt disgusted to see them not doing anything to save their skin.

The pub was run by control of the safety unit which was called soon. The pub owner had already brought them in alert and they started to do the common process to have scrutiny. One look on the floor said that the bomb was powerful though it had been of low calibre or it could have blasted the whole place out. They checked for lost paper, and any missing links and finally decided to confiscate the bag that contained the bomb to check its wrapping and any technical wires to control the weapon still lurking inside.

No bag in his hands sir, I have checked the camera, the IT person said but he was still not able to find out why the camera had 15 seconds of footage not available to them.

This may be a high profile attack, the bag is also kept very strong with the bomb set on a certain time limit, the other security person said looking at the sounds coming and they decided it was time to call Vedant the security agent to find what he may make of this. Only he can help us to figure out why this bomb blasted here with its purpose, they said and the staff waited for him as he agreed to come after a short while.

However, a person called Sehgal was feeling relaxed after he heard the news that the main bouncer died of the surprise blast. She used to be his girlfriend but it was her in this pub that she started to date someone else and refused him. You don't have riches to take me to such places, Why should I not go with him? She had commented and now it didn't pinch Sehgal as her betrayal had been settled and he had simply escaped the fire as he didn't wish to see her dance and had been drinking beer on the lower floor.

As the blast took place with a booming sound, the person decided to run upstairs for his friends as he knew the explosion might bring damage and take lives with it. NO, Not you, Please Vindhya, he heard someone say having a final glimpse of the girl who had been onto the floor but he didn't shout and the feeling only sounded inside his forehead as a few more people came ran to drag people away from the flames with shouts coming from all sides and the person decided to help those who were going to survive it despite best efforts of the villain to kill them all in one single shot.

There were at least 8 people who had died in the fire caused by the blast and 15 members had been injured due to late realisation of the burning mass. They all had been a gang of performing artists who used to perform for the public on party nights and the pub owner confirmed that they do choose this place for every Saturday which means that they had come here 1 day earlier this time to plan something big. As the security of the place confirmed it was Friday, they couldn't think what may be the cause to come early and face the price for it.

Yes, we needed to come to see a prior rehearsal as one of us had a birthday coming this Sunday' a remaining member who had been injured did agree but he was still not ready to believe what had happened here. Do you have any idea who is going to be your guest? The Pub security person asked with some suspicion. The other injured person said that it may be a famous personality from the commercial sector who would be honouring them with his presence on Sunday.

Madhur the family broker, is it? A voice said as the security people were arguing with the injured and they were happy to see Vedant coming with spring in his stride to look out the case. He tricks people into being commercial grace and then blasts them using a bag ruining their functions simply. It is one of the known traits of his, Nobody had seen him coming but it was his style as a detective where he enters quietly and steals the show by his smart gaze and intelligence on the past cases.

Here is the photograph sir, If you can start the case, one of the security members said handing him the chip Vedant smiled with more purpose as he took out a photograph from his purse to show and they all felt cheated as the photos may have been matched. I am sorry that I had to come late but if Madhur is involved, It may not be easy as he is supported by higher people in the gang, the detective warned but assured that he would be traced, which brought a sigh of relief to the injured people hoping for justice.

It's time you are taken in to have medical help and get heel as we look over the case or you may become the focus point of the visual media, he said, calling an ambulance, and those who had more severe wounds were sent from the pub for treatment as the owner apologised them for lack of safety measures and they shrugged being taken off with some care by the medical helpers coming onto the spot to help them with support.

We have lost Vindhya, I am not sure what we will do for bouncing anymore, she was the best, a girl said and others shook their heads with fear and pain not willing to talk about the mess they had to actually face in the pub. As the ambulance went taking them to the hospital, more news of crime committed by Madhur came to the lurking spy and he was fuming to find how easily he was able to execute his so-called deadly plans in such a highly safe place with such accuracy.

A board has come outside the pub showing it to be closed for 1 week till the next party as the owner assured the performers that they will get their chance once they recover. It may be helpful to trace Madhur if you ask me, Vedant added to those who had left behind and they all agreed. However, the troubles were soon going to increase for them as a news headline was shown on the TV and also being shown online. It argued about bands that show themselves to be under the logo of victims but had been responsible for blasting or causing mayhem and it did make the pub owner feel disgusted not for this team but for the news people who highlight it in different ways.

Another case has come to me which considers this headline, the detective said standing up with a word of seeing them soon. It demands of a band leader who has stabbed one of his members before running away, he said looking firmly to find the connections and the pub owner looked concerned now. He checked for the band and found that the team did perform on stage at his pub last Friday and the day had been certainly pinching him now as things were happening here regularly.

A man was sitting on a rich sofa couch as a few servants helped him. He had marks on his chin, a small face like a rat and he wore certain clothes that resembled him to a shopkeeper but in reality, he was a mastermind. Madhur may look like a chubby person, but when it comes to offering milkshakes and fruits at his official shop, the man doesn't look as frightening. But the place is perfect for marking people and he is specialized to do that as a professional who likes to take lives for his pocket by claiming them.

I told the man not to argue for the higher rates or there will be an issue, he said to one of his servants as a few more nuts were added to the milk pie to make it delicious We started it recently, boss. The visitors may feel it to be of their taste, he said looking at the senior who obliged with a smile. After His job in the musical pub, he must be paid and he had added this sweet dessert with a liking after committing the crime as a gesture to his success.

Three men came to the glass jar where the curd was floating inside and they smashed it without Madhur getting to notice it. After 10 minutes of a scuffle in which a man had a cut on his cheek, two of the men on the floor, and curd splashing everywhere, he came to see it and started to shout for it. There was a sound of a gunshot from behind, a man fell and Madhur saw one of his serving people as dead. Before he could see or speak anything, the man who did most of the damage was gone. He was feeling miserable as he collected the remaining curd to be put into the filter hoping that customers would like it later when it would be sold.

He was more powerful than my men? How could this be possible? He thought as a few orders of pies came and his other workers served them. The jar counter had been closed as Madhur observed the person dead and wrapped him with honour. He has brought these people from outside and he takes true responsibility for them as they were involved in his crimes as a partner. It may be someone from the police or secret spies and Madhur felt anguish as he prayed for the spirit to be pure and thanked the dead man for his services.

A call came in the evening waking him up as he was trying to have a short nap. Mr. Madhur, I am from the Legends band. I talked to you about the deal of 5 lakhs last month A voice spoke and he stood up in fright. He remembers this call from an unknown person who claims to reside in Dubai. He has asked to pay him 5 lakhs in advance if he wants to see all his men working safely or they shall die by his hands. Dubai is the place from where Madhur gets most of the orders to simply bomb public areas with crowds and he fears the people of the city the most.

For some moments, he quietly thought of it and replied, Sir, I am still arranging the money you asked for, please give me time for 2 days more. The voice felt pity for the man and laughed telling him that one of his servants was already dead. If you delay again, I am afraid that all of them will die and you shall be left alone to lead the shop with your fair kind, it laughed more terribly as Madhur begged to listen to him and asked for some offer so he is could at least pay them him advance by committing the crime and the person on other side agreed getting back to his normal voice.

I will send you one more task. Same place, same time. Can you do it? The voice sneered as the man on the other side agreed. Arrange the ticket to enter, I will be more than glad if you do, Madhur requested and the voice wasn't worried about it. You think about the crime, not the links to which it is connected sir, it rasped and the call got disconnected as he thought of doing the cremation of the curd counter servant with a promise to finish this man once and for all.

A message flashed with a ticket for the next day's evening ceremony at the pub where he had plotted the bomb last time causing deaths. He looked at it with some surprise as it already had his number registered and the audio message came onto the phone. Do not enter the place from the front door, it is sealed by spies. Just go through the backdoor and I will be glad if you do, it said, also sending a photograph of his cart servant who works outside with a warning that he shall be dead if he doesn't follow his word and commit the crime on his actual orders.

A horn could be heard as the afternoon turned into evening, police were making raids at every shop and it forced Madhur to put the shutter down before they came to catch him. It has been the grace of these people from Dubai that they don't like to raid him and he hasn't served their monetary demands in the past either. Just like the other day, he went inside, changed into the clothes the man on the voice note had asked for and he was off holding a knife in his hand with practice on the move to finish the night with pure joy.

It has been told in a sticker attached with a ticket that a person who belongs to the band must be killed and Madhur is ready to do the honours for his men. The camera traced him once more but he has done the trick similar to last time. He had to hide his face this time too which was covered in a white mask and he had gone in welcomed by people who had the cake ready to inaugurate a certain moment. Few People were singing around with music once more and Madhur hates it to be a celebration when it is planned so well in the background to kill someone.

We will cut the cake once our drinks are over, the pub owner said feeling better that the police had lifted the curfew from his place and he approached smiling at the masked man with some mischief. Here is your favourite one, he said without a gesture and Madhur felt strange that this man knew his drink made him feel a bit awkward. For 10 seconds he got time like he had been told in the logo attached to the ticket and he stepped forward taking the knife out.

As the man was ready to cut the cake hoping to be part of a good memory, he had got his chance and he let the knife go smoothly inside the belly, turning it with a flipping sound. For some moments the people around him couldn't understand the look on his face as the man shrieked with pain and started to feel terrible. For Madhur however, it was time to go and get his men safely home as he had done it right as it was asked by the unknown foreign voice involved in it.

With lights coming back and everyone shouting, It was a strange mess heard loud as he ran away. Vedant was called again to check for the leads and he smelt Madhur may have been involved. He told them to call out the police to inspect and they do need someone strong to solve this or the pub may become popular for crimes soon as more cases have been coming.

The voice felt delighted to hear the news of one more death as he went through it on an online new streaming place with glee. He released the man from the grip his fellows had caught in Mumbai who belongs to Madhur's milk shop and told him to be careful. He was sent back with it being a perfect joy of crime being successful again as Madhur asked for mercy from his other workmen or he may not be able to recover from it. The voice laughed more peacefully in the call where he told the Indian to have sent his man back and 2 lakhs had been brought down due to two top-notch crimes done by him.

A warrant has been issued against Madhur to search and arrest at his local place by a police person. He comes by the name of Siddhant but mostly his junior calls him Sid' due to his calibre to trace people. He knows some outside people may have been involved and wishes to settle the crime. Sagun, Did you prepare the call log connected to the pub owner? He said looking inside his place. He had keen eyes and a tall figure and he was around 6 feet which suited his physical stature with the official dress making him look like a decent person.

I doubt he is involved with the foreign people sir, a voice said Anirudh the junior inspector had come in with a call log in his hands where he had also been able to trace a close by PcPO in connection to crimes. This caller ID is used to be in touch with people abroad sir, possibly Dubai and you may feel who may be involved in this directly, the junior inspector said that brought a smile to his face. Yes, Vardhan, the old musical criminal. I feel he may be connected with this, the chief inspector sighed looking closely at the PCO details.

Set a trap for the pub owner, We need him before more crime news comes to us, the official call rings and a voice comes from the other side. Hello, my friend, how are you? Wanting a hand to catch criminals? It was Vardhan and he got wind of people looking for him to arrest somehow. Not interested in you right now. You save your breath, Siddhant shouted and the phone got disconnected as they tried to trudge along towards the pub to set a trap.

The pub owner was resting in his room when a call rang on his number to ask for service. Yes, what can I do for you sir? He said, hoping to get more money from outsiders by planning one more bait. I need a meeting to arrange as we are civil servants holding a party, Anirudha's voice came from the other side and the owner agreed to it. He called for 2 men who used to look for his security as a cover-up and thought this may be the best deal he could make by people and the police team had gone in civil dress.

One photo sir, the owner said as Madhur was not called this time and he was trying to do this on his own as the voice had told him not to expose the secret person all the time. Yes, I want to stand next to you, Anirudha said, looking to finish this quickly. They raised glasses and said cheers' but Anirudha didn't do it as he decided to surprise the pub owner as he does all the people at his place. One for your last smile, sir, shall we? He said, throwing the owner down and he was stunned by surprise as he was pinned.

The other men who had been called put their drinks back and there was a blast that took place inside the owner's wardrobe where all the certificates assigned from Dubai had been carefully preserved for his goodwill it went in total fire as Anirudha showed him his list of crimes as a digital records done already by Vedant when he visited him last time with very few chosen words spoken and they took him on point of gun to the station as their work had just begun with this capture.

Madhur was hoping to get one more contract so his debt may come down but it didn't come. Instead, a letter was delivered by one of his working staff. Sir, it was by the police, he said looking grim as the owner looked at it and felt since when the police started to send him summon. He thought it may just be a prank and let it stay on the counter as the evening progressed and people started to go away with his milk pie sold.

A call came in the night from that strange voice just as it comes on most occasions. You are lucky Madhur. From now onwards I am not going to give you a contract of killing. I have been traced by the Mumbai crime branch and I am going under cover, It made a feeling of disgust and sadness come to Madhur as he wouldn't be paid by foreigners anymore but he was fine with it as it meant no more loss to his workers and he thanked the man once the call was dismissed making him feel better to hear it.

We are thinking of going back sir, If you don't mind. Our time in India is over, three men came to him the next morning as he sat silently at his front shopping store in calm. Yes, your passes, just tell them it has been sent by Madhur so you can't be stopped at the airport, will you? He said giving them back and they smiled as he also held some money to give and he went in his secret room where he keeps it locked by a gunshot which he hopes that it's not known to the police. I will be jailed forever if they find this out, he whispered to himself, came out with hands filled with notes and the men had gone relieved of their duties.

Vardhan was trying to plan for a trap so the crime branch wouldn't be able to reach him by any means. He made a fake video where he could be seen poisoned by his cook who took certain money to act by handing him a flower juice instead and he acted as being sick and then being paralyzed by it. Further, the news started to show that he had gone from Dubai and to make things not look fishy He added his quote edited on how much Dubai had to offer him but he can't stay there forever as a citizen or he may be caught.

It was not the perfect time to do it and something strange happened at his residential place. One of the people who was his daily spy had been found dead inside his building without any hint of how it happened so quickly. Troubled by this deadly assault, Vardhan felt disgusted and ashamed as he couldn't summon the police or he would be caught with his stay here. Instead, he chose to take the help of his other spies but found that 2 of them had also been killed in the same manner. Someone was in the city who should not be and he or she may be killing his men without mercy against them.

They all had died in the same way with cuts below the throat and a bullet clinging close to their chests. The gun that may have the bullets looks Indian and Vardhan is worried as a call comes to him by an unknown number. Terror of the Indians, I am coming to reveal your worst fear, the voice said sounding more familiar but it hardly mattered as Vardhan heard more gunshots in the background with a shoot out of man and the shooter hinted that one more spy had been sent to the heavens by his hands as the receiver shouts to reveal the identity with abuses to which the shooter laughs dismissing the call with glee.

Back at the Indian frontier, Anirudha had broken the barricade that is especially attached close to the secret entry at Madhur's home. He sneaked in with a purpose and had finally found a false gun left there to be protected. He opens the bullet filler, clicks a voice and to his relief, the closely located drawer opens showing the heap of money kept safe there. He captured it, filled the bag, and then proceeded to the next room to open one more drawer. He found illegal Dubai passes left with the signature of Madhur as agent and the larger picture became clear to him.

Sir, You can send our men. We need to confiscate other items too, he called Siddhant who agreed to do the necessary. He simply had sent a team of police staff to collect them before Madhur could reach back home. It was strange that he was not here and hardly anyone could guess why he had been missing from the place. We may find the trickster soon, Don't worry. He won't run out of India in such a critical time, I am sure, the seniors said asking them to continue.

They were assured to find more so they continued their search in the huge home for more clues. They were trying to find what else may be hidden inside with so many pockets and they found a torn shirt with some pills to make people go to sleep. They got more sims with fake identity cards, and duplicate masks to wear, and to grab from the place. A Knife was hidden safely with dried-up blood stains, a lid to load something by it had been poached in a corner and it had been an absolute mess with more evidence remaining in such an open place to latch out.

A call comes and Siddhant answers it at the station. Your man wants to kill me. How fitting is this sir? Vardhan had managed to call him from Dubai and the inspector smiled. You are not on the hit list of people from Mumbai. There are others who want you too sir, Siddhant said laughing as the foreigner understood and the call was over. Last year he did kill a few men in Kandy in Sri Lanka and maybe they might have thought to take pure revenge by killing his men as he was on the run now.

Three hours later, Vardhan was crying outside his building, shown by a camera that he was still in Dubai and a fake trail had been sent by his cook so he could simply escape without being caught. Though the media did feel on what they had found on the grounds, they can't deny that almost 150 men had been killed in a gap of just 180 minutes and the capacity of the shooters had to be of the most daring. It will soon be revealed who was behind such a brutal strike as the leader felt vengeance coming in his heart as he shouted openly to kill the opponents.

I will see to it that he is broken into pieces, he shouted with tears tumbling and the media exposed him showing him right beneath the building which made Siddhant pleased as he watched it on an online platform back home as the chased to find out Madhur was still open. He was not seen by anyone except his workmen in the morning and has vanished from the place. In Dubai, top shooters were given contracts to kill those who had shot the supporters and now it was going to be a true fight on both sides as the storm rages above.

More people were killed by Indian shooters as they tried to run away, hide in secret cabinets offered to them in the past by Vardhan, or in a few cases tried to run toward the desert. The Indian experts tracked them down, simply destroyed those who had been newly assigned and the city became red with blood as more deaths took place. They were unstoppable as they had already taken permits from the government to cooperate and there can be no question the strikes by which Indians were crushing them in the desert. It was only a matter of time when they may reach Vardhan and he may also be under their grip and shall be dead by them.

In the night, Madhur decides to call his working team to ensure his presence in India. I am safe, Don't worry, he said changing his mind by sending a voice message to the group but he did not know that a police inspector had secretly joined the group one day previously as a milkman and now the things were going to be more concerning. He requested to meet Madhur urgently as milk supply may get affected due to people at the borderline not sending the right charges and the boss agreed to find him once the sun rises.

I very dearly wish to find you sir, the milkman said before the sun had properly risen. He had been able to trace Madhur's location at the Juhu beach where he had turned himself to be a beach ball player and was wearing a sports robe to entertain. Let me show you the kind of dress I wear sir, the milkman said, knocking Madhur down with too much strength and taking a badge out from his pocket. Crime branch, its official mate, he whispered, lifting him and throwing the man down with brutal strength. He took out the handcuffs, raised his gun, and took the agent finally under their grip.

Come, sir, I am waiting for 3 days to find you, Siddhant said with a smile as the police inspector dragged him inside with soft behaviour. I shall not take long to find what you may have been up to. Fake passports, sending men from Dubai to India with false money promises, and a lot more. Do you confess it or not? He asked not as a statement but to ensure that Madhur spoke by himself which he finally did agreeing to all the crimes but he also told about an unknown voice who forced him to do all this stuff with details on how his men had been brutally killed in the past.

I know the voice, Let me give you a tip by playing the audio, Siddhant had been recording what Vardan had been saying and he played the last request where he was threatening to freeze the whole plot by himself. Yes, this is the man who tortured me. He is cornered then? Madhur said, hoping to get some taste of the way his man had been committing crimes. Our spies are fighting with his gang as we speak here in India to ensure that he is caught, Siddhant said, receiving the call and feeling better after hearing the news.

Official from the embassy of India in Dubai We are deporting the man in charge to India, Allow us to do sir, a voice message came and Siddhant sent one more document online simply to start the process officially. They will soon catch Vardhan so the actual level of his crime can be traced and be exposed in public. Tell me, sir, why did you start the milk dairy? How long have you been involved and what was such a huge amount of money in your drawer? The senior inspector asked as Aniruddha had brought the bag in which he had filled the money.

Madhur wanted to deny all the cash but he saw a dotted file alongside the bag and he started to speak out. He talked about the illegal business of sweet powder, the profit of gold lining in curd, and the secret process to get milk cheap and transform it into certain chemical products sold in Dubai. All the missing clues started to be revealed and Siddhant finally felt peaceful to find the whole list of crimes he had once attached to his official file with his wish to catch the culprit one day and he did it now as it was a severe scene of uproar.

I didn't intend to kill. It was the result of the wrong content I was supplied, the convicted tried to skip off from all such charges but he had no room to spread out. We have direct traces of you doing all those crimes. We have also taken out the secret pills you had been using in the dairy products sir, Sagun said commenting on his case as he looked sadly towards the members gathered in the place. Yes, a man is caught red-handed with red marks all over his shirt. I should say your torn cloth was enough to show us how much damage you did to Mumbai roads, Siddhant booked him for all charges.

Now was the time to trace back all the things that had happened to children including stomach problems, fatigue and slip off from dairy items, and people dying due to soft cream pastries and other elements so the cases booked in the past may come to a close as the chief decided to lock Madhur for all the crimes asking Sagun to prepare the charge sheet with all crimes. It was the time he could book him for severe crimes including for charges outside India in connection to Vardhan who had been the main villain causing so much problem to his country.

A vehicle enters closely in the police area with an official horn. It stops with 4 men dressed in white taking a man who had bandages on to his face and he was under their grip. You don't know who I am, I will be able to transfer you by my power, the man said as he was gathered and 2 of the officials kicked him in disgust. For now you are a common man. Come with us, Siddhant is waiting, They took him as the chief came to find Vardhan caught amidst them and he had a huge smile to see the foreigner caught easily.

Welcome to India sir. I apologise for the pain you had to face. Alright, give him some more, the chief said, gesturing a hand in gratitude to the 4 men for their tasks who kicked Vardhan and he fell. Siddhant came close, took out a short pistol, and asked in his horrible voice to him. Do you need an excuse to find who may be behind this? He said, asking him to get an explanation. The gun was pointing towards the person's throat ready to shoot him but he must be told the things that happened first.

Last Monday, We were told you had to empty Dubai and settle somewhere else in a hurry, the chief said, still pointing his gun at him. The people from Candy had run off from the prison and the next thing we found they had killed your men, he sneered as a leader of the group with gang members keeping a close eye if Vardhan tried to run up even in such conditions which he had done in the past.

They hurt him badly as Siddhant spoke telling him about the plan, and how Raw had been involved to keep a closer eye on him. When he had the name, Vardhan's fear became true that his old case of taking money from India had caused the blow.. He can't dream enough that the plan would pinch him as those words had finally come true for him taking him to the doors of death without any certain sound or threat.

Now it is your choice, sir. We already have the formal order to kill him from the Raw, the four men said, stepping aside and with a sound of 3 bullets on their count, Vardhan had been shot dead without any hint of how he was caught and not a word to his supporters in the other world. They will know it someday but till they do, we can live with peace here, siddhan said as the criminal died in front of their eyes.

He had been killed smartly under the rules of the security agency so no one could challenge it even in rule books. The case was at its end after all the efforts they made to crack it from years and the wishes had come true. As the crimes may come low due to this attempt, the officials in white dress congratulated the chief who looked pleased with its closure and thanked them for all the courage they showed during the fight in Dubai with delight.

The file was submitted to the court for scrutiny and justification where the order to kill Vardhan had been attached and the evidence was presented. Alongside the official charge sheet for crimes, the statements of criminals such as the milk dairy workers, Madhur, Shravan the cook, and a hidden spy from Dubai were also attached. The court announced the verdict in the police's favour for its bravery and expressed the view that it did a great job to finish such a highly connected criminal by true force and determination as everything came to a close with relief to the officials.

5
Tribals, Tears, and Truths

It was a quiet evening in a place with shadows of trees that gave a cool shade with a true natural feeling. Things were not out of bounds and people were laughing out loud as they talked about the legend that inspired the lake around which they had come to walk as a tour. The people of local tradition can be seen selling hoods, distributing food, and wearing round neck jumpers as they laugh and welcome people with glee as tourists explore the place and hope they may spend some money to let them have a comforting life.

One for my good health sir a lady said to the owner of a tea shop as they drank hot tea with some Chinese food to give them company to have a true feel of it. It's not very cold but this mist gives me thrills to find what may be the mood like, the owner said, handing the lady a glass of milk alongside some hot buns so she could feel comfortable. I do come here every season, I am deeply fond of the lake, you know, she said, sipping the milk with pure relish with being closest to nature here.

The lake is known to contain a lot of goodwill for people as it lets them give it a pure mystique, hope to get glory, and has its legacy. However, the business owner doesn't think it's wise to use it for commercial purposes or they may be thrown to death by the tribals. There can be a larger number of them who surface from the woods whenever there had been any effort to construct business places close to it and things had only become bloody whenever they came to fight.

I suggest you try other natural ventures. They do bring much better courses to the district, a man in his late 20s said as he came in to ask for his orders with some egg ladened in a basket to help the owner. Thanks for your service. The order is ready if you can take it, the man said, asking him to come quietly without a word to the tourist outside. Both of them went in and the folk came after 10 minutes as the tourist paid her bill to get herself going she lifted a bag and a vehicle came taking her with it.

The tourist watched the scene as she started to take a few pictures passing through the Shilloi Lake and the landscape kept changing. Nagaland had its natural hot spots if you consider them but the natural scenes also hide some secrets in its paradigm. The land belongs to Naga, once that used to be the giant Nagalim but had now been limited to this state as a final portion of land to themselves. That tribals here shouldn't be challenged or you may find your life packing if you don't stay good to them.

They are very productive in sharpening the weapons that they use to kill or grind inside people. It is very horrible for anyone who actually wishes to challenge them as media reports keep coming up with more deaths in the inner portion of the woods. It is forests that the tribal call it to be their home and don't want anyone to interfere with their green life. They can be seen to sacrifice, choose young age children to be burnt if they don't fit their routine, and use smoke most of the time to protect them from any excursions done by outsiders.

It is almost night when a vehicle stops, two men come out and they start to create noises like an owl. It may be part of their plan or otherwise but they wanted to make the tribals angry. One of them threw an empty bowl into the ground and the noise was heard clearly. We warn you not to come to our area, Don't you know who we are? One of the locals said in his own language as the visitor struck a match to burn his cigarette and started to smoke that made the tribal feel disgusted as he shouted for few men to come.

I want my son back and I will simply go from here, the visitor said looking at the tribals who had come with sharp blades in their hands. You demanded the district officer to pay the money and we provided you, Now hand me back my son, he said politely as a few of them gazed into him and recognized the man to be the father of the son who had been captured by them while he crossed the bamboo line and they had kidnapped him as punishment telling that he shall only be returned if the government cover their demands.

Your son crossed our bamboo lines and the other person had paid for it which does not complete the cycle, one of the members from the tribes said harshly to him. Who will stop the parties from breaking into our woods, cutting off the main forest resources from us at such a pace? They said, looking mean at the person. The father knew it may not be easy to bring Rohan back so he thought it wise to try to convince him that soon the process will be over so now they must hand his son back as he needs him for the process.

Come to us when all the demands are met by your side, you understand or face the price, they said, throwing a knife towards the father who caught it and burnt the weapon with his lighter making them angrier than ever. The fact is that they had sent the child somewhere from the state and the leader who had helped them didn't want to tell to the son's father due to which they were trying to trick him every Sunday night when he came to ask for him as they knew its most crucial for Rohan to be back at home for a ceremony to happen next month.

The men had gone after a shout from more people as they couldn't fight all the men and needed to think of a plan to act later. They tried to hire a few spies who could help but most of them refused as people feared the tribals due to their violence. I am sorry, I can be of any help:, the tea shop owner said one evening as he was requested to help to find the son. I don't want to lose my life or it may do more good to them rather than us, he said thinking once he heard the whole case and finally sent the men packing from his shop.

No sir, there is no point in trying to spy on them. I am afraid I have lost my wife already so I can't take the risk, one secret spy said as he was offered the contract to search for the son in the woods with crucial information. You are so well connected, I am sure the police can help you. Why not try them instead, they had taken that option also to find 2 of the policemen dead in the process to trace with their guns taken with bullets package as well that showed they may also know how to use guns in the wild.

I am asking it one last time to help me sir please, the official said with wet eyes as he walked to the police station with some hope. Tamang the inspector looked at him not with pity but a hope that he may be able to solve the case. He hasn't got much knowledge of the case as he had come here a few weeks earlier except that 2 police officials had been murdered which makes him feel angry to hear it. Don't worry sir, I am with you. My previous seniors may have been in the league, but I shall help you the police inspector said to him with true confidence.

He asked the juniors to bring the report as he was going to make a plan and started to consider the trial. It is not possible for tribals to run away with a son this long. Any grudges they had with you in the past? He asked, offering a cold coffee to the official who felt a bit calm after it. I stopped them from expanding the bamboo line as usual, he said, showing it was ordered by the government and the inspector nodded understanding the backstory but there was something still not perfect for liking of him.

Tamang was not just a genuine person, there was a reason why he had been sent to Phekh district as he was one of the experts in alerting people. He charges to cover them before the tribe can attack and cause huge damage to the city area. It was common in Nagaland to have fights between the people from the woods and those who lived in the city. It was essential that people living below must be given tips earlier so they may somehow escape the brutal assault of the severe locals.

Most of the time the tribals had been repulsed but in a few cases, they had also been dangerous which had led Tamang to act as a thin but fat man of around 5 feet who is agile and knows his duties well for now. I do fight them most of the time so I do know they can be terrible, he said looking at the official but he still felt there was something that lacked information. I have someone to help you. I have heard you need a spy so I can get you help by the aid of Lesoro, if he can come out, a thin man came to his words and it was somehow coming back to the track with the help of better people now.

I was reading the case as you talked through sir, He said to Tamang opening his pocket to show a pipe and started to smoke. Mind you he smokes a lot if you can see, the inspector told the official who didn't have much problem with it. The thing is your son must have been returned up till now if he hasn't been then or he must have been sent outside too, the detective tipped as he had a stocky profile of someone who likes to crack hidden layers and the unfinished cases for his own standards.

It can be clearly seen by his sharp eyes, thin mouth, and the face of someone who likes to do things under cover and Tamang tapped him to show that the case had just begun. Lesoro, It's not what we can see through, it is what we have to chew for, the official said, giving him a photograph of his son, a past file of people missing and the role of tribals in it with brutal slashes. You wanted to close the past cases and fell in a trap with your own son out of sight. Sir tells the Meghalaya team to be on alert, the detective said, standing up and willing to go now.

It was not just tribals who had been involved in it. The official didn't know it but someone from their side had also been playing as the ceremony is of utmost importance to him with a lot of money to offer in it. I can see entries of new people in the gang, alerting the wild beast to thrash them. The traitor sent a message to someone who could spread it amongst the tribes. It had been delivered and things may now become messy as it started to get dark with evening almost turning to night with some personal affairs to score between the officials.

However, Tamang had caught the movement in the wind and someone was struggling with pain as he crushed the person onto the floor with pure delight at his work. Nice to see you, Mr Poppy, you were known to commit certain crimes and today I have caught you, Let's go back to my home, the inspector said, taking him away as the plan didn't go the right way and the tribals got half a message of what to do next. Tamang took the person inside a cabin to lock him and then started to hit him with a hockey stick so he could express all the things that had happened till now.

I was told to take the son to Manipur, to send him to Arunachal and then to China by border, the person said in pain as more hits came with bruises on his head. The head of the dept. Of culture told me that the son may be pivotal as he can play a part in ceremonies that may happen both in Northeast and China, he squealed in more pain due to hits in the station. What's the ceremony after all? Who organises it and how many players are involved? Answer me, the inspector took him down and he felt worried about seeing such a fierce strike.

It's something to do with Chinese New Year. Every year they chose a child from Northeast India to show that they do have the strength to control the region rather than India, the man said making a frown come to Tamang's face as he heard the words. He did know of the rumours and now he feel they may be true if the son had been taken. The Chinese ask for the harmony of cultural bonds and ask a child to be chosen. This year Nagaland's official son was chosen and the child may be there by now if you ask me, the person said cowering with pain as more blows came and he was finally onto the floor not speaking much to the inspector.

A phone rings and Losoro is on the other side with briefs on the latest movement of tribes. I have connected to the circle sir. We may get a tip on the outpost soon, It hinted to Tamang that the spy had already found out about the ceremony to take place in China. I shall be trying to figure out the outer powers involved in it sir, he sent a text message expressing the concern further as Tamang sent him a photo of the Chinese lunar calendar and asked to find traces of the yangpis' in the regional territory so they can try to connect the case.

Vardhman, you are new to the city. May I ask you to keep things up to date by handling the documents? Tamang asked one of his juniors who was best in shooting but had been kept quiet out of action for some time. I can act in many ways if you ask. For now, I shall do the duty as You ask me to keep the updates live, he said with a kind of expression that he doesn't like Chinese to trick his land and may wish to finish a few of them if he gets a chance to do the honours for his country.

Medha, I would ask you to check for any recent hacks done by the yellow men if you please, they all laughed as the phrase revolved and the IT head started to find what Tamang had asked for on the web. I can find 2 hacks done but they were not successful or detected early sir, she said, looking closely at him with interest due to his guessing skill. She sent him screenshots of the efforts by the Chinese and Tamang looked at them closely as they referred not to Kohima but to the natural areas of Phekh and its outskirts which made him feel more curious to see it as a lost trail from the past.

I knew this was coming. They will send tribals to launch before they do the digital strike, he smiled, checking the Ss more closely as Lesoro sent one more message on the son being sighted at Manipur last week. The inspector told him to connect to spies who can send details and things were connecting faster with the turn of events in the guidance of the right people. As the official worked with huge pressure in his sight, he does trust the police now and hopes that his son may be revived soon from the grip of the wrong people who were behind it causing so much pain to him. It may only time that may tell whether he shall be pleased or not?

Tribals started to howl in numbers again but Vardhman had been sent to handle them with a group of policemen to control the gang. They did face a few scars but the main leader had been fine as he revived the wound to heel with a potion after coming back alive with others in his backdrop. Good job, I can look at the bigger cases as you can handle them well, Tamang said, handing him ore potion and started to look worried. The junior said it was all part of the fight, thanked him for the medicine and it was somehow getting in the right direction for the team.

A message flashed again, not by the spy but by someone who doesn't belong here honestly. Stop searching for the kid or he will die, you get me? The sender wrote as Tamang looked at it. Warning me or trying to trick us away from the borderline? He sent the message back and a photo of a child inside a bathtub was sent as a response that didn't make him worry but felt they were close to the case. It looks like India so the ceremony is a false trail, the inspector said and now his mind was working things out as he brought the wounded informer back who had been put into custody after an enquiry in jail a few days earlier.

The facts he revealed this time were more than shocking to the inspector as he started to talk. The captive said that the official had tricked them due to which the earlier cops had not been helping him. There were two sons, both born to him as twins one was in India and the other had been sent abroad to China. It made Tamang fume with pride but he may think he has a different scheme to search now. He sent the details on to the spy who was at the site and had somehow skipped out from the bullets fired at him by a few hired personnel as he realised the involvement of the father in it.

He started to run at top speed not for his life but to prove them wrong by his skill and shot two of them dead before they could try to converge, returning to the station with glee. Here we go mate, I have them. Those who wanted to clear me off first, he said, coming in a hurry to join Medha who had finally traced the actual case of three years back in reports. It was in Manipur where the son had gone missing for the same cause and has helped to connect it with the new case in light of the events folding to them.

Tamang started the scrutiny as he called the official to come urgently, tricking him as he told him word had spread regarding his son and current location. It made the official feel calm that he may be released from the grip of the Chinese who had been tricking him for years as he took out his bike to go back to the station quickly to find more on the progress of his son's trace as the inspector did have insights to share besides inquiry to him about the twins and how they had vanished without a word to the public.

Come now. We can't wait more, Vardhman said, asking the official to do it quickly. The person left his bike in the courtyard, stepped out, and found the main inspector to be waiting alongside the spy. Welcome sir, we have some good and bad news. What would you like to eat first? The Momos with chilli sauce or hot spicy hockey stick of our place, he said smiling as the official felt a bit worried by his tone. True to his word, Tamang shared news on the son being witnessed in Manipur but also said that he needs to ask a few questions.

Where is the other son? I have true information that

you did have two sons, the inspector said asking the direct query. The official looked baffled at first but then handed him an envelope to open a letter. A word by the Chinese, you can go through it as you know the secret, the official said as the inspector read it which mentions the new year ceremony, his son being selected and keeping the other one inside a bathtub all the time so the process can be fulfilled. You are biased sir even after being ranked so high, what got into you? He felt disgusted to get the final proof of prejudice with the locals even at this upper level deeply rooted in them.

Tamang said all the words in fury and he couldn't believe what he was witnessing as the other child had been pushed to a worse state. Vardhman, go to his house. Release the son now, he ordered not listening to the requests of the official. For you sir, it is time we teach you the lessons of the law. We are in India or if? you may have been killed by now in China, he said closing the first part of the case. Lesoro handed him some more information on the letter and they decided it was time to crack the circle once and for all, sending a few secret agents to find the child traffic gangs.

In the evening Vardhman had managed to reach to let the child come out. He had to open a few locks before he could get there not to mention he also had to destroy the false security link so no one could easily enter inside. He traced the child in pain, let it come out of the boiling water, and wrapped it in a cloth. By the looks of it the days had passed since it saw anyone or any light with the child's eyes not able to recognize a person in front For a moment and then he tried to skin back but Vardhman helped him to stand, took him, and told they had come to save him that made it felt comforting finally.

As for the official, Tamang has filed a chargesheet of false information, putting a trap and a case was lodged as he was also taken into custody. The official saw a man behind bars and he felt more worried as the man had been connected with the conspiracy to send children to China. He understood where the information came from and now he thought the other person may also be caught by the police. His fear came true as Tamang managed to capture one more official closely connected with illegal supplies of rock gems to China and he revealed that he had been tipped by the official to help in his son's quest which led to finding a Chinese and he started to make it count.

Tamang was getting angrier than ever but he kept it quiet for the right time as more people were caught selling fake drugs or losing money and he wanted to close out the whole mystery of the son's case as the Chinese New Year was coming closer but they may have to let Losar go first being the Tibetan new year and a trick came to the inspector's mind for a grab. Medha, check for tickets next Wednesday, he asked as she obliged with information on them being available. Lesoro, you will go as a mascot to the festival abroad, agreed sir? He said and the spy felt delighted. He had a look at both the officials and decided to play a game with them.

As the carnival in the local area approached, a few outsiders started to gather selling fruits, garlands, and even small crackers. Tamang had a close eye on them as they did damage to fragile children. He had sent a few men to the local hospital to bring reports and had suspected that the medical place may also be involved. The plan was to send both officials as working people in a Chinese company. They are already aware of the language and when they share a drink, the inspector would tell the public that they are from India and their son is missing.

It would be a trick or a huge uproar which will bring the crowd into action and mostly they will be stunned or probably be killed. Why finish them so badly sir? Surely they are of some credibility? Medha asked him as the inspector told him that this would anger China which may not be able to complete its ceremony and the official plan may come to reality but he fears about the child that is still in their grip. I have talked with Norbu, the leader of the secret society if he can somehow help, Tamang said as the other men of his command looked at him with some desperation and he knew what to do next at the right time.

The reports proved true as there were cases mentioned in the last few years of a high number of children sent to China from the Northeast to make the sacrifice and it made Tamang feel disgusted. He told his team members to stay close to the hospital wing as they found an underground tunnel where all this activity was happening. The leader asked them to charge and the place was filled with smoke, flame, and bursts of gunshots as the whole team had launched themselves on the doctors who were dead before they could ask anything for an excuse.

The mission was a huge success and the children were safely brought back as Tamang distributed sweets amongst them trying to calm them down. I can't bring the people who left you but can assure to punish the culprit, he said, asking Ven Zao to be taken alongside his 5 other Chinese who were involved. They were booked under the Child Traffic Act as they were forcefully brought by Hye Yang, the person who is called a secret agent to Tamang and the Chinese felt worried about finding themselves on the trace in India.

Lesoro took on himself to go with Vardhman on one more secret mission as they found Men Zao, a Chinese who was known to trace human bodies and had been involved. Furthermore, the official who was behind the bar was traced back to the hospital as his photo did serve as inspiration inside the tunnel that was taken down, and more charges were attached to his name. Things were happening so quickly that the Nagaland crime branch was surprised and the higher-ranked official felt great to see Tamang living up to his name.

A raid happened in the financial office of the Tibet

cultural group and it was organised by Hye Yang on Tamang's official orders. They found a huge amount of cash not for the Losar festival but to have exchanges as the trafficking of human bodies that was planned. You all are under arrest for exposing the pain and worst case scenario for the children in Nagaland, the secret agent said, dragging 10 men by his arms with true power and they fell onto the floor. Within the next 15 minutes, a van had come lifting the false people and they were taken to police custody.

All to be sent to the heavens on the day of Losar, Tamang said, feeling elated to find more crimes simply covered. I may need to ensure that you all had been seriously involved before I send you to death, he said as there was a tradition to throw out bad spirits on the new day eve and he was looking forward to it. For now, he asked Medha to look for more web crashes and she informed him with the latest snippets so his mood was perfect to think about how to plan it well so that it can help in recovering a child from China.

Tamang was ready for the moment coming soon with the festival. He told a few men to go to the lake area to check and he updated him that preparations were in total swing there. Good we need them to help for the destruction of bad spirits once and for all, he said as he had got orders to arrange or look to provide special service for the people who are in custody and the officer looked in true mood as he thought according to his plan of action.

Hye yang speaking. I have got the link between the secret pavement that leads to the Chinese outpost, a voice said, making the inspector's mood more pleasant. This may be the place from where the child had been sent. Please oblige me with the right photograph, he said wanting to get a better click to track as Tamang sent an HD image that had been taken of the child who had been rescued so the other twin could be located easily while the spies searched all corners of the borderline.

Tamang had been at the field too. He stopped a few people from Tibbet who had come from the other side and asked them to show an official card to do business in Kohima. They provided him with the right documents for the trade agreement so he was satisfied and let them go without asking for any charge. It was a trap to keep the bigger power confused as Tibet was on target rather than China as it worked to give an advantage in tracking the child.

He kept looking for false drills, and things out of place to bring order and also visited the prior hospital so he remains to be in check with it. Lesoro had been on the other side and he brought him perfect news on progress. He had found a trader from China who may come to India next week. The thing that made it more interesting was the fact that the trader was looking to get a brand new cloth supply as he was going to design the suit for children selected for New Year celebrations and this could be more than delightful for Tamang who was waiting.

I have more for you sir, Another spy responded who had gone with Lesoro to trace out the process. We were skillful enough to oblige the cloth trader to show the image of the child chosen after complimenting his ability to craft suits, the words made the inspector surprised a bit but the phone got disconnected and an MMS had come showing an image of a child in a bathtub but not much burnt in recognition as a twin rather than feeling grateful to be there for the moment coming next week.

Lesoro sent a text mentioning his presence at the celebration as a secret agent who wishes to find more on cracking hospital sources. One that is involved with child traffic as you know sir, the text read and Tamang smiled that multiple crimes may be traced with one single event. Losar was coming soon and he was going to be on the guard for it closer to the lake so Tamang asked Medha to choose the cracker that may be suited for its welcome. With the help of Dahlia, one more junior in the branch, it was all set to destroy the criminals before the lake round the festival in the city.

The night before the Losar had come, Tamang walked up to the official who was the father of the twins. I am sad to say that your sons would survive but it's your last night, the father smiled as He realised that life can be truly cruel sometimes if, to be honest. You had helped me to figure out how to tackle the crimes. I thought we have to be part of it to resolve them, but you proved a true person, I can be thankful to the mother's sons, the father said, requesting to send them to her once the other twin is safely brought back from China and the inspector agrees walking away as he closes the gate.

There came a movement from the woods at top speed as it does every time and Vardhman was ready for it. Leave this to me, I am more than prepared, he said charging with his team of officials who controlled the gang from the woods as the tribesmen scattered with gas and smoke swelling into the air used by the police harshly. The public went close, feeling blissful by the fact these men helped them to arrange all things in order and they were thankful to them as they flashed and Vardhman smiled looking at the musicians with joy and true fervour.

A few of the group members started to go away laughing as they thought what may be displayed as bad spirits in the evening for fun and the time was coming closer. Tamang went towards the station to bring the men for their final evening as special honours and he took them with all of them being handcuffed in the celebrations and people watched them with awe and fear of what may be coming too.

I have asked them the last wish folks, Tamang the inspector said as he had got habitual to giving speeches in certain places wherever he was posted. I am going to show you that their crimes are enough if we have to consider them as bad spirits altogether. They are some of those who had been involved in the worst you can imagine, he called Medha to be on the stage and all eyes turned towards the projector as she started to show a presentation with names of the people in handcuffs and the crimes associated with them.

People started to hush, then their voices turned into whispers and they soon started to go wild with their voices to finish them off. That had brought the chance the inspector had been waiting. He launched an air weapon into the air and he flashed with sparks. In the next 5 minutes, the people who had been handcuffed didn't even realise what had happened as half of them were dead from the light produced by force.

For The next performance and public murder happening openly, Tamang displayed his skills in firearms as he threw grenades at such speed that they hit more people with true force. The victims recoiled in the smoke spreading and further of them were finished as the crowd started to roar with pure delight. More to come folks. The show is not over yet, the inspector said and the crowd started to become large to gather and witness the procession of it with true joy and pleasure.

It felt like they may be the victim of some sort of tricks but in the next 25 minutes, the people caught for severe crimes had been killed as the leader sent them packing to the heavens after they all had died. The crowd was getting more fierce but the policemen were ready as they didn't allow them to cross the marching entrance of the lake forcing them to turn with louder vocal efforts. The music kept coming from the speakers as Tamang felt pleased to fulfil his duties once more and now the only thing is to bring the child back home from China safely.

The news was coming on TV that suggested a flood had hit central China taking many lives. Tamang watched closely as the Chinese reported to change the child who had been brought and they were planning to kill the son they had taken from Nagaland. Tesoro came in time to find the mess and decided to fight for the child. There was a smash from behind that kicked the spy off guard as few kung fu actions accompanied the move and both sides engaged in the battle with strength.

There was a strike closer to their eyes, Lesoro threw a man onto the floor and it was too noisy outside as he went away cutting loose with an explosion that circled the whole place as the spy took the child crying with the noise of fire behind. This is China, You can't escape, a man rasped as the spy started to run towards the border. He thought it may not be safe for the child to come with him so he simply summoned the other secret agents as Norbu appeared and it was the perfect time for his act.

I will take care from here onwards, the man said who was strongly built and his undercover cops started to fire as the child was simply taken inside the Indian border with high profile security. Tamang was called to be at the border and he deeply expressed gratitude to his secret team and the Indo-Tibet border for covering up the child and bringing him home back safely as gunfire kept happening fiercely at the backdrop.

For the Nagaland police, the case may have been solved but the officials know that the Chinese will come back, they might look for the son and they may be biting time for their revenge. Meanwhile, The inspector thought to help both the twins come together and he was feeling happy as they created similar sounds while trying to recognize each other as they started to feel easy with handshakes.

The police staff watched them both with pity and curiosity as the women felt more attached to the children asking the inspector about the plans. I will take the duty to protect them. It was my fault somehow that his father is no more in this world, Suddenly he remembered the person's wish to send them to their mother and he thought it may be his job to do the honours for the remaining family in his strides.

It's better we do it soon sir before anyone starts to claim the kids are there. You know the mood in the state, medha the assistant said, lifting both of them together and touching their cheeks affectionately as they felt a bit warm trying to be calm under the female gaze. Yes,I am doing it son, You shall keep an eye on them as I do my best to find her, she nodded and Tamang had been off trying to locate the mother.

Tamang had sent informers to find and Hye Yang had managed to search the mother who used to work in Tnanti National Park as a medical staff but had been last seen outside a cafe. She was in bad condition after losing her both sons and she may have taken time to recover after she had stopped seeing them for a while. With hardcore investigation, Tamang finally reached her and handed the baby twins and her expressions were great to watch as she welcomed them back, and finally, the case was closed.

6
Clockwork Chaos on the Rails

It was a noisy place as people walked across a station to find their place. Few trains may go late and some of them were making an absolute sound. Those who may have to get their first experience of traveling by train may feel it irksome as the voices were heavy to cover their ears. The announcer kept speaking of the trains to depart or come to go as soon as people started to look for their traits or check seats on the chart hanging from the ceiling.

Carts can be seen moving around the platforms as people keep filling in to find their train, checking for arrival and the time to depart on the train clock. A few of the children who had seen the 24-hour clock for the first time were perplexed as their parents told them how to consider it if they had to know the time. The voices were getting louder than ever as an engine ran onto the track and vanished away with a lot of children asking why it did so.

It was a usual test on how the main vehicle shall carry the other bogies during the journey with it, a parent told a young kid of around 9 as the train had been inside the yard with its engine running on the track at top speed. Do they give the details if any accident happened at the place? The kid tried to ask but the question had gone out of the parent's hearing due to a loud siren made by the engine itself as a few men started to find their place fighting for the tickets.

Calm down. You were waiting. now the chart has been pinned so you can see how much waiting has come down with the crowd filling so much, an elderly person in white clothes said to the man who was arguing for the birth showing the ticket to others. We shall talk this with the TTE, once he arrives, alright? Get a seat yourself to share till now, the elderly man said as the other one got quiet after he was openly offered the seat.

Few trains did pass through as people fought for birth in one. It has been a routine for those who work here with total confidence as they know that people will fight or argue for the best seats to get a perfect experience to fall asleep. Night trains offer sleeping berths to let the travel become more prudent as with the luxury of the government's efforts, things have come to a proper fold. Now people do get better ways to entertain, the internet for their devices inside, and a proper way to enjoy meals with fresh water supplies on a regular basis.

People comment on the new process but somehow they are getting proper comfort with a better life and room to spread out for them than ever. Nobody thinks of life as it works, they only complain of it once countless are torn apart but soon a train incident will make them feel how much they miss out on the portion to live a happier life as it is cruel and hardly gives you proper chances to do so, you must enjoy actual moments with pride.

Hi, I am Vaidya, the TTE, Your seat has been changed, sir. Come with me, the ticket checker had arrived talking to the man who had argued. He may have to adjust to the berth he assigned as the crowd had got in with more people. While moving away the man saw a few bundles of certain materials were shared by millet traders who had to sleep on the floor without a proper berth as they had no registration.

The TTE took him by the next corner and asked to step into the next bogi where he saw less crowd around the floors in numbers. The man thought for a while checking for seats and he had got what he wanted to have a perfect trip by night. a perfect low berth was in the order for which he paid as they asked for the price on offer for this particular night with it to let him have a happy travel and he has finally got settled in it.

I may tell you the bathroom at the other portion of the bogi, Vaidya said as the man took out his luggage and started to feel better. No chain snatching while we go in critical areas? He asked with a smile the TTe denied and he had gone, allowing the man to be at his most comfortable now buying tea from the passing vendor. I need some information, Anyone help me with it? He said, giving a large amount of money to the vendor and he excused coming in the next half hour to talk with him to help out.

The train started to move slowly as they could hear the whistle of the guard. It may become the journey of the future whether this whistle should be the last time from his mouth or not as he plays it happily making the sound go loud. People inside the train were still fighting as the tea vendor sold most of his tea and had come to talk. Hi, My name is Magadheesh, I come from Orissa, the rich man said, looking at him with some joy to share. What's the final destination of this train, surely from where I come? The vendor nodded and it was not clear why he had been asked to provide a tip.

May I know what kind of help you need sir? The tea vendor asked as the man did like the approach by him on the subject directly. I am providing you a tip being top secret instead of what you do, the vendor felt a bit serious as the passenger said this, taking out a silver metal from inside his bag to show him. A date is written in it honestly. The date of an accident. Did you get me? The vendor was perplexed but waited for more to fall upon as the man spoke in true grace affirming words told openly by his side.

This time the train may survive, but when this express goes to Orissa the next time, you will find a huge accident, it made the vendor feel strange as the rest of the berth had people asleep and he didn't dare to have a gaze onto them. This may happen as multiple trains may clash into each other on the same railway track taking a lot of lives with them, he smiled, throwing the silver metal back in his bag and asking the vendor to go who thought on his words with a smile.

His feelings were deep down connected to the motion as he did want something to happen that could crack the past open. The torture of the main officials, lack of money, and all the pain his struggle saw including his brother's death on the railway track may be covered with things out in public. If this comes true in some form as the rich man had said, he may get his revenge back somehow from those who hurt him the most while selling tea.

As the train moved in top speed, Magadheesh had taken his expansive blanket out to have proper rest. He didn't care whether it might be snatched while he was asleep or whether it might get dirty due to the wind blowing with mud from the open window. A few bridges came in the way of the train as it made loud sounds but the man didn't feel much for them. They all are part of the journey until he continues as he knows if the train collides, the voices and their movement will somehow also change which he does not want to see.

This is why he wanted to have someone for help but he may not be supported in public areas by outsiders. He feels sad even being so rich to help the workmen in his city with pride but unable to do it where it is needed the most. Life will take your test and in some cases, you just have to let the timeout or things grapple with pain and effects of the past. The man may feel out of panic as the train may complete the journey this time but he can't change the destiny by his financial strength or public influence to control the time.

It is getting late honestly. I want to get out of the train for now, a voice said that belonged to a young person who may be aged around 25 and was small in stature when it came to physical appearance. As it can be seen, He may be around 5 feet in height, did carry a cotton bag for travel, had sharp glasses, and wanted to be on the train to find any tricks happening in the backdrop. He had been tipped that people may try to sneak illegal goods as they get a chance to load while others fight for berth or try to complain about the quality of seats.

The spy came by the name of Ranvijay and he stood up planning to leave in the next station as something caught his bright eye. A thin bag was lying on the corner, as he went close enough, he could see some documents were thrown at the top of it and he didn't dare to check what they meant at first. His curiosity as a detective took over however as he found out they had names and as he crossed check, his fear had doubled just as the train stopped as they were death certificates of unknown people and he had no clue of it.

I can't stay here taking things off, the spy said, stepping down from the train at speed as people surrounded the bag looking for money. He had somehow nicked the certificates off as he knew they were more connected to this place rather than to the people on the train. He tried to see through problems, stepped in the crowd, and finally arrived at the place talking to his relatives who he had spotted in the crowd with ease.

What kept you that late detective? I was starting to get worried, his mother said as he touched her feet and others welcomed him with delight. The train had got late, This may be the first time it has happened as it is one of the best, the younger brother said making him feel bit comfortable that his word of spy are taken out of the talk. He asked the mom to come out in line since it was crowded, took the bag in his hands back and they had gone with certificates still safely preserved by the spy.

Back at the train, a guard was fighting with someone to check for missing documents which he thought belonged to him. What bothers you, sir? I can't see any problem, Vaidya had come trying to see the matter. The documents, one for the last journey. They are not here, the guard said with frustration on his face as the TTe checked for the thin bag which had certainly been disturbed from inside. Who caught them, sir? I won't report it to the boss or I shall be dead, he looked at him with some fear turning away from the crowd filling in.

The station master had come without a hint as they stood there captivated in fear. Vaidya changed the mood by asking why the train was late to which the guard showed mist in the visible weather What kind of season are we in sir? No excuses, the master said smiling but his voice was strict. It was almost May and it can't be foggy as they complained. The loss of documents secretly was hard to swallow for the guard and he went away curing the master as it was he had asked them to create fake death certificates for his future plan.

Vaidya too feels the effect of it as it can be a huge gap. Now they may fall into the trap if someone from the security agency finds it all and it has happened similarly as Ranvijay had gone straight to local police to enquire about these cases. He showed them some documents and the police started to expand the network of spies to find out whether such people had died or not recently in the area. The case had been found closer to the station that involved the death of lower-class men who used to work as salesmen in trains, but the rest of the critical documents did prove fake.

The police wanted to act as they were under pressure to consider due to frequent train accidents from the past in the area. I am not going to see it away as nothing but a story of dreams but the word is crucial, Mohapatra the chief inspector said as Ranvijay thanked him for help. It's just a simple case connected with a lot of multiple ones, the inspector said as the spy went off handing the documents to be in police custody till further updates are related to them through the network.

Bishan, I may ask you to go to the station if you can? Mohapatra ordered and the junior inspector simply agreed.

Can I take Vangar with me sir? He requested and the other man stood up ready to go and the senior obliged. Try to find out the plan, what is the mess, and why it's so urgent to have death certificates, the boss told them and they were ready to leave the place as the wild clouds started to emerge in the sky signaling for something bad to come very soon.

Back at the station, the master was sitting with someone who looked to be from an elite family. I have paid you for the last 3 deaths, I am not going to pay you big money if you don't have the right plan, he said threateningly with his finger inside his pocket where a gun was safely kept. You promised to fix the leads to have the larger crash take place but we missed on it last year sir, the master squealed in his babbly voice asking him to have some more portion of the drink. The man looked from a criminal background and he paid the master some money to start the new scheme as they were going to plan something big this time.

Bishan had been walking along a glorious railway station, one that is renowned for its food service and he looked to have some food before he started the search. Vangur, his supporting staff, told him to be careful as people may misuse the taste, inspiring it with something else. The junior inspector had an eye open for the tea vendors who did most of the tricks as he was obliged to pay one of them to bring some fresh news. Hello sir, yes I will help you, the vendor said, selling out his tea shouting it at low prices to people on the train with pure delight to do it as he saw the inspector coming to talk with him.

I have seen the master plot some old business with Mankhade if you ask me how things are happening so fast, the vendor said, coming back as he feared the gaze but had gone as Bishan didn't ask much this time and felt grateful to have some good words. You think it's enough to get things cracking bro? Vangur asked but stopped as a few railway police cops had been passing and they shook hands as they took off at speed, smiling at the progress of the things around.

Sir, Mankhade is back, were the first words Vangur said after coming back to the place with a report. They told how he had been again active with the station master helping him with some money as told by the inner spies. He is not known to do smaller bids. Trace the actual call for which he had been sent again by the goons now, the inspector said to his staff. A few months before this Orissa had a train accident that was plotted by members of the gang to which Mankhade belongs and now they may look to do something similar like it for their pleasure.

He had sent them on purpose to first pull the chain, kidnap a few members, and also damage the main gas pipe that had caused a serious problem on the track. Unfortunately, the police had not been able to catch the mastermind and now he has come back to do some larger trickery. Bishan said that a few unknown masks were also roaming the platforms today asking for the right doors and gaps of tracks if certain trains come face to face. This made Mohapatra worried as this was the exact thing Mannkhade's men would do as they like to cause mayhem.

I smell a plot here. He may be involved. Let's try to find more stations active with clans Ranvijay said as he was called by the inspector to discuss the matter. What's the stage of gages in Balasore? I figure that it can be a hot spot if we keep things on track, the inspector gave it a thought and asked Vangur to bring a map of the whole state for scrutiny. For some time they all kept trying to plan and then Mohapatra's eyes fell onto an outer junction where trains can be tricked if multiple vehicles come at the same time on track.

Sir, I have been able to locate a driver who is known to run in trains loaded with goods locally. He can be part of it., Marudha, a subordinate at the police said, showing the history of nic incidents by the goods trains to them. It has done damage I guess. How will we stop all of them if we presume there is a plan to create an accident? Bishan said, looking closely at the records and thinking the way out as it was certain that something was going on quietly.

They were just thinking of taking the plan forward when a call came and Vanguur was told by local police that a few workers had gone missing from the workplace so they must trace it but they had fallen for the trap set by Mankhade as he was behind it. Vangur told the team to keep the trail of the train plot as he may handle the case by himself as it's his duty. The senior felt pleased as he sent Marudha with him and he was still there with the spy and bishan to consider how the plan may work.

They decided to set a trap for the station master where they must catch him before the actual plan commences. Ranvijay was told how to deal with it and he planned to be another station master with an official dress challenging the person for his actual status. That shall do for us if you ask me, hopefully, we may get him soon or it may be too late, the inspector said and the detective had gone smiling on the progress of the case open in front of them as it may be a huge task.

Mankahde had gone to Balasore, a place that is more known to have a heavy Muslim population. He is welcomed there being a prideful person with a lot of cheers happening for him. Usual taste to have with you sir, Amir the local juice maker said, offering him a glass and he didn't say no. Their plan was almost close to the finish and the boss didn't want any errors this time. Are you ready to crash things out or have any fears of being caught? He asked the juice maker who shook his head and told him that he had been awaited by Abbas bhai inside.

The criminal went to talk with the main leader and he welcomed him too with glee. I wanted to know how it would all go so I thought to call you back for a tip, Abbas said with the smile of a professional killer. I don't have much details to share but your men will take over once the collision takes You get me then? Abaas nodded as the criminals gave him a portfolio that explained how trains may catch into each other at top speed and what they must do to run off.

Keep a secret, Or you know what can happen to your family, the main culprit said to the resident as he decided to go. Your biryani sir, don't you want the taste this time? A servant said as Abbas agreed but the visitor had turned back with interest. Keep it packed, I will sit and eat with you only if my mission is completed with a coalition of the trains, the servant agreed to pack the food and he finally decided to leave hoping for some good news.

I am changing the plan sir, he called the station master like he had got wind of police trying to track him either by force or rounding his followers. The station master of Balasore would be more fitting as he is your neighbour, what say you? The master said yes on the phone as Mankhade told him the change in plan and they were certainly going to rock the tampo with their crucial scheme in stations. Bishan may get right for his guest but the lateness of the police that is famous might affect the condition here.

The guess came true and Vangur had managed to grab hold of 5 members of the gang who had been involved in theft and robbery while trying to snatch purses in the train. He took the people who claimed themselves to be workers earlier but now work for the main villain as they were tortured hard before inquiry at the station. What's the plan? I may like to ask you one more time, come on tell me, Vangur said as the other working staff watched him flare for the first time.

He was trying to get the information that could prove useful so he had been able to find that trains may be colliding soon. I know the primary part. Three different trains will smash into each other when the next arrival of the Coromandel express happens in Balasore, the man said, feeling a lot of pain but Vangur was not satisfied and he thought it was better to keep them in custody for further questioning and Mohapatra agreed.

Make a team of a few members so we can keep an eye on the trains moving in the next few days, the official said and Bishan agreed, raising to have an action plan. Few of us shall stay here in the capital station to watch things over, got it? Mohapatra said, Who shall be where for it? Bishan, you alongside Vangur Shal go to Katak for the extreme inner circle plan, agreed? The other team did say yes hoping for everything to be in control. Ranvijay, your job is to track me for all the movements happening in Balasore and I shall be there on your signal, the spy agreed and they were ready to go for it.

Mankhade had still not gone from the place of his royal status where the event had to take place next week being one of the worst of its kind. He was talking to people who were in the most severe pain, unhappy, or not supported by the government. He distributed food to them, talked about why they were stressed, and told them of the misuse by the local community that hurt him. It will be taken over soon as their men will lose too, he promised with some hope in the faces of ladies of the stress clan who are tortured.

He feels for them as he can take care to arrange all things for himself being a criminal but to be honest, these people have nothing to do with the way they were treated and it hurts him more than before. I hope a lot of people die in that accident. That's the only thing to justify the pain of conquering it by giving it to others easily.' He relishes such a feeling and has been waiting for the fall. He did fail in the last two attempts last year but this time his men are ready to do the damage with all preparations done.

Marudha had been in the act as he had managed to catch a supporting member of the person who handled the goods train. Come with me, I need to ask a few questions, now, he said, shooting him in the leg as the person was running. He calls for the vehicle, lifts the man, and takes him to enquire about the accident plan. He did agree that his brother had been involved before but Mankhade had killed him as he was going to tell the police about the whole blueprint revolting against him. Who else is involved then? I am sure you know the new pawn? The subordinate asked, throwing him down on the floor after questioning him.

More people had died falling from a certain place inside the station where the clash had to happen soon. People were somehow unable to figure out who was trying to trick them but more news of the deaths came and the state government decided it was better that the fact shall not go outside or it may be an outrage or pure laughter on their face. No news on how these people died you understood? A railway police person said as the man had watched him from afar and felt good for the moment coming soon with its horrific reality to bare out of bounds.

It was total darkness as a technician sat in a corner reading something. He looked to be a man of his word and had been inside the plan to let the trains crash into each other. Sir, I have fixed the mess, it may work to let the trains get confused if you ask me, the technician said in his lazy tone as the main villain agreed to find a trace of their skills and the technician was sure that it may not b easy to find for the police once they start the mission.

I don't trust in rash words. It is my duty to find out whether we can be caught or not, the juice maker who comes by the name of Amir told the technician. They need to be spotted so when the train collides, no one shall be able to find them at such a tough time. Abbas bhai has graced us to use the equipment well. We shall make it count, the technician said as they were talking on a conference call arranged by Mankhade who was smiling as they all argued on how to make the collapse successful in the right steps.

It is up to you guys, how you can hide or reveal me, the boss said with everything going quiet For a moment The leader of the Muslim gang hinted at the deception by equipment but the other cut across saying that police can't be intercepted and they may get caught at the end. Who cares, I feel its a true honour if we are caught after doing the crime for ourselves, The technician finally spoke and mankhade felt them to be committed as the call was dismissed with smiles from the gang members still smirking.

Amir had a word with the boss personally in the night about how he could stay back serving people juice by his hands if he allowed him. Your job is to be on the platform dude. Ah yes, you can sell the juice there, Mankhade felt blissful to see the plan going with a bet of spirit in people and it was time to fix the case which he couldn't in years. He had been finally on the course to settle the old scores after being rejected by Railways, insulted for his talkative nature and he shall soon be reprieved.

Mohapatra was on the run to search for more men as he tried to raid the main Bazar at the place of collision that is just 3 days away now. He tracked an online operator who was giving bribes to the station master asking him some tough questions. I know you belong here, what doesn't stay with the time is required to be known. Tell me the time of the collapse, the person started to stammer as he heard the word from his lips becoming worried with his involvement being minimal.

I can't be sure how many of them there are, sir, the person said, now collapsing himself on the ground in fear. A huge section is connected to the plan making it come true as the police search around and it looks like they are confirmed as they have the word of things being put into action in this place coming soon. No news from the central area sir, one of the policemen called Mohapatra as he kept tracing more people, hurting them badly or taking them back as he drove them in his vehicle for custody.

I am still in charge. We can, however Scatter and find what we can do for the missing links, he said with a fierce voice. The chief saw something fishy with a man pushing a cart of food. He decided to question him and took the man under custody for selling food without a permit to do it in trains as he told he was allowed by men who belonged to Mankhade. A criminal helped you to establish sir, good for us, the chief said, taking him by the scruff of the neck and ready to book one more case against the local.

The leader doesn't have any change as he knows the police can only catch the lower men or those who are not directly connected with it. He stays at his place, eating biryani, smoking, and having fun with the poor families of Balasore at a camping site with pure joy. Thanks for making us at home sir, we are grateful, an old man said as he had his life's first outing with the children of the village in a rich mood feeling happy for the arrangements. It was a kind of festive morale for everyone and other people looked equally joyous too.

I shall be more kind if our plan comes to fruition by the blessings of all of you, the leader said thinking whether it may come true or not. The old man bled to be on board and they felt cheery as they enjoyed the food and talked about the actual tales of past incidents against them by the officials, police, or even locals when they travelled by train which made him feel sad but he knows the time is coming for revenge.

Who had to lose his leg during the late delivery of food on the train? Mankhade simply asked as a limping young man came in front. One who had to lose the whole cousins in a delayed cramping of the inner bogies? One more person came to the front as he asked. Good, all the problems we had to bear shall come to rest in peace on the day coming, the crowd cheered as the leader stepped out, shook hands with tormented souls and he had gone with them, closing the camp with one final look on it.

The people were not sure how many of them may feel sorry for this but one sure thing is that there are more who are going to join their ranks being in pain or having to face problems or losing their families. The source of the criminals only expands when the emotions are burnt to the level where hurt minds try to control their pain to use it more in society. People like Mankhade know how to choose men from this condition and it may certainly help to make their mission come to reality through such schemes.

The moment was coming as voices started to come from a train where people were fighting for food service inside it. There was a very loud horn from the engine as the train tried to avoid a false trap. The whistle of the guard was heard loud on the top and the train suddenly stopped in an outer station with a lurch making few people feel surprised by it as the fear will overtake their smile soon.

What this hell for us now, I need to get medical support and it may miss out if it doesn't reach there in time honestly, a person said looking impatient as other people started to look out from their windows to check. There was one more loud sound, movement on the floor and the train had started to rattle again at top speed going away from the outposts. As most of them felt calm to feel the wave of its sound, there is something hidden waiting and it may stop the pace of it soon.

Now I can get the cool wind on my face to get fresh feelings, a girl in her late 20s said as she was missing her fiance and wondering what he may be doing back home. I like him to see cooking with such a level of business he commands inherited from his father, she thought and more such faces could be visibly worried about what lies in the future as they don't know the fear looming in current and keeps thinking of their dreams, challenges, and pressure in life as humans away from people who like to share pain to kill or get their scores settled planning the bigger picture.

Another train was coming to a certain track with no clue of where the destination may have been. The driver of the train was a huge fan of sports as he was watching cricket instead of focusing on the train. Bet me, the team will get out on 235 or I may give up on sports for my life, he said, turning the steering wheel as the engine kept pulling forward onto the track. There was a signal to stop at a certain place, but the driver didn't respond as he kept lurching forward at top speed with no idea of what may happen next.

From one other side, a train was being loaded as most of its bogies were in the yard to lift. Hurry up, the boss will pay us a very heavy price to do this, the driver said, checking the numbers of bogies that should be missing from it once the crash happens. Are you alright mate? It may be the last day of your life if you ask me, the driver waved to his friends with the air that he was not afraid to worry as he bought tea from a closely-going vendor and felt pleased to be part of the actual scheme.

The express was going up in level, the flow was absolute and the passengers were busy playing cards, munching food, and trying to laugh as a few jokes were cracked. This may be their last moment to enjoy before the horrible moment rises so they must get together to make it worth it. Old people can be seen complaining about life, its miseries, and why it takes so much turn. The doctors on the train were talking about the hardship of serving the public with the blame associated with it. The mood had somehow started to become grim as Balasur was not far now waiting for the destiny of the train to come and let the strike happen simply.

There was a huge sound of an uproar, people were on the floor and suddenly the train crashed. There was the sound of horn from the engine, whistles from the guards and people shouting but it was all becoming a mess in the moment of it. Three trains hit each other without a hint of the time coming and the bogies had got separated from each other due to fierce strikes. The main express felt being hit at top speed by the other one and the portions had toppled over.

The sounds kept coming louder as people started to just realise what had been happening as they had lost too many lives. A few of them had been lying on the floor but had no voice as they were dead from the severe strike. many of them had got injured and it was going to become one of the worst cases to remember for those who had been part of it. They can't believe that one of the most popular trains, one that is best for Eastern travellers from Bengal Orissa and is known for its service, had collided with unknown trains without a hint of it being a possibility.

The government took action against people who had been the main culprits. Mohapatra was first in shock to see the collapse with his eyes but then decided to act fast to round things up. He traced Mankhade with the help of the national investigation agency and brought him over for inquiry. In the lock-up station, many inspectors hit him with severe treatment but Mohapatra's feelings didn't go away as other members had also been caught including Amir and the technician for their crimes.

Any idea how big this had been for us as a loss as servants? The inspector asked and the culprits smiled at him as they now realised how valuable life is no matter how much you make it worse but the people who died are not going to come back to their relatives. The officials had announced financial aid for the damages but it won't bring the dead back as life is already in its severe stage in a few of their relatives and it may be close for now as the closest have died in the train clash.

We did succeed even though we are in jail, I am pleased to be part of it, Amir said, shaking hands with the elated boss who did smile. Our revenge, the people we had lost, is equally settled as they have damages too, they went inside the prison to face charges for their crimes but had no guilt for what happened at the main bazar location. Their plan had come to actual reality in the form of the train clash as they witnessed it all with their eyes truly satisfied by the result.

Time smiles on everyone as it has seen it all come and pass with effects on life. NO one can consume the severe effects with one being the ultimate observer but time knows everything, what happened, who was involved and why scores were settled by both parties onto each other. Families had been torn, dead bodies were set for last right ceremonies and the media as ever continues to comment on railway safety but it will not restore the damages and the pain shall stay forever making its final remark on hearts.

7
The Flute Seller's Truth

It was a calm day with a lot of people being out on the shore playing with fun. The sea was vivid, blue with its quiet waves and people splashing in the waters with pure happiness. A lot of voices were coming from young ones who like to be close to the sand rather than going inside the waters. The parents showed them how to dip in with their swimming suits so they could feel comfortable while going inside.

The places are well known not only for Indian heritage but throughout the world due to their actual influence. Goa preserves certain heritage not only in the blue backdrop where children can be seen splashing water on each other but much more to be seen. The truth is that it is hidden in its palaces, the culture within it as inspired people of multiple communities, and they can be observed while trying to mull over the beliefs as they gather around certain places for their cult.

People can be seen widely in churches, certain groups can be seen with practices of Hindu ideology in the temples close to the seashore with chanting of mantras, and a lot of other groups have witnessed either selling or trying to get their families to stand together in light of what the place offers to them as Goa does hide a secret in it too and it can aspire crimes.

Few people could be seen selling small toys to tourists at low rates, baking on to their cross-coded bakers, or sitting quietly in the sun as it becomes more than warming into the sun for them. It was a perfect day, no clouds in the sky and everyone was ready to enjoy themselves. Goa is somehow always known for its beaches so people like to be part of it touring the place for the best ventures.

It is not just beaches we have ma'am, a flute seller said to people who were talking about the rich Beach culture. We crave to boast few great historic eminence hardly any of the beach area may possess as a masterpiece, he said showing a kind of sand statue in small size to excite them. He said that they are rare to come by, designed by experts and he would be delighted if they would wish to buy one of it.

Do you have one in brown colour? That's what fonds me more than others, a lady in her early 40s said, asking to buy out a piece. For a moment the seller took his flutes down, produced a brown shape from inside the packaging, and handed it to her. I don't belong to your country. I can pay you in a global currency if it's easy, she said in her foreign tone as the man felt gratified. She paid him 20 dollars, checked out the quality of the figure, and had gone to take the small piece with pride.

Many people like to come to the flute seller asking for such packages and the locals had never enquired him what they contained inside them. He says they do presume to have a unique glow that is preserved in them due to which they are sold heavily in foreign currency to people around. Few of the locals had felt suspicious of what he might fill them with but he told them they were not his creations which meant someone else gave him the order to sell and get his or her commission by them.

Drugs, are they inside the piece? A female person felt strange as she thought so. Vimona is a kind of spy, she deals with persons who sell such pieces of carved statues but she has not been able to trace the right trails by now. I may wonder where that lady came from. She doesn't look to be from Abroad, instead she feels to be an Indian Christian, she said thinking to take action and then calling the local police to find or trace such pieces in recent times.

Vimona is a young lady in her late 20s. She is charming by the looks of it and belongs to a mixed family as her mother was a Parsi and her father was a Christian who married after 4 years of their dating life in Goa after a lot of experience of personal life already being together. She was born in the state herself so she knows the culture better compared to what is being told to the tourists outside by those who handle the terms. She has sharp brown eyes, a perfect-thinking brain, and the knack to cross things out without even being described to her.

The level by which she can crack hidden clues makes her special when it comes to serving the police as a detective. She knows how to investigate, checks for smaller details sharply, and is known to crack down on things that come with hidden promises due to which she is interested in the smaller statues. She guessed that they contain some sort of materials in heavy strength and soon she will be able to crack the whole plot down if it goes well with her skills.

A single file told her enough that the pieces were indeed used for criminal activity in the area. The spy thought about the flute seller and was not sure whether she wanted to find him the next day or not in the market. It was so easy to search out selling the statues to people without any fear openly. She decided to trick him if he came to do it again the next day as he may wish to sell it more and the police can take him under whatever section is suitable.

Give me a blue carved painting, Vimona told the man as he came to sell out his final pieces. I have only 3 left to miss, Why not try all of them? Pay me 3k as a discount and they all shall be yours, Vimona had a smile while taking the package that held 3 items in it. A smile came over her as she could see a vehicle coming closer and she was feeling calm to see it.

A look on the vehicle coming and she had pressed one of the items in her hands tightly. Please don't do that. My whole effort shall be ruined from the part as the material comes out, she slapped him before he could say a word and the seller felt worried due to it not knowing her to be a spy. I know what kind of material It contains. I am afraid it can land you in jail, The expression of the person became blank as she said and he was still worried about the strength by which she had hit him strongly earlier.

You are under arrest Mr. Recardo for selling drugs in pretense of the artwork to the public, a voice said and the man tried to run out as an impulse, Great job Vimona. I am pleased with the way you tricked him, Nathidas, the local inspector chief said as he took the man by his grip and dragged the person with handcuffs taking him over. You are just the beginning of the entire chain. I wonder what else the other may do to sell drugs, he said, forcing the man to come with him in his vehicle.

Vimona was content that a step had been taken as she had been shouting about something being fishy in the decorated pieces from the start when she first saw the seller. The police had told her to find proof of what made her feel so negative about them and now she has helped in the strategy. The traces of metal and the forensic test shall tell them the kind of drug inside that is used to fill them and why they are so potent.

However, the lady in her 40s had not been seen ever since she bought a piece paying in global currency for her liking. Neither the seller confessed to containing the money as he had sent it to someone else who had demanded it. Things may be more critical somehow like the beasts resting in the deep waters and the police need her too as she may be involved in the whole process or might be the leader of the crimes somehow connected to it.

I was told to take the statues into the market, Recardo said as the police started to treat him in the jail. I was asked to take them or deport them by the port so the foreigner can take them, he said as he was beaten up but the police were not satisfied. Who did ask to sell it, sir? I don't think you just picked up the package and started to sell it by yourself? Nathidas seems to be in fury as he asks him as he has finally recognized the plot.

A man by the name of Cardos brought the package, the man finally spoke and the inspector felt deeply shaken. Cardos was a man of foreign descent, he was known for his crimes in India and if he came back, then it would be more than worse for the people of Goa due to his grand schemes. When did he give you the package sir? The inspector asked and Recardo said that he handed the package last Sunday on the beach as he was selling flutes. The man told them that Cardos may certainly come back and distribute more such packages at cheaper rates to other people so they get used to it.

The next day one more spy joined them by the name of Vijayan who was renowned for his skill in tracing drug paddlers. We are aware they work in a team, we should separate ourselves or the base won't be revealed, he told Vimona as they planned to watch them with drugs. Sir, I may also like to take my informants on the go if you like to, a police inspector by the name of Kalyan said looking for some trace as he sent a message to find more people selling drugs in hidden form.

The chief felt he had few backups as he engaged in a fierce way to find how things had been folding in the capital of Goa but a new case had come as they went through their search. The chief received a call from the official receiver and he was told that a dead body had been traced on the beach. The informant said they are not able to find who the man may be, but asked police to come quickly to the spot.

Vijayan, are you coming with me? I suspect the case is related, Nathidas said and the detective agreed. They sat inside the jeep honking away and soon reached the spot. Clear away all of you. Please don't touch the body, the chief said, coming closer to the scene as he saw the person was thrust inside the sand by force and he had to remove it to see the closer marks on to the neck that hints at a severe scuffle.

A sharp weapon, probably a knife or a shrewd one, Vijayan said, looking at the body closely. I shall try to figure out what he may be doing here, the chief said, asking the locals when they saw the man first. I was the one who called you sir. I saw the man lying as I tried to collect sand to create a clay toy for my child, a man appeared at the front with goggles and the inspector asked him with benign interest about the way this man had been traced.

Anything else? I mean did he have any bag, luggage, or anything that can help further to know him? He asked for some way to find out any clues. Yes, an instrument. I saw a guitar lying here on the floor somewhere, the man said as the Inspector waved a hand in thanks and gesture they would find it. After 15 minutes of searching, Vijayan had located the guitar inside and deeper and he felt something strange about it.

This is my field. I know what it contains honestly, the detective said, taking an instrument out from his pocket to check. This tracks the presence of drugs it is specific for it, he said with a smile. There was a smoke that billowed, a kind of strange sound, and the strings of the guitar had broken with a zing sound. Something came out from the handle as it broke apart and Vijayan punched the air with his fist as he felt certain that the case was connected somehow with drugs.

Hello, This is Vaidyanath speaking. What can I do for you? The person on the other side said as Vijayan connected in a call. any track of recent drug cases filled in musical instruments sir? He asked with some surprise as the other person laughed. Always on the negative side of the nodes, are we always going to be like this sir? He said as Vijayan clapped from the other side with a whistle.

He told him to be patient and that he would respond to him as soon as the spies may have been told what they were looking for on the beaches. Vijay had problems with time, but he had enough patience as he knows drug cases go long and they may have to be braver to catch the right people involved in it as he tapped Nathidas on the shoulder to get going with the process.

Vimona had also been connected to find whether any new brand of guitar had come into the market. This is similar to the way you caught the flute seller, isn't it missing? Vijayan said to her, calling the spy next. Yes, I know what to do, I am sure there may be some sales on offer, she smiled as the phone disconnected. The police chief hinted that they should take the dead body for forensic testing and the spy agreed. They called the helper from the nearby lab to send the body and the case was getting on the right terms now.

I may ask you to get more men, sir, this can be tricky as we go through the process as a whole, another junior inspector tipped the chief as he tried to sit quietly in the evening after the fieldwork in the fiery afternoon. I may ask you to bring me one more chilled apple drink, the heat gives me some sort of frustration you know, he said asking the person to follow and he took the orders simply. It may be possible that Cardos might be coming but there was no wind of what he may be doing and the chief felt worried he had his hand on his head thinking it over.

As the drink came, the chief felt calm as he sipped fast and felt thankful to the junior who waved it was nothing and they should get going for the case as a challenge for them. I will ask Tushar to be involved in it if he agrees, he used to be the best in the past, the chief said recalling the time when he used to work under the retired person and the junior obliged feeling it may be the right way to settle it.

Vijayan had sent a photo online to the chief showing a man with an expensive guitar in his hand. Trace this if you can. Am sure he is the direct drug paddler in Goa for now, the text message was sent alongside it. I do know who this is,

Don't worry, the chief replied and Vijayan felt calm hoping to visit him the next day to figure out the case further as the battle continued to rage in his mind thinking how to close the actual deal.

The chief was trying to find where the man had gone who he knew well from the past. He tried to connect and finally, after the 3rd call in a row, Tushar answered feeling a bit distressed. Yes bro, how are you? Is there anything I can help you with? He said with a polite interest to talk. The junior told him the process and the way cases had risen and Tushar laughed like he was familiar with how it had been in a Goa-like state as politicians command the whole circle of it.

I am looking to find some of my old friends to figure out a large deal to capture those who we missed out, Tushar told the junior, mentioning the names of Cardos, Banfi, and one other who he had forgotten to be on the top list. I am guessing that Carddos has set a false trail, He will not dare to come to India, Nathidas said with some hint of the deal to be on the right course. The senior thought he had been wise to compare the situation and wished him luck as the trial was still on for the men outside India.

Meanwhile, in the Konkan area, Vijayan had been in a hard-fought battle with someone in the evening. He had arrived here after receiving sharp information on attaching guitar handles with drugs and couldn't resist himself. He was hit by someone from behind as he was almost able to trace the chemicals and felt a bit surprised by it. After two turns of the hit from both men, Vijayan made the other one fall on the ground as he struggled with raw pain from the strike.

The man chasing stood to fight again and hit a hard punch while in response the spy had hit him on the face directly. The fight started to become intense and Vijayan had to take the option as he had no choice left except to kill him. Don't do that. I swear I was not sent to fight with you actually, the man requested as the spy took a short pistol, turned into the air, and before the man could run, he was shrewdly hit. Three bullets went on to his chest, there was a noise and he was dropped onto the floor but dead by the strike.

I don't need to ask who you are, Vijayan whispered into the air with some style. You have been hunted by the Maharashtra police for years and we have all the list of your crimes, he said, sending the photograph to the chief inspector with gratitude from the other side for closing the old drug peddler case with ease. I am on to hunt more if the time will permit, the spy texted him and it was still on as he marched towards the waterfall, found 2 men smoking dubes and he was ready to charge onto them.

There was a flash of light from a metal device and the drug was destroyed which made the men fume with disgust. Where did it go? We bought it at such a heavy price, they looked into their empty hands drenched in liquid and then at the man who had sent the light flashing by a device. They rounded on him as he may be the one who destroyed it. The first man-made Vijayan fell onto the floor while the other one took out his gun to question and wished to finish him off, but they didn't know it was a trick.

In charges of attacking an official and forcing him to be on the floor, You shall be punished, the spy said, taking out his official pass and with some courage standing up as he took the gun from the hand of one who was holding it in open hands. He turned the throttle down, fired two bullets and the first one died simply by it. He rounded up on the other who decided to run but the spy had thrown him onto the floor like they did earlier.

I may like to settle my score if you please Nayak sab, the spy smiled, punching him on the cheek and then they started to fight as the spy hit him brutally with his legs. After 15 minutes of heated battle with wounds and cuts to both sides, Vijayan had finished firing more bullets and he shouted before falling onto the ground to have mercy as he would kill him.

You are also missing from years. I shall be happy to close these cases before Cardos is forced to come, the spy whispered as the man died, making everything go silent. He kept staying busy as people came to see who had been dead and sent more images to the police personnel. The police branches were feeling joyous in different states by seeing them finished as they were all connected to past cases and had been on the hit list of drug crimes from years before they were traced by Vijayan.

I am looking for the man who ordered all of these to figure out the actual damage, Vijayan tried to find more men on the loose as he sent a few texts and he was able to ask the chief to send some men to cover the Konkan coast as there may be more people vanished from the trial. I am sure you will be able to find those who have been on the run and I shall like to catch them off guard, he smiled, sending a text to the chief and it may be on the track soon if they can find the missing links in the whole case.

Far across the sea, it was very close to the port as a ship was approaching it inside the waves. Someone could be seen at the above side of it as a few crew members shouted to get permission and bring the ship in by order of the port. Their word was accepted with the flanks of the flags changing as they entered Portugal so they needed to change. Everywhere when the ship enters into a new country, the flags shift to the boundary and the crew is well practised to do it as they have been with the ship for a long time as workers now.

A man could be seen sitting inside a cabin right behind the main captain's room and he was smoking with his famous pipe. Cardos may look like a known burk of round 28 but his face says it all being gaunt and totally ready to be like a demon who likes to play with his food first. He had already killed 3 other partners in the ship, throwing them into the sea from the top of the dock, and wanted to get more money. They had said no to his Venetian drugs and he had gotten angry and denied such a perfect chance.

I wonder when I shall see home, I want to deliver these, he grunted, drinking a potion he had made himself as the ship was approaching. ah there they are, lights of the home port, delicious, he saw them from the window as the darkness was getting low with the ship coming out from a sea tunnel openly. It rose like a cork, there was a sound of hul being lowered with hard canal-like swishes and the ship had reached the port finally with its horn sounding absolutely to their ears.

Cardos checked for his bag, found the drugs missing to be in the secret pocket, and stood up to come out alongside others as he hit someone to follow on the back by the local boat. I am interested, Just let me come out from the official place, the man said, following him quickly and they went in a rush. Cardos had a lot of followers here and he wore a mask to avoid them and he finally left the port after 30 minutes of hard travel as he reached his place in calm talking to his family about the trip.

What happened to them? I can't believe it's done, he had switched back to English from his country's language as an online call was received by him. The Indian forces have gathered to break the master plan, a voice answered from the other side as Vaidyanath was talking to him. It was a hard fact but the person had been in league with the foreigners for the money or he would have told the guitar seller already to Vijayan. Alright then, I will see what I can do for my followers in a great country like India for drugs, Cardos replied to him with a kind of snarl.

He was in deep thought smoking one more pipe and looking a bit worried as he disconnected the call. He sent messages to South Africa and they told him all was in order.

He sent more texts to Venice and they too reported everything to be safe. He was not going to trust the information as Indian forces can be severe once they come to strike. They may look simple and quiet, but if they start to dare, then the level becomes out of your grip so the man wants to fix the course before his whole business shall be tampered again.

One more phone rings and Cardos is on the receiving side again as there is one more order for him. Sir, I am Kartar from Patiala in India. I am looking for visa help sir, the caller said and Cardos obliged. What shall I get in response If I help you? He said with a sneer as he knew what he may have by conversing with Punjabis in India as they do help him circulate his packets without much checking by the locals at the main places as they switch hands.

The deal to send it to Ottava is ready sir in Canada. You won't have to face any tariffs while they are sent through air rather than ships, the person said with a smile as Cardos too felt grateful. Where do you want to send people with free visa access? Send me details, I will try to fix them up, the Portuguese said with a sneer and the phone call ended as he felt somehow safe that Indian forces were still not after him and he could plan to check for the Gulf of Aden or may think to visit it soon.

Back in India, Vijayan had caught a few People who belonged to Kapurthala but had come to travel around Goa. We are sent by a man on the hunt as a spy sir, a few of them said as he sent them to the main prison for questioning. Todi gall feeki pad jandi si, the chief told them in Punjabi and they felt miserable as few hockey were used before they confessed to being in touch with the drug paddler Cardos who promised them to send them to foreign in exchange for selling his drugs in India.

Very well, we may also have to visit Punjab then. Are you ready to do so Apoorva now? The chief asked and a policeman was revealed wearing the official dress with a cap. Yes sir, I shall be going there, It will be a perfect way to leave then, he said in his strong voice, and the jeep was summoned to drop him off. It shall take your time to simply adjust there, I will find you, my friends to help then Nathidass said and he smiled while leaving the place with some work to do for the police.

Tell the people to be on high alert. Our men shall disturb the surface again with huge ripples in it, the chief told Vijayan and he did as he was asked. Vimona had been able to find some guitar packages in an open street and they were left without a delivery note; she told the boss that they had traced them. Apporva had started to act just as he had attacked one man and with his police movements as more damages were done to the drug paddlers inside India with anguish.

Vaidyanath kept alerting Cardos on how his Punjabi friends had been captured in regular time. There was no news of Punjabi folk as he may have gone underground but Apporva knows how to trap the opponents. Similarly, in Goa, people were trying to hide a few bags which were filled with drugs and the police had traced them. Vijayan was sure that there was someone amongst them who was passing false information and he wanted to catch the person before it got too late to reach him by any means.

A call comes to Vaidyanath by a charming lady asking to meet him. For a moment he felt who may have called him this late in the night but then he decided to go. I am looking for someone to fulfil my wishes as my husband is not in the city this week, she said in a quiet voice and he felt this may be the right time to let his desires be fulfilled. He asked her to meet on his colony's corner and thought to take his short gun with him just as a precaution.

It was the kind of night Vijayan was looking to thrill the man for his last musings. He crept in pretence to let the lady come first who was a spy member from his community.

Vaidyanath came quietly first, checked for any intrusion, and then started to walk calmly. a hand grips him, right from behind by force and knocks him over as he tries to find the lady out. Hello sir, I wanted to see your strength before you meet a hot lady, the spy said, hitting him with punches as blood started to come out from his nostrils.

He felt unable to speak as Vijayan had been on song as he started to hit him and he felt cheated. This is what we felt too. The day I came to know you had been sending all the updates to Cardos, one more slam, on to the forehead and the man was turned over on the floor. My trick shall be over as I wish the lady to finish you out sir, he said, asking for the fellow member to step up. She came out from behind, took her gun and fired 2 times in the sky as her feelings got over her and she killed the informer.

Thanks, sir, he killed my parents and I finished him, she said, holding her emotions for the night. It's fine, I knew Cardos would come again and now It is the time when his story shall be closed once and for all, the girl had been a victim of the drugs case as her family members used to serve Cardos in the past. One day Vaidyanath tricked them to become the most trusted as he took him by the sea, drowned her boat and they were killed as Cardos was caught just after the act.

From that day onwards, she had wanted the Indian dead by her own hands. She knew the chances would come and now she has done it as Vijayan reports the case to the chief who feels ecstatic as he did suspect Vaidyanath too. They had gone into his room, had taken a warrant of the search for police-level investigation and they found evidence clearly that suggests foul play by him expressing and exchanging confidential information abroad to help someone.

Vijayan got something that may help them with the case as he opened the inner hidden drawer of the owner. It was a secret number written on a file, one that belongs to boats that are not registered under legal rules and there is not much left here to worry about. He called the ship authorities and was in a much better mood once they assured him that the number belonged to boats that were not registered in their system. As the process became final, he was ready to help his country and this may be the last dice to the throne.

This will lead us to the main villain, I was hoping to get such a fact somewhere, he whispered, taking the lady with him so she could be cleared from legal charges and be allowed to lead a happier life. They collected all the items to be sent for lab testing and wondered whether there shall be anything they had missed. Are you sure the boat belongs to the heir of Vygaudas? She asked and he raised a hand feeling that someone may still be here so they must keep the information private not talking on the subject as they walked away.

The morning was very pleasant for the chief who ordered his favourite breakfast. People from Punjab had been taken into custody, Cardos may have to face pressure as he might cancel the plan to visit the Gulf of Aden and they have all the tariffs received from the boats they had sent to search under waters in the night. Vijayan had got the job done by finishing Vaidyanath and the case was in their grip. They are indeed closing in somehow rounding up all the agents involved. Will they succeed or will Cardos trick them again with his skills?

The time is ticking as it watches over the process and slightly people are in a happier mood as they come and go around the famous tourist attractions. Vijayan alerts a few people on the short that they remain away as there may be heavy rains on the shoreline. The weather was clear with no clouds but they understood what he meant by the code words. It may be some sort of plan he is thinking as he discussed it with the chief to send extra men the coming night being their best plan to catch the boat bobbing in the sea.

If you predict this, then I am with you bro, a voice said from the phone as the chief was talking to Tushar. Yes Vijayan, I will send them as my retired senior also agrees on the plan, he said, looking at the detective coming to talk and finish the case. They sat thinking it over and decided to make a secret raid no matter how many people may be involved, firing them from the other side of the encounter as these men were capable of clearing the blows.

Take some extra bullets, just for a round-up the chief told Vijayan, filling up his gun and taking sea grenades for rapid fire. We are on the coast soon, better have life jackets too, they switched the protection and counted the striking weapons. It was about time that they got involved and let it settle with their strength.

Apoorva made the feeling better as he had finally caught the Punjabi inside a hotel as he was trying to offer drugs to a servant for long-term business benefits. He traced the man and made a strong plan to come and it worked for the team so he sent his photo to the chief as weapons were exchanged at the station for scrutiny. Here more serious things were going in current through feelings of nerves by two strong fighters being heard for one single cause as they prepared to capture the main drug dealer.

The fishermen were reporting news of the water level rising to lower police members as they didn't want them to go there at night. Informers of course. They are paid to do the foreigner's bidding and have to be in their control, The lady told the fact to Vijayan who had killed Vaidyanath and they were trying to make this a short-time affair settled once and for all. A few other team spies had also come who had lost their family in similar ways and it was going to be neck to neck inside the sea in the battle as it rose with waves making a crackling sound inside the calm waters.

There was a voice from a boat, horns of the moving paddles, and one sound that pierced the worst. Vijayan had blasted a vessel, hitting it directly with an underwater motor bomb. OH no, they are here. What shall I say to the master, a man said looking at the destruction as the whole vessel had exploded. Vijayan was not going to stop, there was a smash, the sound of boat guns and people were dying more easily than they could think as the forces started to emerge under the waters swooping on their prey.

I have not come here to let you destroy, one more man loudly shouted as he was sent into the deep waters head first as the chief shot him without much trouble with his gun. Search for them. It's time we bring things under control by our grip, a naval officer wearing Indian robes commanded from the top, and more blasts could be heard coming from the patrolling parties. Oh yes, I have got the machine, Vijayan said as they kept firing on the opponents inside the waves with pure strength

There was a count of 3, a sound like something launched from the machine by true power, and the raft coming towards them with drugs of extreme cost had been destroyed by the strike that happened due to its light. I demand you to stop this or I kill the men I had sent from India under visa abroad, a voice note spoke in the chief's phone who smirked as it came and he played it for everyone to hear inside the waters fighting hard.

He decided to reveal the master plan to everyone as they watched both in fear and glee. You don't know what we have in store for you, do you? He called a secret inspector to come forward and he wrote the text as a reply. The inspector dragged a man by the scruff of the neck who had been captive for days in the prison and forced him to speak as Cardos was soon falling into their trap to settle things off.

Uncle, I am sorry. They had caught me and have kept me here, Cardo's lungs were empty and they had no air as he heard the voice. It was his nephew, Ricardo who was a famous musical person from Portugal and had gone to India.

His team had sent him drug packages and Vaidyanath had told him that he had been missing but now he knew where he had gone. Come to India, Cardos to take him back sir. We are not cruel like you. We will keep him safe as you come, the uncle felt worried for the first time in his life and decided to take his revenge in India.

He sent a group message for all the people to come back, dropping the fight. Few of the boats that were on the surface were gone out of sight and the deported luggage had returned to the Gulf of Aden for exchange. Indian forces wanted to finish this but they wanted it by word of one who is behind the whole process to end this finally by their skill as the leader shall be in their strong grip soon.

Great job, Kushal. You stayed behind and ensured Recardo can't escape, the chief tapped a junior inspector on the shoulder who had a moustache and felt calmly pleased for the process done till now. He reminded them that this is Cardos they are dealing with and they must be prepared as a secret boat had come on the shoreline demanding to find his old friend back in the group and strike with raw power.

Vijayan was there to check on the receiving end and took out the secret number he had got from Vaidyanath's drawer before they had gone for the strike. As the details matched, the change of schemes started to happen pretty fast. He felt the frustration in the air with true hatred of the person as the gaunt and tall bulky figure stepped out with the true purpose of killing everyone. There was a billow of smoke, a strange metal cling, and the sound of guns as he had killed a few informers who couldn't update him on time for his nephew.

Vijayan had hit him fiercely but he hardly moved, throwing a fist towards him fiercely. A roar was heard from behind as a naval officer pulled the man onto the floor. My wish comes true, Cardos. Last time you tricked us, but not this time, it was hardly any worry for the spies as naval forces had caught the man they had been hoping for years and Vijayan was asked to leave with gratitude for his services as they would deal with it from here.

No problems this time Cardos I have permission from your government. They too are not happy with your crimes to tell you the truth, one more officer stepped in and showed him the official documents to proceed. Any other statement you have before we do the honours? Three of the naval officers stepped as they showed the track of his illegal drugs at the Hambantota port, the Guardar port and in the Malavi basin that made him feel shocked on how much they knew about him.

Bring Recardo. He has been part of the whole treasure, the leading officer said as Kushal came in holding the man with him brightly. The nephew saw the uncle surprised and then fearing for what was to come. The last 2 members of the family if the data is correct, the officers said as they raised something in the air. 3. 2. 1. Fire, the anti-aircraft gun launched countless blasts in a few minutes and the drug dealers had been finally sent to hell with their crimes settled by the official course.

There were noises louder than ever in the naval basin as all the men congratulated each other. The chief was recommended to have an award for cracking out the whole case and the mood couldn't be better there. As Vimona and Vijayan were blessed with recognition for what they did during the process, the case had somehow come to the close with its impact to stay for long in the society.

8
The Forbidden Waters

It was a dark evening, clouds were hovering in the sky and so it was filled with rain. The sea was opening its arms wide with water pulses, ready to strike and no power could control its fall as it is known to bring huge waves. Fishermen were still on the shore trying to catch fish for their children as they may wish to earn and this is the only way they can do it simply.

The lightning flashed into the sky as they saw a strange image like someone had made it occur without making much effort in the sky. Few of them didn't fear what may come as they tipped their fellows to go across and try to get a hideout. They were ready to lift the boats, hang on to the life, and simply sell their fish out into the other section of the islands. The only trouble is that they were not allowed to do trade or even enter those boundaries.

I suggest we take a chance, that's the only way we can survive, the man on the lead said as he let his boat sail around and the other men followed him with impatience. If we are caught, I should say that it may be worse for our families, forget to face or weather the storm coming, he said without a fierce look but the boats in front kept moving so the other fishermen had no choice left but to keep following.

Just take my word, when I say you have to hide, do the same and we shall be safe for a longer time here, they did trust him as he had protected them in these islands before. This was not the first time they had to cross the water territory and thrust themselves into a different place. On my word, keep your boats hidden, he said as a few men started to emerge inside the water jumping in and out to check any movement as spies so they could report to their officials.

Sri Lanka is a peaceful place, You can see the best views that are visible from the sea being the best but for outsiders, rules are tight, especially in the marine waters. The government is strict about giving any rights or allowing people of other countries to do fishing, even if they don't leave any stone unturned, taking the order seriously. They had taken steps and had arrested Indian men in the past due to fishing close to their waters and kept protecting the boundaries with pride.

No men sir. I checked the strait from where they come, a young man of 25 reported to his boss on the phone. Check the hidden sale boats, and connected ivies and I shall be fine if the government punishes the intruders, the senior said with a smile as he looked bemused but totally on course for the government. In the past few months, the problems they had to face have come down to being minimal as the internal pressure had been deduced but it doesn't mean that they can allow India like bigger neighbours to do direct fishing in their territory.

Dhamika, This is Vudaru speaking. Any certain trace of the fishermen from outer countries in recent times in our country sir? The senior had sent a call to the other naval official who was on the shore checking. Sir, I am keeping an eye, there is some movement from a few people underwater. I shall be able to track them and report to you soon, finally the official felt pleased as there may be few people for him who can be captured and taken to the courts to arrange the trials.

The head fisherman had stopped looking for a place to hide out. This looks like the right place to cover ourselves for now from the threat looming, he felt pleased asking the others to go in as he said the words and they had simply got themselves covered. The voices became low as 12 fishermen went in following the leader and they had managed to find a way till the storm became quiet in the sea after which they may go back.

What if they catch us, We don't have any choice? One of the young fishermen asked as the leader shook his head sadly. No choice except the trial by the court. You have no lawyer to defend. No choice to escape from the place and even the tagline of an Indian is of any help as they simply send you to jail my friend, he smirked with his pointed beard getting drenched which he cleared with his supple cloth with some hesitation in his face.

I hope we can go back or it may not be good for our families if you ask me honestly, the leader said and told them to get some rest from the tiring efforts in the waters done a few hours ago. They may need to think of the returning plan as the threat is not too far from them and spies can make their life worse than ever here. It is prudent to have a cover as they report the officials first and the leader told 2 men to keep an eye close to the entering stone from where they came to this place.

Fear of being caught is worse when you are in someone else's land. The leader had lost his elder brother the same way last summer when he had travelled with him to cover the souring storm. They had dipped in, turned their boats, and had almost been trying to get off when a Sri Lankan personnel had caught his brother. With no choice to leave besides where he may face the trial, Vyangar had left back to take the duty to do for his family and it pinches him when he remembers this from the past as a painful face-off.

The pride in the country is not the only thing for which fishermen have been taken from other countries. They are matters of money involved in it as People who catch them are rewarded. This is not much known to other countries but people in the Lankan court are taken with trials and as long as they are held hostage, it does give certain officials get in touch with monetary delights.

This is so complex that the country's highest court has not been able to trace out the inner layers connected to it and people like Vudaru do feel pride to gain by its effect. They do capture fishermen from local countries demanding them to connect to a certain inner circle where they can ask for money. A case from Thailand did take place where the officials failed as one of their supporting men had been killed, but apart from it, the other element has been working well so they continue to plan further with hopes that they will remain safe under it.

Officials like Dhamika are fed well by the stronger circles so they can't raise their voices high. The legal process is complex and does take time even in this country the corrupt officials take advantage. They gained a huge amount by the inner fight that happened last year but now their banks are not in the vision to gain more so they need remittance to connect. However, Dhamika had been given 2 flats for his family so he is not going to complain about the things that may be going on here simply.

I suggest you keep quiet about our deal or you know what can happen to your family, a person had told him as he was thinking of turning over the records of captives despite being paid so high with touches from the benefits people get under him. I honestly don't like it. The day India will know what we have done, he is looking into revolt but then his land and the people to whom he is responsible don't allow him to turn over to a native country and he keeps his mouth shut being closer to his birth land than ever.

He keeps the records on track as Valemalla has called again to send documents containing the recent arrests and the value it may prove if they are taken to prison. Sending in an hour, please wait sir, he texts the person feeling a bit relaxed, and sits there smoking a cigarette as the puff of some dust rises and he clears it. The man looks to be pure but has a weakness that lets him serve those who want to continue to commit bigger crimes openly using him for their benefits.

A phone rings on the other side of the shore as Vallamala tries to figure out the number on the device. He couldn't trace it but thought it may be from an official so he decided to pick it up. Come to the dock quarters in Room no. 27, It's urgent, alright? He heard the person say, sounding like a fisherman who could be a spy, and without thinking the receiver stepped up and simply left as the file was shown in digital format sent by Dhamika online to him and he sneered at being able to take a close look at it.

Welcome sir, I have some good news to deliver for you, the person said as he approached the room. He asked Vallamala to come closer to the room so he could show him some details. What kind of people they are? Means Which country do they belong to, the person smiled as he took him quietly inside for a talk. The visitor still didn't realise it might be a trap and simply stepped in getting habitual to dark in the room to get some unique clues by the person himself.

The man gave hardly any hint about nature. There was no news on the number of fishes caught either and Vallamala felt strange to see him standing there as he let the things fold over. The place was quieter than before with no certain case to argue, hardly anyone talking and they could be only men who had been standing here gazing into each other for further statements as the one who had called started to move trying to start the conversation with some strange anguish on his face.

The news is sir that you will be leaving this world today, the man said, now taking advantage as he hit Valamala from behind with a sharp knife. I may be not familiar to you but my family does remember the night you caught them, the man said, sneering better than him as Vallamala felt pain in his neck being hit by a sharper weapon. Soon the official had been thrown into the floor and the man towered on him willing to finish the person making it happen in this particular room.

Do you know this room, sir? It's the place where my cousin was sentenced by your evidence after you caught him on the shoreline. I am glad to finish you here in the same room, there was a final lurch from his hands, a shout that made the room's calm wind rattle and Vallamala was no more dead by an unknown person in this room with one of the simplest tricks ever known to cause such a murder.

The fisherman looked at the man dead with some contentment, thanked the heavens for making him fall for the trick, and had gone from the place. Before going he had rung the summoning bell so people could come to find what may have happened in the quarters and can do scrutiny. This place arranged the process to call people by a bell that is directly in touch with the main officials but Valamala didn't get the chance to ask for his trial. The case had already been decided and all he could get was the final sentence that ended his corrupt life through the possible act.

A horn had sounded in the area as the fisherman went away without any guilt. He didn't surrender to the police as there were more cases he wanted to fix in the country. However, the tunnel where the Tamil fishermen had been resting had to face sudden smashing as the men tried to catch them for money as the fishermen tried to run off for their lives against them.

Vyangar was a brave man and he struck the men coming by with his fists telling others to go as it was his orders or they would pay. They didn't wish to simply follow his orders but he chose to fight with the officials inside the waters rather than go quietly like his brother had done when facing the court trials. He was going to ensure to do maximum damage so the trap set for the fish wouldn't prove of enough golden treasure as the corrupt official considered it.

There was a strange light as he gripped fist to fist fighting with 4 men together. Three of the men scuffling were taken back with some brutal force as the secret member reached the spot after killing Vallamala. He punched one man to fall back and kicked the other 2 and now Vyangar did have company as he joined the secret keeper breaking the jaws of the men quarreling with him as they shouted with agony inside the waters and the action was raging further becoming more wild.

One more time. For the true Lankan heritage sir. This is not the area officially ruled out from the past law, the secret keeper said, taking his harpoon with the purpose of killing which he had sneaked straight through the throat of the first man with no mercy. no, please, this is not my time to fall on. I will be deeply insulted, the other person said who may be the leader of the pack and the man was killed simply trying to avenge the damage to his fellows done by the killer.

I can't be more than thankful to you sir, honestly you saved me, Vyangar said in Tamil as the other one obliged with the right phrase. This is not the area that is restricted but they do crimes to get money. I am trying to make a better Lanka if possible, the visitor nodded with gratitude as the Lankan helped him to take the boat to the other side of the waters, and with a huge relief on his face, Vyangar was going home finally having someone who protected him and this will be one of his sweetest memory to cherish in life.

Travana speaking sir. There has been an uproar in the sea if you ask me, A spy informs the officials as a call rings and Dhamika picks it up to find someone had been killed. He was informed that 4 of their best naval men had been missing from the spot after they tried to capture a group of Tamil fishermen in certain waters and had been under high command. Hours later the 4 dead bodies were recovered from the sea and they were confirmed to be the same men who had gone to capture outsiders inside the sea. It made him feel angry to find his men dead but he can't do much about it.

Dhamika was also told of a dead body publically found but the officials were not able to recognize him as the neck split had made the face miserable later. The chief scoffed on hearing it as further argument kept happening on who he could be. He was found in the inquiry area and they can't identify who he is? Disgusting, he said that he was coming soon and would see who the person may be as surely it must be from their side again who had done the damage or could be worse.

Half an hour later Dhamika felt disturbed with huge panic as he had identified Vallamala to be dead with brutal force. His best friend's face was crunched, there were spot marks, and the neck was broken. No clue may have done this but it gives a possible hint that someone from the secret group might be involved. Dhamika knows the intelligence group that works to protect national pride but he still stands here with guilt about whether to join them or not after seeing all this today.

A phone call confirms that this is not the act of the secret society. The informers have told Dhamika that someone from outside is involved in this to crack the whole mess. He feels more worried as he hears the report and a message flashes. It contained details of someone who had lost his family at the hands of the Lanka judicial trials and Dhamika felt somehow calm as the threat of his security service had gone over and he was ready to take charge of the actual case.

I wonder how you escaped, sir? A few fishermen came with delight to see the boat coming closer and the cloth banner on the top suggested to them who may be coming. Vyangar had reached home as his boat sat down and he had a huge smile. This is more than a miracle, surely someone did help you as they say? The boat owner agreed as he stepped down and handed that the knot to the junior so he can tie the boat from the close by stone pillar carved in his name years ago when he used to be a competitor of river boating.

Thanks for the soup, I do feel drenched after all such mess happened inside the waters, he told his daughter as his wife sat with not many worries to see. Your prayers did work this time, I assure you, he told his wife who had a smile and lot of people had gathered to hear him. He told about the sudden person, one who claimed to live in Sri Lanka and as they were not in restricted water, he survives from the threat without much surprise in his recovered voice talking to everyone.

In one more country few horns could be heard with softer noise, the nation is very closely connected to Sri Lanka but doesn't have such hard restrictions on the fishermen especially when it is warning of a storm. It looks to find solutions rather than capture or kill people in the process to look but there is one thing that can be tricky here. Thailand does look beautiful as it is closely linked with culture and heritage however it has somehow inspired the thought of people to be part of it.

A young man of around 20 had been told off as he was looking for a service which is such that people are not going to talk about it openly in the streets. The massage helping team refused to have him be settled for the famous snake massage and he looked furious to have been refused to get it. A few days earlier the shop owner had promised him to get the massage and now it looked like it had been the word of ages to him as he relished the feeling of a female onto his body honestly.

If you succeed in the task I offer you, It is promised that you will get a massage of high quality, the owner finally said as he stood for hours there with nowhere else to go for the service. The bloke looked perplexed but then thinking it may be once in a lifetime, he agreed to help the owner who told him to be a spy, to bring him some information and ensure it was done without being caught by the officials.

He did not know what to do, be it here or to be in another country as he does have some experience of it from the past with bad memories. At an early age, he had to suffer a lot when he used to spy on outsiders as they may only give him food once he proved them wrong by his spying tricks. Due to the 3rd son in the family, it did put a burden on his parents who were just simple wage-earning middle-class people with not much to share in all 3 children in the home being hungry for their dismay.

He did have the luxury to be convinced quickly by such tricks and managed this habit to be ferocious as he was surely able to earn a lot of pride and food. By his stronger skills, he made the other brothers happy and they had started to make a pack for success. First, the facts were shared and passed through and the spy would crack the doors open of all the complex concerns to finish the task so he could be honoured. This time however it is tough to be on such a high level but he is ready remembering those happy days from the past.

I learned what I am asking after sneaking up on the neighbour's windows in childhood. It won't be tough for me if you ask it, he said, marching away with a paper in hand and pondering over it. Indian men in the Lankan waters. No this doesn't look fitting. I guess this one is more suited, an Indian man betrayed by Lankans who wants to get revenge for the past, he whispered, talking silently. He stopped at a bakery shop, asked for fresh hot buns, and was obliged by the shop owner.

He paid the money from the notes handed by the owner at the massage shop in advance and he felt to be on the actual trail as he smiled taking his order back from the shop. He gazed at something lurking in a clear blue backdrop as a poster for a wanted person, but he didn't feel much interest as he may somehow find out the truth later. For now, he only considers the missing identity of a South Indian who might have committed many crimes to take revenge and that shall be it.

More news had come on how the murders had been rising in numbers. The visitor had killed a lady in her kitchen after taking her purse out in which a photograph of a few people laughing on a court trial was closely preserved safely. He did manage to sneak into an official's room while he was drunk badly and shot him without a word just for the key purpose of revenge. The man was becoming a kind of fear to people as they were not able to trace him by any sharp means and he was taking it as a chance to make his wishes become possible.

Satellite images do help the authorities to get his identity but the face was never clearly visible and he had become a kind of threat and cause of fear as people in Thailand laughed at the news coming with their old rivalry somehow at a better level now. The appointed spy was trying to guess why such a man may look to kill unknown people as he started to search in old newspapers or diaries. He was not able to find much as he asked for old libraries and paid them small tokens so they could be of help to figure out a case that was missing in the past years.

Sir, I have found a case for you, a call rings as the spy is in the bathroom after having a nice shower. He was feeling much better to be on the updates and couldn't resist. Come to the library this evening is a secret story I know but anyone, to be honest, a man said with no fear but a true wish to tell him why the case had been missing. The spy was in a hurry to find all the details but he had to wait for the evening to come as he went to the bakery again and munched a few pastries to fill up his dull mood before the coming moment.

As it struck 6 in the evening, the spy took his hat, put on glasses, and went to the library in a changed identity for a surprise. The man met him on the same pillar where he had been told to come. He gestured to sit with him, and have a cigarette and they both started to strike matches. The man didn't tell his name as he wanted to keep it a secret. He just told him to consider as an informer who was helping him and the story starts as his eyes never went away looking at the spy directly with calm.

The man was simply impressed by the skill of the spy and told him the links connected to the marine places. I was born in Sri Lanka, but my parents took me to India for the visit and I started to become fond of the country, he smiled as the spy looked at him. He told how his childhood was truly inspired by blue scenes and nature being closest to him. I gradually started to hold the culture of both places aloft and My emotions took over, he expressed the fact that he decided to go over to India and live there for the rest of his life.

Why are you telling me all this? I mean how it is connected to the present anyways, there was some impatience in the spy's voice but the man raised his hand for quiet. He continued to explain his case and how he got in touch with Lankan fishermen and they promised him never to reveal his undercover identity serving for their safety as the present spy understood where this may lead to the end once it finished.

We were caught by our people one day you know while on a trip living the rest of the day happily, the man said, taking a newsprint out from his pocket that says the capture of the local fish guards, betrayal to the country' and the spy had got what he wanted as a final verdict of the story. This is what you were looking for, aren't you? What do you think of my case now? The spy checked for the image and he looked up at the man with a fierce gaze towards him almost similar to the young lad in the old photograph.

It was a strange feeling as the young lad of 20 was now clearly seen behind the memory in the eyes of the man looking at him. Both of them trace each other's pains, the past they had struggled with and they sat for a moment in the dim light of the open library. I wish they could have made the trials easy, let my parents stay alive. They didn't do it however, I still regret it, the man said as the spy felt certain that there was not much further pain than your own family dying in front of you and he dared to speak to him.

I am with you. They shouldn't have done this. How will you prove that it was done by the criminal's mate? The spy asked, thinking it hard. You are a professional, it's your job to see how I am going to do this, the man said standing up to leave. He gestured that the person had got what he wanted and now it's up to him whether he wants to reveal him to the police or not. The spy shook his head, let him go and he didn't feel more miserable than before watching the photos in the old news rag with wet eyes.

A horn sounded as the spy came out, police had come somehow as he could see but the man had gone before they could reach here. It may be possible that the massage shop owner had sent them as he was tracking the spies' location by some technical method. The person looked for the man, felt pleased that he was not there and the police had entered. Check the whole place, we got news from Lanka police to find a man on the loose, the Thai guards said as the spy shoved himself to a secret passage, turned right, and went too.

There were sounds of gunfire from somewhere in the night, the man had confronted the secret spies of the Lankan gang and he was on the march. I am known to do the damage before it comes to reality, he sneered, punching a pub manager who was handling the spy network. After 10 minutes of rapid fire, 7 men were knocked onto the floor and all of them were dead by his hands before any other battle could rage against him.

The visitor thought it may not be good for him to have further stay in Pattaya for longer so he decided to take his boat and he shall vanish before anyone came closer to him. He let the waves ripple through his skill of paddling the boats and he shall soon be gone from here as more men tried to search him with his posters circulated by the Lankan police for capture and awarding the one who does that being prize money.

Back in Sri Lanka, Dhamika had been removed from his official home offered by the corrupt group. He had been told that they needed to do renovation until he could find a new one by himself to settle around. I'm not in a position to buy highly accustomed flats sir, he shrieked as the senior came with the documents asking him to clear out the place with his family in the next two days. You have disappointed us, there are not many cases to come. Besides with the murder of our gang even in Thailand, it is getting worse, the senior said handing him the papers and he felt disgusted by it.

I am going to the other side now you have removed me from my place, Dhamika warned the man and he tried to fight with him. I am clearing in 2 days, what's the matter? Can't even wait for just 2 days? He said, throwing the 3 men away as he was known for his physique and the best of their officers was no match against him. They can't allow this to happen but if he goes over, things may not be what they like to presume as he was one of the best fighters in them.

The secret assassin had arrived in India as people were grappling in Lankan waters. He dismissed all the strikes from the elite group, had a close eye on the waves at higher levels, and paddled his boat safely inside the Tamil area to spend some time. He does have friends here, those who welcome him with his favourite masala dosa and he was hoping to find them so some of his time could be spent together.

After 2 hours of inquiry and search, he had located Vyangar and they shook hands as the Tamil welcomed him with true joy as he saw him coming and recognized the man.

He brought the woollen mat so he could sit on it, feeling comfortable, asked him for a meal, and told his daughter to bring some coconut water to drink and feel fresh. It also meant a bond of new welcome or a gesture of greeting as he had come to their place for the first time.

The agent expressed gratitude and told them a few tales of the old water rivalry as they kept talking during the meal and fell asleep after a lot of laughter and jokes amongst them. After 2 hours passed, the visitor felt something fishy in the area as a trap from his own country could come to the surface. He decided to move forward as Lankan spies may come inside India in the form of local woodcutters or other ways so he can't let others be threatened by them as these are his friends.

I will take care of them if you ask me. After all, you saved me in your waters, now it's my duty, the visitor said no as the resident offered it showing a great source of gratitude for the past event. You are aware bro that's how serious they can prove in combat. I don't trust the way they operate and shall not risk your lives, he said to the family who had to agree as they were ready to bid him farewell. The man simply stood up and he was gone before anyone could come with a promise of his return, thanking them for their great service as he was a guest.

A phone rings and Vudaru answers it trying to talk out further. This is Matheesh speaking. Clear all charges from the man on trace or You shall be removed from the inquiry office, the voice made the official feel frightened as it ordered the man to drop it. For a moment the person couldn't understand why the order had been sent but then the official document had come to him online with mention of clearing all charges and Vudaru felt more worried than ever reading it.

Who cares if the higher people are involved? We can't stop minting money from humans, he said to himself as he wrote a document of his own, copied the signature from the higher-ranked official, and made a digital copy of it to proceed with his false scheme. Vudaru was soon going to feel that he had made the biggest mistake of his life as the document sent had advanced software that was tracking his movement and one more call had come.

I need to meet you outside your office, it's urgent, the voice said as the official inside couldn't recognize him. How come, sir, what may be the purpose of talking now? He responded but the voice could be heard getting angrier and he felt something fishy in it as he threw the written note into the bin and proceeded to face the threat of his life looming ahead.

He didn't have to wait as Matheesh was standing there in his official wardress. He was one of the commanding leaders both for cyber security and integral forces who kept track of piracy in the Lankan waters and beyond. His attitude was calm as he wore a simple dress with glasses in his eyes twinkling. I have been waiting for you for 5 minutes. Why did it take so late? The junior saw him fuming with lines on his forehead and Vudaru felt a bit surprised to see him as he rarely comes out of his offices to check for the patrolling or other aspects.

You didn't accept my word. I am known to command huge respect here, the commanding officer said, slapping Vudaru without any response from him. I come here sir, what else can I do for you with my best efforts? The junior tried to argue but Matheesh looked fearsome to his junior as he had loaded his gun. I am not known to take orders but as you have forged my signature in a false document, this may be your end if you ask me, Vudaru covered as the gun was put onto his temple.

The officer counted for 3, 2, 1, and with bullets getting louder, the junior fell, unable to speak, and simply dead on the floor. The officer wanted him for weeks as he had stopped to join meetings, and may only have talks with those who exchange checks of financial leverage or accounts and the officer had been able to trace his misdeeds. After he was able to recognize 5 trials being false where people had been sent to prison to get money from the department, the inquiry panel finally accepted the officer that piracy had happened and he wanted to catch the man who had led it all.

My order to protect Vardhanesh, the officer said, looking straight into the dead face. He called for a person to take the body and do a formal ceremony for the dead who agreed. We did well sir to keep a close watch or they would have sent all people visiting our nation to face the trial and earn from them, the person said as Matheesh called someone to connect to Vardhanesh who was in India and was happy to receive so well by honest people of Tamilnaddu helping him with water issues and how to crack wells.

A message was sent that Matheesh had closed the main case which made Vardhanesh feel calm but not pleased by it, he had made it much later than the spy had expected him to cover the whole course. I may have to go back for now my friends, I am so grateful for your help in tough times, the man said, shaking hands with the best family one last time before leaving the tamil shores and feeling truly connected.

Before going back to his boat, he waved to all of them with pure joy and they smiled a bit painfully as he took off with no water threats coming this time for him. They all felt a bit sad to see him going, but it had been a kind of rescue they had been involved in making him stay safe from the intruders in the forests and come out on top. He shall never forget what they did for him as a complete group merging their strengths to help him as he goes back with dignity to his nation.

Dhamika is happy as the main culprit had been destroyed not by political ways but through the actual order. He expresses gratitude to Matheesh but may have to face imprisonment of 2 years due to taking money or he can be convicted which he accepted. People in Lanka arranged for a corresponding meeting and the high-level talk finally resulted in fixing the whole matter after both parties had settled to tackle the false tricks of the underwater tricksters and the case had been closed with captive fishermen from the past sent to the home to relish true joy.

9
A Man's Double Life Unraveled

It was a blissful night, a lot of voices were coming and they all had laughter in them in the backdrop. It was a friend's wedding and most people had come to welcome him as he had just come from abroad to settle and had decided to get married simply. People were wishing him on arranging a best mate and he couldn't be happier. He was a thin person probably around 28 years old and belongs to a rich family who has the tradition of sending people abroad before they marry their chosen person in a ceremony.

The person's mother was scolding someone for not arranging the party in the order they wanted. The mother called the son to form a procession, follow her, and take the ritual to the next level before the wedding could be over. The son obeyed her, walked forward to take the step and after the round of ceremonies, he had made everyone laugh by his words. His would-be wife was also thin in stature, may reach around his shoulder and their faces were somehow identical.

Delhi is known to arrange cultural bonds as a lot of weddings take place in certain weather. This one was no different from the one that happens with ritual colours and traditions held amongst people. At the heart of the capital, people come to form bonds and get together to be part of custom and it hasn't changed. However, there are few other elements to it and that can also perturb if you know a place like Delhi which has beauties hidden on both sides to balance the cores.

Poornima got married to a man who is loyal to her but has some of his tastes. They say in the family that he may not be addicted but he drinks at parties and on a specific day, it may go out of his usual standards. He lets the day come with its readiness calling his wife earlier and she may feel miserable for the moment coming. It was a kind of routine for him that every weekend he had started as there was no other chance to go abroad and have his leisure activities. The wife started to feel something was out of order and asked someone to help her in her quest to find what her husband was up to late at night in the pubs.

The informer was not sure but he started to work as a spy. I may need regular updates on Saturday as that's the night he is not coming back home, the wife said with a diligent smile paying him some money to start. As you say so, is it sure he goes to the pubs at night? She nodded, handing him a paper she had managed to steal from her husband's purse and it was a duplicate card, one like the many he holds in his pocket for entry in the pub. The spy nodded, took the card, and left before anyone could see him.

I am here, bring my towel please, a voice said, giving a kind of surprise to the wife as the husband emerged from the bathroom with glee. She went out to bring his clothes and the man looked calmer than before. I am thinking of searching for a better company so we can go out together, he whispered as the wife raised her eyebrows but he had gone in without saying much to her. Poornima packed his food, offered him a cup of tea and he picked up the box in a hurry, stood up, and went smiling to someone from a distance.

It was Saturday and the noise was getting louder from the pub as the man entered it quietly. Prachurya as he was ced showed his pass and he was allowed without question. He has a lot of connections both in India and abroad so they can't deny him to go and he asked for a beer to settle his mood. For a moment he showed like he was simply looking for someone but had then got settled with the drink as he couldn't see the movement outdoors.

Any help we can do for you sir here? It's a special day tonight after all, the receptionist said with a smile as he smirked at her. Search me for a secret message delivery, it will do me a lot of good, he said as he had never told his family what he does in these pubs but he has been working as an agent for the nation. His job was to track rich people who don't hesitate to cross their limits and report their movements to the security forces before they act against the country as they can be terrible if they are not stopped by the secret teams around them.

Prachurya raises a hand to someone to come forward and offers him a drink. The man looked familiar as he had been the person hired by Poornima to look for her husband. Give the tip to my wife that I am secretly dating someone, he said with an image of a rich lady and the spy smirked. You already know that I am hired to do that, how come? Prachurya waved his hand as 2 more drinks came for them and they chilled having the true fun of the pub with the night becoming louder and dark due to certain noises.

A lady had certainly arrived in a rich sari, her eyes brimming with joy and fashion of top level. She passed Prachuryar and the spy as they let her go in and settled on an inner room that is used for conferences. There she was joined by 4 men of high level and they had started to discuss something. As the group was talking to plot a school to go for the attack and despite being the Indians, they hardly had anything to lose as they had enough money to sustain their lives which makes Prachurya feel sad for the victims to face the price later.

I want to hear what she is telling them as a main plan, the spy said as Prachurya stopped the man from going to fight with them. You can't go in just by your wish to stop them, You needs to get an official pass or an online link, he said smirking the spy had sat back as the agent asked him about his wife, what she does in lonely afternoons and why she is feeling uneasy with all the movement taking place in the pubs.

She is your wife, sir, at least you have to spend some time with her, the spy said as someone brushed Prachurya from behind and he could see that it was the same lady who had just gone in a few minutes before. I see the conference is over, I may have to report it before the time gets over, Prachurya said and he stepped out shaking hands with the spy as they both had gone away in a flash of a moment.

Yes, what's the news? Our lady shall be active on the public streets again? A man spoke from the other side as Prachurya called him from the inner place of the pub. He didn't speak for long as the noise was deafening and it may not be clear so he only said Schools are in threat, take care, he spoke the words and saw someone standing on the backdrop from where he was calling to the secret agency but the agent is habitual to do violence whenever he feels something like this and he was ready.

There was a sound of the glass breaking into pieces as Prachurya was pinned into the wall by the visitor and he let it happen simply to give the other one advantage first. The man was one of the 4 who had gone in with the lady and he was trying to keep a close watch on him, which is why he was so interested in the conference in the first place. After 5 minutes of punching and severe fighting, Prachurya had come back to what he was known for and was well-appreciated due to his raw skill.

Another sound of glass tinkling took place and this time the man was on the floor not able to stand up and badly wounded by the strike from behind. It was not going to work for Prachurya to leave him lying there alone or it may raise questions by the public. He takes out a whistle bomb, blows it and the place and the glass case were sent flying as the man was dead with no more sounds. The music was coming loud as it was almost midnight and Prachurya had no regret as he was familiar with taking such steps in urgency whenever he was in threat of being captured.

I didn't get what you were trying to say, can you tell me now, a call comes and Prachurya receives it where the senior is asking him what he was trying to say. He had come outside the pub and was walking quietly so he could explain to him. The lady brought 4 men to plan a school plot. One of them died by my hands as he was trying to find what I may be after in the pub. He simply spoke and the senior felt pleased that he had confidential information for them. The lady had been missing for 4 months now and finally, her sighting was big news for the whole team.

I am sorry I keep it late again, you must be tired he said as he reached home around dawn and Poornima opened the door for him. I am sorry I put a spy behind you, it was so stupid of me, were the first words she said and the husband smiled at her. You are my wife, you do have the right to find out what I do, but It's better you keep quiet, She nodded, bringing a glass of water for him as he felt refreshed and had gone to change after arriving.

Poornima felt better that her doubts didn't come true and Prachurya told her that he put a false trail for her spy to tell her that he was dating someone with a laugh. He didn't get time to update me yet. He was with you the whole night wasn't he? She laughed as they both sat on the hall's sofa munching breakfast and things were coming back to normal. A message flash reporting the last location of the lady by his boss and he didn't worry about it. He knows what to do for such a high level of criminals and he shall soon be on the track with details on how to crack it.

False documents, acting as a secret spy or a criminal, how much It may hurt his followers? News was coming on the TV as the couple watched it. Prachurya looked closely as he recognized the man whom he had killed as a false person to the report. We urge people not to hand over their details or more people can have forgery as it can cause a lot of damage, the reporter said as they changed the channel and songs started to play instead. The husband was not in the mood to talk about crimes or how they have gone recently.

He was thinking about spending some time with his wife at home or outside before he leaves as it may soon be bleeding and messy with strikes. Are you sure? I didn't hear about going on a tour recently, she felt surprised as he packed their clothes for a personal evening and Poornima was excited taking out her camera from her bag pack as they had some joy to themselves in the Humayun tomb with true laughter and melody. It also proved handy for Prachurya as he got some secret information about the case and he is prepared to find more clues.

Is that helpful for any further work in the inner kitchen? His wife asked him to buy clothes for home jobs and he nodded. The man asked for two cups of cold coffee to enjoy in the outer sitting area and they sat there as a few men crossed by looking closely. He can imagine that the other members of the team might be in to find the secret information including who killed their men and they shall soon be tracking afterwards for the case. He heard a child talking about some sort of infection as it cried not to be sent to school and Prachurya let the child go without a word with its parents.

This issue would soon arise as a few other households may also start to report their children with some sort of infection in them. As a secret agent, the man did have the idea that the sharp brains won't plan a bomb or a serious crash but may try to execute their plan. They work as slow poison in society and the response shall soon start to emerge as people can be seen taking their children to hospital who complain of some spots on their arms and chest making them feel weak due to the way they surface along.

What happened to you dear? Poornima asked a child as she visited a hospital for migraine and saw a few of the children were still on the bench waiting for their turn.

I am getting nervous, feeling so weak as I don't wish to go anywhere, forget the school, the child said as she touched them and their temperature was normal. It's an infection of some kind is it? She asked and the helper from the medical staff agreed as she had got her call and she had gone for her check-up thinking to update her husband about it in the evening once he returned.

She didn't have to tell him as the news had already started to surprise people as a headline that was on display. Children out of bed sir. Children do not listen to their parents if they are sad. They complain of something that disturbs them and they are found infected with rashes, what could this all be? The news reporter asked as her husband came back from work tired, opened the TV and was busy eating the evening snacks sitting on the sofa as the newsreader continued.

I did see a few children with the same marks in the hospital, struggling to come out of the pain, she told him and he was not worried as he knew there may be some plan to captivate attention. Did you? Were they looking worried or confused due to the problem? The husband asked her straight away as he handed his empty glass back to her politely. She told them they were not very warm or it seemed to her like their temperature was getting low due to the effect of the infection in them.

He told about three raids, two of them being a failure and they did find something in the 3rd quarter after he was done with his work at his company. He opened his bag, lifted a file, and showed her something that was related to the cases. This may be of deeper interest as I feel it is connected, he has been able to identify the records and feel this key may be the reason for the infection. What would it be if you could show us? She said as a call rang and it was from the chief who he keeps reporting to about the concern.

Key detected, she will be in our grip soon if you

believe it. Alert the main gang for the process, the husband told the chief who smiled with some hope on the progress as he explained the condition of the criminal. She tricked us last time too very simply by swapping them with her skill. I hope she will be in our grip this time, the voice said from the other side and Prachurya felt calm despite all the pressure from the working staff as he did have news to cover things.

We didn't manage to touch her men in the past, to be honest, This time we had already struck 2, the chief felt surprised as the receiver said that one more person had been arrested with his help this evening as they talked. Let me confirm, shall you? This is perfect news my friend, For a moment he didn't believe it but a message came in the backdrop from the police team that made him feel elated as he disconnected the phone to confirm it with the official staff at work.

Gurdeep speaking sir. Have arrested a man for illegal medical kit after a tip from Prachurya, a man responded as the chief called, giving him a sense of relief by the news. I wonder what he contains. Check the kit and update me on the proceeding he ordered as the receiver agreed, sending him the images of the kit he had confiscated as the man was taken into custody for treatment and inquiry of the police standards in the jail. It was common to have raids in places like Delhi where cases also surfaced regularly and Gurdeep was not worried by the level of it.

The chief sent a gratitude message to Prachurya as he was eating but one more message had followed behind it. a kind of warning from a group who may be trying to look after his movement. You don't have children yet, It will be a huge ask once you have them, it read and Prachurya smiled tracking the sender to whom he had sent something as a bug on the chat online making the man pay for his trick as he smiled once the dinner was over accomplishing the task and looking for the next one coming soon.

A pub was running with music as a few battles were taking place in the background with noises. It was Saturday again and Prachurya knew what may be coming here. The lady with a unique blue sari could be seen going into a secret room as few people fought in the actual backdrop. However, the agent had the upper hand as the spy who helped his wife had come to his aid. They sat there acting to be serving the cold drinks and sneaked in to find the reason for the fight being in total swing with a lot of shouts happening around them with buzzes.

They were fighting for the key which was not in anyone's control and the punches kept coming hard on each other with true strength. Prachurya surprised the one throwing the bottle down after putting his drink as he was hit on the nose directly. There was a voice, a horn, and the music had gone silent as the police came. Suddenly Gurdeep was in front leading the charge and his men were capable enough to handle the case as he ordered them to catch the gang involved with a surge of infections to which they were somehow responsible as criminals.

You are under arrest, Great job Prachu, he said looking at his old fellow from the security team who smiled too. Take them before they change out their faces, the agent said with a broader smile. Amandeep had come to gather the lady before she could sneak away and this time she had been caught. They were not my men, I don't know them please, she shouted as the lady constable took her and they were all thrown in the jeep to be taken for inquiry at the police station.

I have no idea of the plan, Believe me, please, she said after being taken for custody by the ladies at the enquiry place. One more time, you dare to say no and I shall tip you how hard it is Amandeep said smiling with her stick she finally said yes talking of a master plan on infection and sending children to death by it. The police were shocked to see how long they had planned but things were coming to reality and they had to track the bigger parties truly involved in it as they do have their plans to execute it currently.

Who is Magar lal then? I may like to know more about him and the past case of professional murder, Amandeep asked the lady who shied away but she may have to reveal it to them. A secret person who works mainly as an adviser to figure out how the plan works. He may be in custody but someone visits him in the Lucknow jail. She smiled like it may not be easy for police to track the actual mastermind behind the scheme or even crack it whole.

The lady constable smiled at her with some playful manner like she already had some clue on this. We will soon be able to catch the bloke, I was waiting for you to track us like this, she hinted at hitting her and the lady felt the pain of her brutal assault. My men will play more with you as long you hurt me, she said in pain but the constable didn't care as she wanted to hear something more interesting and the lady finally told of the device, one that comes with a key and they were not able to trace it so they planned to capture children and ask for it instead.

Gurdeep sent his men to Lucknow jail to find Magar Lal and they confirmed his presence. The spies also said that someone visits him every Sunday as an actual token of gratitude. Sir, the person may be connected to the whole case if we can track but the main scheme is still not known, a spy said and Gurdeep agreed as the guess may come true at the right moment as the device was also found under command of the headquarters as a susceptive one that can cause deaths easily rather than just spread the infection.

His chief called him asking him to go to the mohalla bazaar nearby to find a certain crime happening there as someone had alerted them and he responded to the boss. He saw few children were left in the open and they were crying openly in the cold with people watching them rather than trying to support the needy. With the help of someone to make them happy, they were looking to find or to know why they had been left so lonely as the jeep arrived and Gurdeep stepped out to investigate the scene in his manner.

I called the main inspector sir, a man appeared showing that the children had been left outside in the cold. Good on you, I think this is a certain trap if you ask me friend, the inspector felt it as the man was hit by someone from behind and the officer jumped at the right time to protect him. Thanks, sir, How did you guess it? What shall we do now? The inspector told the man to come to his jeep and he is taking the children in it so the assault can be restricted to minimal damage by him.

A message flashes asking for instant removal of the Madam in-chief from the jail or more such children shall be left on the streets with their parents dead. This did make Gurdeep worry as he forwarded the message to Prachurya who was still at his company office but he responded to it somehow. Yes on to the course don't worry folks, Gurdeep took the children with him trying to find belongings as news of a couple dead in their home started to stream on TV with their four children being left in a public platform with people watching the scene but not helping them.

A man had come holding a torch in the night walking silently. He quietly crept inside a cramped jail and vanished before anyone could try to ask. It was night time so the jailor and the other staff were asleep as the man quietly turned right, inside a pocket of a ceiling, and had reached the place for the purpose he wanted to fill in due to the tip of a police person who needed to kill someone to close the case out.

The Lucknow jail is not much different from others, it had the same wind of being kept with tightness as people were of the same calibre and Magar Lal looked old and weak as he coughed from an inner prison cell where he had been kept as a criminal. It had been years since he was taken for custody, had been enquired and after his laugh that his conspiracies won't stop, the police had sent him to prison being convicted for 14 years by the court for the crimes he committed in public.

He had been living here in the jail ever since and wanted to fill in his desires to continue the drug racket he used to hold before being captured as visitors kept coming to meet him, helping him ensure that tests on children were regular. His gang used to capture newborns or infants to be tested with a severe medical supplement and had caused a lot of serious deaths. After a huge uproar from the public, Magar Lal was trapped by the help of his informer and was taken to jail.

The agent has no wish to kill the old man, it won't do any good as he only advises people. The main plan was to catch hold of the person who visits him every Sunday as it is a few hrs left now when the sun will come as the person may visit. The visitor took off the lid of an inner sitting place, quietly lifted the cushions, and hid in it as people started to talk with the sounds of birds in the air coming with a change of mood within them.

The prisoners were laughing, some were complaining about the tea being of less quality and the jailor had come wishing Magar Lal morning as he smiled with 2 of his front teeth not anymore as they may have been broken in a fight in the past. It's Sunday, the moment for your actual tea to drink out, isn't it? One of the friendly prisoners reminded the old man and he wished the person to come early as there may be a few hidden secrets he had to reveal to him with their time limited as he was aware of captures done by police in the public recently.

You sure they will help you get exact money for the tests if they succeed? Another prisoner asked the old man with some interest. I am not much into the chemical, but I want to know how the response comes and the image is of most importance for us, the old man said as he felt someone may have kicked him from behind but it was not so harsh or he may have turned to retaliate. The old man has some strength left for one last fight and no one in the jail wants to go for the hits as he can be severe while fighting in a battle as he had proved many times.

There was a knock from the jailor as he told Magar Lal that the visitor had come. The agent who had been hidden moved without anyone being interested in him to see from the back gate and the old man waited for the person to come. He was not surprised to see a security agent coming with the person and the agent was surprised to see the visitor as he was none other than the son of the lady they had captured and the agent was feeling more than disgusted as he may have to report this to Gurdeep.

Nice to see you nephew, I hope there may be a lot of trial left for us to gain positive news, the old man said hugging him, the agent didn't act as they started to talk and he listened to them without any movement talking about the master plan where they had to send few children to other state or to kill so they can grab hold of the insurance policy. The killer slowly moved without a hint and took the hand of the security agent on guard with a gesture that he came from the jail and wanted to have a word with him.

His mother commands huge respect, I can't withdraw the duty to which I have been handed, the security person said, answering him before he could say anything to him. No, you didn't get me. We have caught the mother, she is in jail, I presume you can switch sides if you like my friend, the agent who was a visitor showed him the papers of the arrest, making the person surprised by it. What's the plan? I am not sure I can be of any help. I only fear her political nature, he said with some sort of guidance to have for the plan.

Back in Delhi, Gurdeep had controlled the case. He was happy that opponents did set a trap and had used it to his own advantage. I was waiting to see how you all were taking children, he laughed, throwing a man onto the floor as he tried to run into an outer area. These people had been helping the gang transform as food delivery agents and as they delivered the food ordered by parents who had newborn children, they would simply take them away, confusing the family of the low taste, food offers, or other ways around which Gurdeep had taken benefit this time.

He punched two of the other men taking pizza boxes inside a quarter as the men went into the lift. He sent his juniors onto the top floor and the food agent was caught without much effort. Come with me, I will take you to the supreme boss, the men said, throwing them inside the lift and dragging them by pressing the button to go down. Gurdeep was waiting and together all the 8 men were taken into custody being involved as traitors.

I don't have much to tell you like You know all the details now, the politician said as more documents and calls came for her release but none of them were accepted as the policeman didn't care of what may come for them in future. I shall transfer all of you if you don't release her, one of the texts was sent but Gurdeep didn't care. Amandeep also told the lady bad news that her son had been sighted and if she doesn't reveal the further mess, they will finally decide what to do with her.

Our agents are active madam. Your son shall be in our grip soon and so will be the junior assistant who works for you covering your crimes, she said with a smile as one more call came. The agent sent to Luckhnow had some but good news for them as he had convinced the security member of the other side to become part of their search and the other men had come to give the leads so things could work in order.

Sir, go to the Patel chalk, you will find three captive sites there in the old factory area, the agents told Gurdeep, looking impatient as he nodded. He stepped out without any fear and went to find the trace. Half an hour later Gurdeep had a quarrel with some men, arrested them for illegal capture, and had taken 15 children's bodies from the inner cell as he felt dejected that they had been late or they could be saved by simple tricks.

Amandeep had been also informed of some nurses active in the Raghveer hospital and she sent her female subordinates to bring them to custody. They didn't make it late as 5 nurses were taken to the police for illegal use of medical ointment that expands irritation in infants and makes them feel uncomfortable. The positive news was coming fast and it made the politician feel worried as her heartbeat started to go up. She was a patient with high blood pressure herself and with the son out there amidst the fear of other members being caught, she may succumb to the pain too.

Back at the Lucknow jail, the old man was happy to get some money from the nephew as he asked the security person to come and they started to move away. The agent had tipped the person to keep moving as he may be closely coming with them too. On the visitor's order, the nephew's agent drove him to a different place than he had expected, asking the old man to be picked by someone else as a police jeep appeared. Where the hell are you taking me? You are bound by my mom's orders, the man shouted but the agent kept driving with no words to him.

Hello friend, why not tell the boss where you are taking him now? The other agent said, keeping with them as the bike swerved from behind and he gestured to the security person to open up about the movement. We are taking you to the custody where your mother is currently, the agent said, making the person fear as he felt no trick had worked this time. No bail order had been received and the threat to police had also faltered with no effect as the man kept driving on the highway faster than ever.

We will be released soon, I will see you all are sent to hell, the son said as the car kept moving and the agent had finally reached the place. It had been a tough drive from Lucknow to Delhi but they had made it without any threat as no secret men had come to stop them and all of them were tipped to side with the police. Gurdeep had done this well and hinted to the madam that her son was being brought to make her feel worried more than ever on the news as the time for their punishment came closer to finish the mess.

We have a few kids who are under our grip. I shall tell you their location if you let my son go, she still had the daring to talk even feeling this weak. No matter, we shall get them without your son being released or maybe Mandeep had, the female inspector said as a message flashed and she was confirmed of what she had just said to her. Now what shall you do madam? Your men are under the grip, the threat is no more, and political glamour is all simply gone, she said looking at the rich lady with some glee and disgust.

I have something for you, tastier than the soup your officials serve in the pubs to let you get rich, Prachurya said as he entered the room with some relief on his face. He had something in his hands, it looked like an order and it says to finish the political crap within the prison ward itself. No, this may not be possible, they can't turn on us, she felt deranged to see the political order and this could very well be her end as Gurdeep wished Prachurya to be at the right time and arranged the official document to proceed the legal process.

My wife helped me, she also had some grudge against the lady in the past, he said, holding another document for his efforts with mention of the government for his skills as an agent. Great job, where they are now, Amandeep said, tapping him on the shoulder. Two agents came as a car stopped and they brought someone to the point of the gun as the lady behind the bar saw them coming quietly. She looked at the man in that familiar blue t-shirt and goggles, witnessed him being lowered and the curtain had finally fallen.

Take them, sir, we are under the order to take the process going, Gurdeep said as the chief was called to the spot and he arrived as the offenders had been finally held as victims by the officials. We faced your reign for the last 8 years, it is fitting that it ends at the hands of one who was mostly hurt by you, Gurdeep said and he handed Aamandeep the honours of taking care of the lady to be punished.

My whole family was destroyed as you plotted the trap, killed my cousins, and also took their son away being just 3 years old with no mercy, she said, hitting the lady with her stick to make her confess and the politician accepted. She was looking to get a better hold on her political seat and money was not enough to do so which led to crimes. The police started to note down all the statements and it was soon going to be their end done by their hands.

The questioning kept taking place as the son was enquired about who told him about the plan of insurance, to lure the people and earn big by grabbing hold of the children openly. Gurdeep asked about his role in the whole case and he agreed, telling how strongly he supported both her mother's political status and the way they were getting rich. This will all end today, I am afraid, the chief said, handing the official order after reading it. Prachurya felt pleased to see the capture of those who call themselves to be pure but have been involved in crimes all the time doing them openly somehow.

By the permit of the government, we are allowed to take whatever action that is fitting, Prachurya said, asking Amandeep to finish the lady. She took out her pistol, fired 3 bullets and the rich politician cried loudly before falling onto the floor and dying. Gurdeep turned his weapon towards the son and in the next 5 minutes, all the culprits had been sent to hell including the pizza boy, food agents, secret spies and all were punished for their crimes at last by the officials.

The dead bodies were sent for the process that is well-known in Hindu customs always. All the team members congratulated each other for their role as the chief announced bravery awards for both police persons from Punjab who joined them for the specific mission and made it count. Congratulate the agent who made it possible, well done Naveen, Gurdeep said as he was the one who convinced others to come with him and be protected by the whole carnage.

He smiled broadly for all of them as Prachurya hugged him being his cousin and all the things had come to being safe in the local area. However, Gurdeep feels for the children who have no parents to go to anymore as they cry loudly while the inspector watches them with wet eyes. There must be something for them to call home and he was thinking that he may plan to make a strategy for them with true joy and become part of it by making a public call to protect them.

10
Dakshika's Fight

It was a strange sound, like water falling from some stones in rapid flow and that could be heard very closely as it continued to fall from a stream. People could be seen looking at the water falling from a distance like they had witnessed gold and smiling very fondly to have it collected. They felt that gold had struck as they bent low, raised their tin jugs, and started to fill in so they could at least have proper water for some time in such heat getting better by feeling fresh.

Few of them could be seen trying to stop children from going closer to the falling stream. They don't want them to throw stones into the water like they had been wishing to do and ask them to stay with them as water is rare and they must conserve it before everything has been gone. Things are not as good as they must look and the dry weather has made it worse with everything on some sort of stop due to thirst, lack of water, and its pain amongst the people.

I wonder what it has gotten lately for them to collect water? A lady in her late 20s said to her tour guide as she could see the people trying to gather water in jugs and also having a fight on who may get how much. It is not easy to have fresh throats in this part of India, people even can kill each other for claiming it, a touring guide said as she looked into his eyes with surprise but then she understood as he gestured towards the sand dome approaching as they trundled away from the people in search for certain water location in the sandy area coming to make them realise why it costs to be so desperate.

I knew she may listen to our problems. We are not mad fighting here just for water and thirst, a girl of around 11 years said to her father as she shook her head in disbelief. They slowly walked away to gather some food and went inside their small home and a camel could be seen tied to the inner yard as they approached the place. It rumbled in the drifting wind of the evening and the girl went to help it get some water to feel calm from this heat in the place and it had been fed with it.

Rajasthan had been like something to exhibit upon with its rich culture and people to make it glorious as they do believe in hospitality and serve it well. It is certainly the biggest state when you go by the area and its expanse in the region but the trouble is that a large portion of the state is covered by the Thar desert in its backdrop. Those who live close to it have to face the challenge of dry weather with less water which brings with it the harsh nature of the area.

People can be seen searching or creating underwater wells by help of outsiders, waiting for once-in-a-year rain, or trying to find sources that can help for their water coverage simply in the raw heat. It is not easy to collect it when the amount is so limited and they do wish to find choices by which they can get fresh water to sustain their lives and make it simply better.

However, there are some crimes this place holds too in the backdrop and how they open chances for constructing the plans would soon be revealed by their smart ways to negotiate it. People can capture lives using certain places, kidnap the young children, and use the desert very well for their advantage as it helps them disappear. They can be seen doing illegal activity, running off, or even welcoming intruders that do most of the damage to our cult, its faith, and actual beliefs as the gangs scuffle and take riches away.

Tell the master that we have brought water if he likes to, the father told the girl to go and she simply went to speak to the son as she feared that they might not be allowed, Tell your papa that the water source had been found as we bring water to you, she told the son from a distance as she had some sort of fear in her face. Rajasthan is known for one more challenge, the weddings of girls of very less age and it may be a kind of feeling which she may try to avoid at all costs.

I may not be interested in what your papa wishes to offer the boss, the son said, going away as he is not interested in such tools. We do serve you after all but it is not going to work, the girl whispered in a taunt she had run before the lord's son could try to grab her and had been panting as she reached home telling her father that she had informed them about water.

The lord had come last week to talk with the father called Mahant who is a small farmer working for him. He had been interested in his girl marrying his son, providing him with some money but the farmer had refused. I can't let her get in the fold so young sir, I am sorry she is the only one I had, the farmer had said as the boss asked him saying that this could be the best deal. Think it this way Mahant, you will get rich, I will be helping you with money and this can prove a life-changing moment for a small farmer like you, the father shook his head as the lord tried to figure things out in anger.

The girl felt miserable as she heard this all from her bed acting to be asleep and the farmer denied it simply asking him to give her some time as the lord went away closing the door. I won't hand you to the devil, don't worry, he assured Dakshika who had been feeling sad ever since. He said that there was a way to figure out, how the family could be shifted and he had not recovered from vanishing of his wife who either died or drowned due to lack of money for her treatment so he must arrange for some way to fix this whole mess first.

It was almost night as someone came to the lord for a word. The knock took place so suddenly that the lord was surprised and sent his son to open the door. Mahant had not been in his place, nor his daughter. They both had been missing for the last 3 days and someone entered to cover them. a man quietly came in as the door was opened by the son and he latched on to him first. Stop, who are you? Don't you know my father? He shouted as the man lifted him without a word and there was a shriek piercing the night as the son had been killed.

The lord felt angrier than ever as he lifted his axe to face the intruder being ready for it. Why did you kill my son for true fun? Who are you? He leered revealing himself out from behind as the man celebrated the assault in his style. The revenge of the past. Mahant was not the only one whose daughter you asked to marry, the man laughed as he turned and kicked the lord with a harsh tone in his nature willing to close the affair with his hands.

I am someone who you insulted while creating the public well after your son was engaged with my daughter who you offended after it, the man said, hitting the lord with his fist and one of his teeth had come out broken. Oh yes, the teeth of my son, how much pain he would have when he tried to protest your crimes? The man said, hitting him one more time and the lord felt worried more than ever. It looked like someone from the past had risen and he had no choice but to fight with him openly here at his own place.

The man started to play with the lord in his courtyard as he tossed the son's dead body in the air, hit him from behind and the lord fell asking for mercy. Apologise to Mahant and all the other farmers who work under you. Provide them money as they are hired labourers and then I shall have mercy, the man said, taking out a coin to open a drawer close by and removing all the money inside it by his smart trick.

I am going this time with this bundle of notes to help them, especially those who need it the most. Next time I shall finish you if you don't learn from your mistakes to be honest, the man said and the lord fell onto the floor with pure disgust and rage for the future as he could see his son lying in a corner unable to be recognized and dead by the hands of an intruder. I will take your revenge on my son. Is she engaged? Don't worry I will show them my power and strength, he thought as a strange feeling of being alone in the night grips him making him feel weaker than before with some bad memories of the past very clearly in ears.

There is not much to say here in the village as the news spread like wildfire and the workers had been told that someone had brutally hurt the lord. Few of them felt pleased to hear while those who were paid in certain moments felt disappointed that the lord was not capable of protecting his son. However, those who had been feeling joyous had been paid by the man the next morning as he asked them to meet him in secret going away from the place.

The lord wanted to find him so he had shared money with the paid workers to track any kind of local movement, but they were not able to search them. There were a lot of voices asking for the threat to pass by and the smoke had gone from the wind blowing away. Before it could be caught, the men had been adjusted by the community with both sides being dirty with crimes accomplished in its actual course.

The night was coming back as the man came out from behind. His name was Vimlesh and he had to face a lot of problems at the hands of the lord and he was looking to settle things with him. He had arranged for Mahant to go to his old place in Bikaner till the matter settled and had now called out the man back. I suggest you work for me instead of the lord till he recovers, the man said, offering him some money so he could look after his camels which he uses to attract desert rides for the tourists in open areas.

My daughter still does not wish to go to the school, I am sorry, the farmer said as he allowed Dakshika to get habitual to the large farm area where a few camels could be seen moving as a few tourists came to Vimlesh asking for the tickets. 150 per safari, If you ask me, less than what you get in the inner area, he said as a man came with his family asking and he had sent a man with the camel to let them feel the best comforts by moving in for the tour.

Mahant was joined by another farmer who came by the name of Dushant and together they started to help Vimlesh to handle the farm. The daughter got more comfortable as a few days passed by and they were having a certain time out being in a group. One night however when she had been asleep, Mahant stood outside listening to some words and his ears stood up as Dushant was talking to the senior in the courtyard.

They were making a plan to track bigger households and Vimlesh must be the one to lead the trap where he must attack being the stronger one. It was simply a clear hint that they didn't have enough money or men left to handle this place so they wanted to snatch more places from where they could get hold of it. Mahan felt worried as he forced Dakshika to wake up and better be off before they ask him to join in the whole plan which he did suspect in the past while coming here.

He took his money left, wrapped all his small luggage in a pillow cover and they vanished in the night. However, he didn't know of the threat waiting for him in the night as bigger parties were involved in it. There was a sound of something torn apart, his money bag fell and somebody had charged him from behind. He told Dakshika to run but a female had caught hold of her. The night snatchers had caught up with them from the village and Mahant's throat was ripped apart as Dakshika shouted for him to come back.

The newspaper next day gave a hint on a farmer being killed by night snatchers and the lord opened it to see Mahant's photo being visible in it. Poor bloke, I offered him to give his daughter to me but he did have to face his end in such a manner, it's a shame, he spoke with sympathy as few of his supporters had a pure laugh. It may be some of them who work as secret agents and the rift between rich and poor farmers is something which Rajasthan do witness in often cases openly in public.

Vimlesh woke up late as he was not able to find the person first. His ears did get the news finally and he felt sad but he couldn't wonder where they may have taken his daughter. Nobody had any idea of the whole mess as the morning took place at a close by locality. The female who had caught her took the child to someone, offered a glass of milk, and after it, she told Dakshika to live with her till the people were able to recover her father as the men had taken the man's body with them without a hint or trace.

I may not like to stay lonely but I can be happy till he is found so I can feel to be with the family, she said knowing that he may not return to her. You can call it a home as we are happy to raise children here, the female who may be around 24 years of age said as she looked after them. She is generally an informer, one who works for the police and they have been tracking people who like to work as criminals either sending children from one place to another or being involved in mass murder acting on someone else's orders.

Do you know how those blokes look like deer? The female asked, looking at her closely with interest. I can't see their face, one of them did lower his hood down for once and there was a scar on the forehead visible more clearly than anything if you ask me, the girl said with a smile as he found a ball on the floor and tried to kick it but failed in the attempt. Good of you, this is all we have then. I will try to help it get settled, the informer said, turning away as the child started to feel better.

Dakshika got a few friends to know at the place as the day progressed. She shook hands with them, seemed to be cheerful to find them and they started to play hide and seek as a few official men had come talking to the informer on the further updates. She told them about a new case, the death of Dakshika's father, and the police personnel looked at more children with some plea to the heavens that they needed to stop. They asked about the process and she told them about the same man with a scar on his forehead being the leader that made the police worried and they want to close this soon or it may become an uproar for them with public pressure.

It was a fresh day again, few people were walking on the side of a lake as this side had much soothing weather compared to the desert side. Udaipur is known to bring delight, to let people feel calm and people like to visit there as tourists to have a fresh weather experience. A man could be seen holding a box onto his head as he sold pastries to the visitors. He offered them the material at a low price and they enjoyed it as a woman passed into the open street and out of sight in search of someone in need.

I can't be that desperate, he was already an idiot who I married in the first place, this woman considers herself to be the wife of someone who used to work in a desert area. It was presumed that the man had gone away taking the only child they have, making the pretence that her mother had died in a flood that happened a few years ago. They never had proper relations which meant that her life was totally rough. God knows if he may be dead by now, I am foolish to search for him this far in urgency as it's not his place, the woman thought crossing the main road and reaching the bus station preparing to leave finally.

A man in a police dress spotted her and requested to come with her. What now? I don't look like a criminal, do I sir? She said as the man shook his head thinking the face may look similar to a child they had seen in a care taking place in the recent visit. He requested her to have a seat, offered her a cup of tea, and took out a photograph to present his words to her.

I feel she resembles your face in stature if you ask me, he said, handing her a photo of the child called Dakshika as the name struck her. She felt her missing child to be safe somewhere and it was strange that the wife who was thought to be dead to the world had to feel for the child who had been taken away from her years in a quarrel. What happened to the man? The one who may be her father? She asked, feeling sorry as the policeman told her he had been killed in a snatching battle.

The policeman requested her to come with him as he may visit the safe home the next Monday which was 2 days from now and he could take her in his vehicle to meet with Dakshika. He suggested a place close by to settle in where she could have rest of the gap with proper meals in 200 Rs and she agreed. It was time to meet with the lost child, one she belongs to and there was no difference as Mahant had died now instead of telling everyone that his wife was not in his support as she thinks back to the old memories and his dominant voice.

Status is not the only thing that hinders the gap between farmers here, but the right to own a family and who shall be the main leader is also a concern. This is what cost Mahant his position as people who supported him did wish to be in close touch with his wife instead of him in the village. Varuna as she was called was asked to contest the village elections back when they used to be together but Mahant had said no to it. After a lot of arguments and fights, they decided to leave the village and settle in a different place to nurture the only child they have for themselves.

The lack of money and shortage of health facilities in other places made things worse for them as they tried to struggle with it. Finally, the flood came that took Varuna with it including other village women and Mahant said that she had gone with it, probably dead, though she survived the force somehow protected by the immigrants in the time of emergency as help came during the effect for all of them.

Varuna tried to search a lot for her husband and the only child but she failed to do so. There were stories in the village that Mahant may have got some other lady. There shall be someone more close to him but the wife didn't believe in them. Trust is very prominent in ladies of Rajasthan as they feel more than connected with bonds of family ties. She started to search for him, worked in a local dairy to earn money and now she is totally recovered and prepared to meet her daughter who had survived the community threat somehow from the past.

There was a sound of a police jeep as the children ran away to meet. It has been known in the care taking place that they do bring sweets with them so the children can't resist. Varuna was told to stay in the outer area as the policeman who had brought her offered her a seat and went in. He told the informer that he had been able to track someone who may be connected to Dakshika and told her to bring the child outside. The little girl had been more comfortable here and didn't wish to go away but she was requested to meet someone from her family and she agreed finally as the policeman handed him a cookie.

She may know you dear, why not just have a word? The policeman also urged and Dakshika came out walking like a small child. Varuna had a gaze on her from a distance as she was refusing and felt that strange relief seeping through. For a moment the child and the elderly person looked at each other and then Dakshika ran towards her like she had some memory of her pale face from the past. Is this you? How did you survive the past? The daughter said, running towards her and she felt more calm than before.

The mother took the child in her arms and hugged her and she felt very quiet to see her again as the child felt closer. I did get help from people who may have wished to meet me with you again. I am sorry your papa is no more dear, Varuna said to her and she agreed. The policeman stepped forward with some tips on the gang that tricks children after killing their parents and he told the informer to find the trace between Jaipur to Ganganagar to which she agreed with a word as she also wanted to help close the whole case by her skill on the show.

The spies had got active and they wanted people at all costs who were actually involved in making things go wild. Raman the main inspector had been called and the policeman who dropped Varuna off asked to stay here as it may be comfortable We have enough space to let you be adjusted with Dakshika, the informer told her and the policeman had left with a word of gratitude by the mother for all the efforts he did to trace, identify and help her meet the child.

There were more calls as Raman was talking about a secret gang handled by a farming lord close to the desert area and they may have to track it so the spies had started to find the main cause. They got word of an early-age children's wedding in the border area, knew it was against the law and it may be the reason why Dakshika was attacked by them in the first place as the police investigation continues wanting more tips on the way the gang members are trying to trap victims offering them touring packages.

Nartak speaking sir. Our tip is confirmed but the network is spread much bigger than we expected, he said as the policeman fought bravely with some people. They look to be outsiders rather than Indians and the inspector recognized them where they do belong. I see you export human bodies to saudi, it's your main bait as you fix out weddings here. Is that true? He said, thumping 3 of the men as a police jeep arrived at the place looking to get the action going further.

Three men came out from the vehicle and they started to brutally fight with the illegal persons who were caught and were taken into custody for their connection with the whole case as they shouted of having no role in it. Every criminal denies he or she is not involved with it, Nartak said as he filled them into the jeep, collected their Indian passes, and asked the spy to trace their link. A few hours later the suspicion proved true as the men had been linked with a gang who looked after sending people to Saudi on honeymoon trips and the police started to charge the men in the station.

Raman speaking, I need to find Armaan on the border, he is the main person connected with the lord making this all stuff happen, the chief said to Nartak who was still on the search operations outside. I may soon be able to give you more tips on the progress of the case sir, he said, asking the female informer to report she said that some movement was taking place in blue vans close to Jaipur which they need to keep a close eye on. A few juniors were sent to the place and they started to track the other activities happening around them with fierce speed.

It was a dark evening, strange clouds were hovering in the sky and a man could be seen with a torch light in his hand getting brighter. He crept in quietly, opened his home's main gate and he had come in. Arman looks to be a man in his early 30s with his beard covering most of his face and eyes peeping like a mask towards everything that happens. He is well respected here in the community as he has a lot of supporters and they were the people who helped him do all the crimes.

Get me my biryani if you like, he commanded one of his servants with a smile on his face and he went in to bring him food. What's the news on weddings in Jaipur? Is any new couple in urgent need to get tickets, he asks one of his other servants who brings a card and he looks over it. Ah yes, there are 3 new couples, did you offer them discounts on the tickets? He asks and the servant shows him the online message to which he smiled as the food arrived at the table.

Some bad news master, We have traced out people looking for us you know, one of the other servants called Raheem interrupted the process as the master was cutting the bones out and shoving more food for his liking. What kind of trace, surely the police are not interested in having wedding ceremonies for themselves? A few of the other people in the large house laughed as the master said, making fun of it generally as the chef brought him dessert to feel perfect.

He knew how police traced him and had managed to tip them off whenever they came closer to his place to search him; he was already one step ahead of them. However, things are folding faster and this time he might not be able to predict the police movement. Nartak had already sent someone to the main city of Riyad to find more details and the man had been cut loose with information for the Indians. Armaan had no clue of him, nor his servants, and things may come to happen faster now as the spies were getting together for updates.

Arman slept quietly at his rich place as people were talking for his safety from behind. They were discussing how the leader has been less informed and they can't do much about it. I am sure he is not worried about the threat of police as he has tricked them so many times, Raheem whispered to Kahrtoomm, his wife who had been the washer at the house helping the master. All of the servants do have some sort of panic, like they were being watched by someone and the fear would soon come true for all of them.

In the night a strange voice had come from the upper floors like someone had broken the security cover by his hands. It didn't wake Armaan up but the protecting guard at the top floor felt awakened. Who is there? I demand to know why you are here, there was laughter in the air as someone came and punched the first guard. As the man fell, there was a sound of a crash and more guards came running to check. There was the sound of a few bullets, a fight had broken out and an intruder had come in looking for more clues to help the Indian police with it.

You won't be able to get that device, you get me, another guard said as three bullets hit him and he collapsed. There was a roar from the remaining people as they took their knives out and lunged at him from all sides. There was a count of 3, a strange whisper in the wind and all of them were dead and destroyed in the blast. One from my side for your master, he will soon know why I was here, the man said, taking out a device from the security camera network as the man had gone taking what he actually wanted after the fight.

He had wished to get his hands on the camera footage that captured wedding couples in the topmost building. This was the place where they came from before having their travelling cards for the rest of Saudi by the master and he got his hand on them. I have sent you the whole digital track record, I hope this shall be enough, the man texted Raman with polite influence and the chief thanked him for responding to it. We're just on the beginning line sir, the man texted back and they wished each other luck in trying to find more from the place with their skills. However, Raheem had been informed of all the security men dead and the device missing from the camera network which made him feel worried.

I told him to be on the alert, he said at the morning breakfast table. He is not going to be affected, only the visuals are gone. We still have videos of the couples enjoying the desert safari, the other servant said reminding him and he felt calm. The food servant obliged the master with his usual cornflakes and the master had sensed the trouble, What's the mes folks? Is there something out of place sir? He asked, looking towards the servant who was arguing with Raheem and they gestured that something had been taken from their place by force.

Armaan left the table easily, finished breakfast early, went to the top stairs, and saw the pool of blood with certain damage to his devices and he felt miserable by it. There was a strange feeling of being unnerved that made him get angry looking at it. Indians, they are back with their force, Who else can dare that much, he whispered to someone. Trace the spies on the loose, I want them in my custody, There was certain agreement from the other side, and the call disconnected as Arman wanted to find out who may have taken the main photograph and for what purpose at this place actually.

Back in Rajasthan, a jeep had come to the outskirts of a huge farm as the place was visible from a distance. Vimlesh could be seen talking to the men who were asking about the farm lord and he tried to explain it. He is not always at his place, you need to form a plan before you think to go in, he said as the policeman shook his head. He had come in a civilian dress rather than an official one and the jeep was white which had confused the farmer first. I shall see what may be wise for us, the man said, stepping out and walking away with his jeep still at the threshold of the farm.

The man at the lead told his juniors to stay there as he knocked on the main door for help. What brings you here sir? I am the lord's servant the man said with a pointed beard as he wore the local dress and looked to be a workman. I have come here to look for an offer to the lord. My daughter is 15 years old and I shall want him to search for a person for her, the man in civil dress raised his face with mischief as the junior in the backdrop smiled on to it and the workman went in all for the boss to have a deal.

The lord asked the chief to sit as he gestured to another to be the member of his official party and the lord didn't hesitate to say yes. He had no idea what may be happening outside his yard as few of the men had been taken by officials. The chief confused the lord to ask for a wedding proposal and he called for more men to cover the area. Another jeep had just come as they had crossed the farm and the policemen first took off Vimlesh and others in charges to plot a conspiracy that speaks of monetary gains and killing people who have younger children.

They checked for other farm workers and found them to be part of certain crimes so they were also taken with very little noise due to the sand moving in the area as the chief enjoyed buttered chapatis and his subordinates smiled with joy. Pure taste, he will be into it soon, be ready for the fall off Nartak tipped them as they were keen to see him moving to find the strategy. The lord had opened the gate and started to walk towards the yard where no one was present and the chief thumped from behind as he felt cheated for the assault.

You are under arrest for bribery and crime to force the weaker farmers to marry their daughter to your closely connected circle, Nartak said, taking him by the shoulders and forcing him to come with him. The white jeep was ready and the men had caught a few more people who had got wind of the raid trying to run off. We did get them to sir, Now we need to trick Armaan to finish the course, they said laughing and it was somehow under control in India now as they count the men arrested and only 4 were missing from the Jaipur gang.

All clear sir, we have apprehended them, Raman was informed as he asked about the progress. Tell Vidyaman to do it quickly in Riyadh, he may reach the main tunnel by now, the chief said, asking for things to move at a better pace and they agreed. A call came and Vidyaman told of getting hands on the video data to be presented as evidence before he brought Armaan to them and it was perfect as Raheem and Khartoum were also taken away by the spies tricking them and they were dead as they tried to fight off.

My men, who are taking them off? I can't believe this is happening here too with such ease, the master says talking to the food servant who looks a bit ill and under fatigue. I may not be able to come the next day master, I am sorry either you kill me yourself or let me get treatment for my weakness, he says as Armaan gives a brief gaze at him and the people who are sitting in the inner room feel worried sharing a few words. They were talking of the trap, how the boss had not been on the mark and there were a lot of noises as a few young ones were crying to go home.

Armaan decided to trick the police again as he called someone in India asking for a table to book. I shall be going to India, what else I can get at your party table? He asked as the man felt elated being an informer of the police back home. Last time we served you the lower buffy, this time we will give you quality taste, the man said and Arrman smiled like he had made him fall for the trap. A call comes to him however just as he had disconnected. Sir, do you fear me so much that you're looking to go to India or it's just a trick for us? The voice looked familiar and Armaan felt worried hearing it and he was the person who almost caught him.

Don't try to leave the house or you shall be dead. I have official orders, the man said and the master felt more frightened than before. He called someone in the ministry and the person didn't pick up his call. What this could all mean, is he really in trouble or these people are just whispering behind his back as they do all the time? I have a ticket for a camel ride for you sir, a message flashes with a ticket attached and Arman feels concerned either to go out or not as the sender asks to come quickly or he shall lose the remaining member inside his place as a bomb is also planned.

As soon as Armaan comes out, Vidyamaan has reached his place smiling with triumph. Come, sir, I shall take you for a ride, he said, dragging the powerful man by his shoulders as it was not easy to fight with Armaan in his own place. Vidyaman didn't take much to think what to do and had indeed booked a camel ride to take the person back. We want to show you what happened to your men in India this is why it is arranged, the Indian agent said as the Saudi could see people on the floor, injured or dead as they proceeded within the borders which made him go through true pain.

I am afraid your cook was the last to die sir, the Indian said as the tears in his eyes started to bloom wondering how much he had to pay for this business that may finally come to a close. My family, where are they? What did you Indians do with them? They must be safe at least? The Saudi asked and the high-profile official told him that they were in India awaiting their trial with him as they were also involved in the grand scheme.

Raman was waiting on the other side as the camel ride came to an end for them Nice journey sir? It's been years since your tricks started to get popular and they might end now, the chief said smiling with a word of gratitude and an official document to the agent who took it with pride. I have rounded the men in India for your team to clear off the whole mess, the chief of the police said and the intelligence officer agreed to proceed with the legal process as they have finally got the main accused.

Soon with the permission of the governor and the documents arrived, they got the right to send the people involved in child marriage cases behind bars and punish them by court for their crimes. The men who were in league with murder and other crimes had already been killed in a fight with police and their bodies were taken care of to be disposed of with true dignity. As they were no more their enemies and must be cleared off in the right ways and the police thanked everyone for their noble efforts in the cause.

For Arman, however, the legal trial was arranged and after he confessed in front of the public, the police took him on remand, launched their rage and he was killed openly by the officials in front of a huge farmer party making it finally come to a close with a positive note. Varuna had managed to get a job in a local Anganwadi centre and she cares for all the children alongside her daughter Dakshika with true happiness for all of them and the informer has been rewarded for her efforts to serve the society in such a manner.

11
Murmurs of the Soda Seller

It was a busy street, people were coming and trying to find their needs and the shopkeepers were trying to sell them the best they had. A man could be seen wearing a pink hat and jewels on his neck as he asked for a few expensive clothes. A few girls could be seen laughing loudly as they stood close to a person selling lemon soda. A lot of them were out on the road talking about the mood of the city. All along the place was packed with people and it could be busier than this as the place holds a huge cultural influence.

A car stops and a rich person comes out dressed in a costly suit. He walks forward to the man selling lemon soda and tells him to meet him personally in an hour. The man takes two steps towards the nearby food stall, asks to pack some potato fritters, and simply smiles at someone with interest. He gestures to a lady of around 30 to come with him as they munch along and she shies with her eyes looking on something else as a drink that is sold close by and the man follows the gaze.

The old one, shall we if you like? She said in the local language and the man walked towards the place with a hand showing to the driver that he shall be coming back soon. The car turned leaving the man to find a parking slot and the friends had reunited. Mazama? The man said in Gujarati as the lady felt fit to have 1 large glass of Basundi In front of her and it was somehow perfect to see them enjoying their taste. Add an extra pinch of salt to it, the man told the drink maker and he obliged to make it unique by adding salt in the drink.

Your son is not back, is he? Why not tell someone to find him, the lady said as they started to talk. We can't convince him. The lad has been in the business of the gems for years. He won't like to come back and settle down here, surely? He said pointing a dot on his chin as a few more friends had come watching him settle there. Let us be gathered too, it's the mood of the evening, they said and the man called Viagra who was rich didn't hesitate to let them join in as they had been missing for some time.

Gandhinagar hasn't changed in years when you speak of the people. They do welcome you like they used to in the past with their arms open wide welcoming you to the food stalls, asking to sit or munch along or pay for you if you didn't have enough money to do so. All that has changed in the years is the level of food, the help of people, and how much the place has developed. It seems that people only used to come here for business purposes, but now a lot of other options have opened up for them to invest and get rich.

The only trouble is that crime has also been associated with the growth of the place and it is not easy to resolve here as cases of kids being hurt or wounded are more than frequent. They mostly happen in mines of the crafts or close to families who practise it so nobody complains about it. The children can be heard crying, their parents in dismay and it was not going to change for them. The payments still happen lately as they are daily wage labourers for whom hunger is still heard more than louder and problems are not going to fly away just with time.

The rich man told the soda seller to meet in the corner so he could talk with him about the business. How is the shop? Is he seen recently? He tries to ask about his son but like usual, the man shakes his head. He is only talking to the people who work under him as an agent sir can't be sure, the seller said as a few more people were coming to ask for some more drinks and the rich man let him go. He called the driver, told him where he was currently and the car had come taking him away with some pain onto the eyes as the scenes were folding outside.

The trouble was that the son was not in a good position as he owned a diamond mine where he kept building up pressure on the working staff. The owner could be seen taunting a few assistants, scolding the agents, and even not sure how much he may earn as he has contracts abroad. The only thing is that he doesn't fear the police or officials due to being rich and he keeps the mess up by not trying to go home or talk with his father about the threats this business brings alongside the riches in the market for the owner.

An old man called Raghuvendra was crying in a small cottage where his family used to live working for the diamond mine. I lost him just like the other weak neighbours, he could be shouting in pain. What's the problem, sir? I can't see anyone else leaving their family? A neighbour came who also worked in the diamond factory but was of high rank and tried to talk with him. You better not ask, you are paid well being on the higher rank sir, the old man said watching with disgust as a few dead bodies could be seen lying on the balcony inside and he was in true pain of losing the people.

I may talk with the owner, he will be helpful to give some concession for the deaths, the senior called Pulendran said as the old man looked at him with strain and hatred. Old talk, like you did have a word with them when my other son died sir. It's no use talking about the problem with you. Get out, Raghuvendra taunted him as the other man had a fierce look at him. You shall soon be removed from the place, I shall see it happening sir, he said as he left with a strained but angry face and the old man was still crying for the people he had just lost due to illness or lack of medical treatment taking their lives simply.

Things were much different on the other side where a man was sitting on a comfortable chair checking on some documents for his clearance the old crap. All the documents in one file. Why not let them be arranged like they used to in the past? He said to nobody but himself. A look at the details told him that more labourers had gone out, which made him frustrated. He may consider to be the owner but he also has to keep their accounts updated. Put the details of removal or the government shall be on my skin on where they all went, the man said, lifting his glasses to read the papers clearly with his eyes.

He was checking the insurance of the dead people if labourers had to face it in some way or another and he smirked to read it. Only 10% of their salary per month? How much they earn 1 or 2 k so that is the better deal for people like me if you ask, he checked for the change of currency, counted a hundred rupees note, and summoned a man called Banwari to be at the desk. The man who seemed to be the agent came in a hurry and received 8 crunchy notes which the owner asked to deliver to the old man crying last evening and the agent left thinking 2 of them to be his being the key person working

This was not going to work this time however as spies were still inside the mine and one of them who works for the government had seen the plot. There was a strange sound, a hand on someone's face and Banvari was slapped by a spy. Likes to take the money of unknown people with glee? Claim it to be your sir, come with us, now, the spy said, dragging him by the shoulder and taking him to the old man asking him to hand the whole money as he is not the rightful owner of it.

After giving the money to Raghuvendra with pure delight on the man's face, the spy took him by the scruff of the neck and told the inspector that trickery had been involved in the diamond mines. What kind of tasks do you do? Nick people's money while trying to deliver it? The inspector who came by the name of Jiten asked as the man was taken into custody without any word to the owner or he may send his own goons to fight with the police.

The trouble was that Raghuvendra's elder son had fought against the corruption in the mines as he was vocal about it. He was so strong with some decent money to his name that he revealed it in public and also asked the police to provide help if he was threatened by the gang. It somehow became an urgent massacre as the son was killed at the hands of the goons hired by the owner without the police even coming to know it. When they entered the place, it was locked up, people were crying and the owner had sent his own people to fight at the station which made the case an absolute one not to forget forever.

Now tell me, who killed the son or I shall pay you hard-core detention, the police inspector asked after beating Banwari and he collapsed onto the floor in pain. I was not present on the day of the murder, I can't say who was involved, he kept repeating but finally, he told him that someone was hired to do the job for the owner himself. Please I shall be dead if I tell this but yes Pragyan was hired to do the job and he must have killed him as revenge, the man said finally on his toes grinding with pain and Jiten felt pleased to hear the name as he knew the killer.

The owner was looking perturbed that his undercover agent had not come. He called Banwari but there was no response as the police had taken it into their custody too. The owner called on a few men to search for him but was not able to find him. Where did he go now, in his village? The man said, thinking of the person as he was most crucial to him and the crimes he committed under his highest level for earning money secretly with them.

I shall kill the men if they have taken my agent if you ask me, he said to a person who was known to take care of his cash and had brought more money to handle his orders. Send some of it to the station, we will see why they may take him, the owner said looking flustered but not dejected. He was somehow able to connect the past and decided to check whether the police had taken him in for questioning about the man dead in the past.

Pragyan speaking sir, I have detected a certain movement of people looking for you from outside and hurting you, the person said as the gang of the business world was also after him. I am not worried for them, right now I can't think of myself but those who work for me, the owner tried to show some majesty as the killer disconnected the phone and he felt amused. The monetary circle has grown up but it has also brought threats with it putting the actual pressure on it as it does bring fears to the owner.

Mandakini speaking sir, I want to get some gems if you have, one more call rings and the owner agreed. Yes, I will send you my agent to choose the right one and you can see the price fitting for you madam, he said with his voice changed. Females are the only people who don't frighten him and he is more polite to them. A customer is a regular at his place by the name of Mandakini who belongs to Lakshadweep and has been here for 8 years now with her taste for rich gems very clearly known to them from the past.

Few more calls to the owner, a word on him shall be soon in their grip and he was still disgusted. The busy hours did make him frustrated as he has to keep an eye both on money and those who provide it. I shall search round for the idiot before they catch me out, he thumped his hand onto a table checking the bills, and filled out a form for an order by a customer from another state with riches accompanied. He smiles as he knows the customer is not aware of the exact price and he loves to trick them exploring his best virtue being money and women to trick with glory that is held by pale hands.

The owner looked for a message by someone with a warning and now his eyebrows were raised with fury as it arrived on the phone. I shall surely not ask you to surrender till I get the exact evidence to arrest you but I am on the right path sir, the message read and it was sent by Jiten who told him to have captured Banwari and the owner felt more than concerned by the way it was sent. The message sounded like a threat rather than information and the owner wishes to fix the matter before it gets worse for him in public.

I wish to find out what may have happened to my friends before I come to talk with you friend, he said, calling another police person as he was looking to get the report. I can't help you sir, they are intent on trying to solve the case, the policeman said and it made the owner frustrated simply. He searched for a purse to pay someone, called a secret agent, and sent him away with a word to do something wrong as he swivelled from the place in a hurry.

The crime had already been done before he could reach the place. Someone was crying, a man was on the floor and he looked a bit old in stature. A glimpse from the agent made him feel surprised to see and then he turned running back. Sir, it has been done already, someone may have killed him before I reached there, the agent scampered through to tell the owner who laughed but with a wind of surprise as who may else be involved is not clear to him.

A call comes and the lady responds from the other side. Send the agent with the necklace I had chosen, I have committed to handing it to my best friend of mine, the owner felt more elated to send it asking for the address as she keeps it changing and Mandakini had somehow been involved in the trick helping the owner. She used to commit crimes in the past as the lady is not of Indian descent. She belongs to a neighbouring country called Maldives and she was well known to trick people back in her own country before she came to India.

The owner adds an extra pearl in the joy of the dead man and sends the package by the hands of the same agent who was earlier sent to kill someone. This shall be a perfect send-off my friend, he said handing the order to him and he assured him that it would be delivered. He proved him to be of his word as Mandikini called back thanking him for the extra pearl and the owner waved the call off asking her not to mention it. He is not sure whether she may have been behind the murder of someone he wanted dead as revenge for his man being taken by the police.

It was here that Raghuvendra had started to drink as he had got much more money than he could expect as part of his insurance. In the last few days, he was also helped by a few locals as police have supported him to recover all the money and they hoped that the old man might help them to get their dues cleared in some way. As a token of looking for help, they have started to hand over a few food packages, early gifts sent by their relatives and it resulted in the man changing into an arrogant one. He stopped to lament for his sons, asked for some dhotis every day, and had become the kind of person who looks for the treat.

The habit has got over to him and it is the way he had started to drink as the owner was trying to find out about Banwari. The factory people had offered him some bottles to enjoy his taste and he was over the moon. Who cares if a man is dead, I may assure you he hardly counts amongst us, he could be heard saying and people could feel him turning just like the other middle-class factory members had. They stopped to send him gifts, felt he may not be of any help, and started to protest against his actual presence in the area the person had said in the past.

I shall live here till I am offered help by the agents of the factory, he claimed as he still has backup of the case and men behind who may have killed his sons here in the factory. The man looked to play some politics trying to get in but he had no response. Raghuvendra hopes to find at least a proof, something that can connect to the deaths, and when he is not able to do so, he obliges by threats that reward him with a bottle but he is never satisfied as his inner pain won't get calm by it.

Pulendra had come to talk with him regarding the money but he refuses to talk about it either. Three men dressed in factory clothes came forward to settle the course but he denies to have any information either. Jiten had tried to talk with him and managed to do it when he was not drunk as he tells how his sons were also put under drinking habits which are not in practice legally. He knows a lot about this place being a pure Gujarati and it is not easy to push him away. After all I know how they trick others to earn big, he may be heard saying a lot of times and it did give a hint on the ways by which the owner had gone on to be rich.

The police are not just after the diamond mines, they also have a sharp eye both for the lower coast and the flights moving on. They have detected a certain movement by people underwater from Lakshadweep to Gujarat and they want to get things going. I shall see why they are moving so late in this weather, Prarthna who is a naval guard tips Jiten on the moment as he asks her not to fire on them, just keep the track and she agrees. The inspector is worried as he knows there is some connection between both crimes and he wishes to find out more about the news.

Mandikini is becoming rich as nobody knows she is behind the scenes acting for her riches and gaining more wealth through such tricks. She has ordered more gems, the owner is feeling perfect to attain it and he has sent some money to Pragyan who also felt gratified. No murder to do for now, keep yourself underground, the boss tips and he agrees as there had been no report of an assault on the owner and his father was not sure what he may be doing trying to watch him from far away as a secret threat looms bigger than ever.

People in Gujarat were not surprised to see more people with gems as it's a tradition but Mandakini plotting something big for herself as Banvari had been released after all the inquiries and he resembles a man who had been well trapped inside a mine with pure grinds. I must shine like a diamond after such hard or beating, he says approaching the owner who was feeling sad to see him in such a state. The man who tipped you about your connection to me has been shot dead, the owner said, but Banvari simply shook his head and wished to go home.

After a request to the boss, he turned away with some money and he thought never to be part of such illegal activity again as Pragyan was called. One more attempt or this time a clear shot? The man said as the money dealer went away trying to leave the gang. He has been crucial to us, we can't kill him, the owner said as the person started to think the plan out. Five hours later news was displayed with a man shown on the street badly wounded, Banvari had been hurt and the money he took shall now be wasted in a hospital to recover as it's not simply easy to part ways with the owner or go away.

More private jets could be seen flying with drones that may have brought some sort of products. Mandakini was on the act of her men kept coming with rich rocks to exchange and she has become a kind of broker to the owner who would oblige her with perfect cuts of the rock pebbles to be exactly fitting into her jewels. She would take them as an exchange, sometimes might pay for the carving and the craftsmen behind it and both of them were on to the course. None of them had any guess that they were being watched or a trap was building where they would be caught by the police for their crimes.

A phone rings and the main female answers it as the client has called. I shall need a few better designs, one that may suit my party celebrations, the caller said and Mandakini said yes, thinking of the pattern for her. Would you like a diamond ringlet or a pure necklace madam? She asked and the person from the other side asked to make a ringlet for her cousin who was getting married. Rachna the informer had tricked the supplier and it may be time to find how these metals are smuggled by them.

Pragyan was told by the owner to make the delivery package as he was one of the best when it came to fighting. I don't need a quarrel as it hinders my name, but if it needs to, keep the gun on, the owner said, packing the parcel after the lady had told him the quality and beads in it to which he had agreed. The owner checked for all crucial details, packed it more carefully as it was costly, and sent the agent to make the delivery without much worry.

A snatcher appears in the road as the shooter walks through a lane of busy shops where the package has to be delivered safely. He looks at him with keen interest and then turns away before he can snatch. A sudden movement happened from behind as Pragyan went away from more snatchers who were looking to get the diamond for themselves. What a day, a rich man is going to be taken care of, the gang members said as they started to circle him without much fear in them wanting the riches.

There was a sound of gunfire, and smoke in the air, and the next moment Pragyan was hit by someone with true force as he was not expecting it priorly. You are under arrest for smuggling illegal supplies of the metal, a man said and the shooter felt tricked as he was not expecting this to come firstly. In retaliation, he did a few gun fires but they were countered as he was outnumbered by them coming from all sides. I already have the permit to find you dead but the only thing is the package, Come with me sir, the inspector said smiling as Jiten received a call that Pragyan had been caught.

They took him to an inner cell where Rachna was waiting and she smiled to see him as the inspector handed her the design. A perfect day, he brought my ringlet then?

Yes, that's the perfect one to suit the wedding, the shooter felt that this was a plan to trick people and he would not be able to inform them as payment had been made by them already to find the metal portions. We need it for testing what kind of metal is used so we can use it for evidence, she smiled looking at him and Pragyan felt more frightened than before as he had no idea of the bigger trap.

The police started to do their routine work as they punched him, the man was knocked to the floor and the interrogation started. Who killed Rameshwar then? If you didn't, the elder son of Raghuvendra? Jiten asked as his junior gave him hard-core treatment in the room. Pragyan was not moving an inch to accept and he was not going to reveal that he was ordered as he was bruised or worse than before after such questioning. You keep punching and the people of the area may suffer it worse than before if you ask me, he said as a retort to which he got more blows.

Leave it to me, I may be able to let him confess, Rachna said, coming closer. Mr. Pragyan, the sharpshooter, known to have 15 best shots under his record, is refusing to do so? I have something that may turn the verdict, she said, taking out a photograph and she handed it to him. It's not just we who are suffering sir, you are nothing different in the dice, she said as the photo was handed and Pragyan looked at him, that belonged to a girl around 18 years old and on the floor dead a secret room without him knowing that she was no more with them.

Your niece, missing for 3 years, we did find her but I am sorry we couldn't save her, the inspector who had hit him said with an apology. Who killed her, tell me then if you have found the dead body? The person said on the floor in pain and apathy due to such news by them. In response, Rachna gave him a ballistic report, bullets of a gun and it changed the whole course. The bullets had come from a personal weapon, one he had cleared for his boss last month and he couldn't be more disgusted than before as he realised the mastermind.

You still want to keep the secrets or wish to reveal them, Jiten said looking into his eyes with sorrow. Pragyan requested a glass of water which they did bring as he was helped to stand up by the juniors. You did your job as usual, it's fine, he said looking at his wounds or lines close to them. He started to speak, telling how it all began and what happened. They were able to finally link the case with the Maldives and now they know how Rameshwar died as he also had come to know about the plan wishing to expose it publically.

Rachna, you do the honours. It's you who had asked for the gems, the junior inspector said to her firmly as the woman called Mandakini again. Thanks a lot for your order, let me know if anything else can be done, the female thought, willing to get more from the visitors as money. Rachna asked to make golden bangles for her as an advance with a tip that she also wished to meet the owner who creates such accustomed jewellery with high rewards for it and the trap was building up further.

Mandikini first thought not to let it do so but then as she was sent in advance, she thought it may be more than worth it and agreed to let her meet when the order was ready. Pragyan, these are reports of the people dead in the chase for the diamond mines, Mahendran the junior said, asking him to recognize the members who were killed. The shooter said 3 of them were shot by his shotgun while 2 of them were finished by the owner after they revolted in the mines asking for a larger amount personally. They were promoted but their salary was not raised which made him feel unhappy at the place so they started to take the goons but failed.

More files came to the surface and the shooter confessed to the murders and it had finally counted to be

15 of them like Rachna had said, making the police feel disgusted with it. The messages keep coming from the naval spies reporting more movement close to the shoreline with cargo boats going away and Jiten looking edgy. Tell me Pragyan, when did you last visit the sea inside? The senior asked with polite interest and he said it was a base to hide out if the owner sent a summons by police or court. He told them the exact location and the police asked the naval officials to trace the place so they could find the exact premises which they did manage to find out.

I am looking for someone to send the island country sir, a naval official responded and Jiten felt calm to see things going in the right direction when it came to acting. Pragyan, you are known to have the best range of shots, will you help us now? Rachna said, asking him to join as she told him they would be sending him to the person who plotted his niece's murder and he agreed to work for them. I shall be more than happy to finish the person, he said with a smile and Jiten had created the document for him to join as a spy who shall be with them inside the sea to counter the opponents.

Mandikini has got a tip however that someone may look to attack her gem business in the waters and she is also making a plan to send some secret shooters who can take care of it. I don't want to feel discomfort. My mind is clear as it always was, she said talking to the person, and the dice were set to roll down. The police know the actual plan, the female majesty is planning her tricks and the owner keeps taking the deal's orders as he disconnects his father's phone without a word and the mood is much worse than it could be in the diamond factory.

A man offers some tasty food to Mandakini as she takes it looking on her phone for confirmation. The person she was hoping to talk with had not called as she was willing to close the deal and a message was flashing instead. I feel you to be in trouble madam, be ready for it, it was red and it was Pragyan who couldn't change sides or could he? She calls the owner to ask about the location of the shooter but he has no idea either and he assures her that he may not wish to change sides as he had been trusted with the hard-core steps in the past and has never let him down.

A stranger had come to the diamond site as the owner was busy inside collecting the bills to find out who else had not been paid. He asks for Banvari, feels that he may have been cheated, and walks past the main gate. After a word of confirmation by the workmen that they were treated the same way, he decides to confront the owner. What are you here for sir? My men are always complaining of low salaries, the owner said as he predicted someone would interfere soon at his workplace and had been ready with documents.

I am not interested to see them, I don't belong to the department you think I come from, the stranger said taking out an order to let him read This is a confirmation of your crimes, sir you are under arrest, the man said without a word of he being an inspector and the owner felt it to be a slap. Come with us sir, I am not alone, the man said, forcing the owner to step out and he was dragged by 4 men who had come with Ritesh, the special officer, to take the man with them.

You don't know what I can do. This is an insult, the owner said as few of the working class could be seen celebrating on his send-off. You all are involved in this, Don't worry my shooter will take care of you, he said as the special officer smiled at him. The side had changed as the officer showed him the signature of Pragyan and it made him feel more than in pain. It was not sure but something had been missing in his records, maybe the murder of the niece and that could be the only way of him going away from his loyalty as the owner regrets it now.

Back in the waters, Pragyan was in total action closing down an old case. Jiten had captured the men who were smugglers and had been selling old rock metal to be polished as new one. He crept closely, fired them on the knee and they fell not being able to find the force from opponents. Time to end this all in one shot, Pragyan said shooting a man from behind and the bullet went straight pass his throat as he fell down. Good job, he was the main paddler of the boat, Rachna said, joining in as she blasted the whole boat and a message flashed to Mandakini again with a warning to surrender or face the price.

She wanted to know how the police had been so quick to trace as it had been 8 years since any case had been lodged against her. India has been a good place for her and she doesn't want to leave it despite the fact she had to lose a lot of money here. She called the diamond shop owner but no response came which made her feel suspicious. The leader called a boat paddler but his phone was also off and he had been killed by cops. The water continued to rage with waves slapping high as more men were taken out and they were dead at the hands of Jiten who had got orders to shoot if required.

One more hour sir, they all will go towards the smaller islands, Vimochan the naval officer tipped Jiten and they combined forces. A bomb sounded harshly from surface to water and a whole boat had been destroyed. No capture, we are here to finish them off, Jiten said as a few men got hold of a jewel box, and on the count of 3 they blasted it too. There was a shout of someone being tricked, a man had come and Vimochan killed him with his revenge finally over. years ago this man had plotted with Mandakini to trap his fellows and had been responsible for killing his nephew in the plot so his wish had finally come true.

Now only Pragyan remained to finish things off and he reached the Olankalon caves to find the clues related to the plot. Someone was hiding there inside a minor cave, wearing a royal cloth, holding a candle, and being dressed with beads on the whole cloth. The neck was covered with a royal jewel, ears too were wearing rich earrings and he looked at the person in surprise with his mouth open as he managed to enter with the help of officers.

You are the one responsible for this whole mess? This is a total shame on your standards madam, Pragyan saw a lady in a royal dress, and his mind couldn't believe it. She knew the shooter might come for her and had plotted a bomb to go off but with the help of the naval team it had been defused and she looked confused about how he had managed to come inside as it was not possible to open things without her gesture or guidance and she wanted to get her answer.

I wanted to find my ways to own the rights and your niece was the only problem in it, she said in a taunt openly talking about the property business and how she had become the owner now with the niece dead. I am not going to get it either as it was disregarded years from me after the business collapsed madam, Pragyan taunted in a local Gujarati style as a few bullets sounded outside the strike and was in an absolute mood in the form of an open underwater operation going as they talk about it inside.

The naval officers were in a fierce fight at the mouth of the main cave and the lady's men were toppling onto the floor due to it. As she watched it in surprise again, they kept killing more people and the place was getting empty with echoes of the dead. One of the men shot from a device with a blue light flashing and it went very close to her face blasting behind. Finally the safe case that protects her in the cave has been broken and she gets furious to see it go into pieces with a flick by the man breaking it by the technical element involved.

Rachna came in with an apology to Pragyan and he didn't mind. She lifted the lady, forced her to come with them, and had been taken into custody as Mandakini got the news of her arrest. She arranges for a chopper to fly before the police can reach her or all the evidence may go against her now her best subordinates have been caught hidden in the caves close to Lakshadweep. A noise comes out of the phone and a voice message comes, making her feel surprised by it as she plans to run away from here.

5 minutes to go before we trace your chopper, take your flight now, she didn't realise what it meant but Mandakini had made her plan, she looked onto the sky, thanked the god for making her 8 years the best and knew her end already. There were men on the dock at the sea, something was launched from another chopper and it sounded like a weapon. It raised like a flying wheel, turned around, and went out of sight as the other chopper took flight in the other corner at Mandakini's place.

After 15 minutes of peaceful flight, Mandakini felt something coming closer to her chopper with total speed. In a gap of 15 seconds of realisation of the weapon on its target, it happened without any warning to her. The chopper tilted in the sky and had blasted into pieces as she was killed by the naval command and they had finally closed the case of the missing lady from the Maldives as she was on the run for years and desperately needed by them for records both in island country and India due to her crimes.

Pragyan was taken to 5 years of jail for his crimes but due to his service in the operation, the police managed it to come down to three years. He felt gratified but felt ashamed to see how people were more than involved in the crimes. The owner was taken to prison for 14 years of jail as his case went separately. He was claimed for the deaths of his workers, plotting a conspiracy, and being duped for illegal mining and exports as the whole news reached his father by informers. The old man felt miserable for it and the owner was taken without any mercy as he used to be the same when he hurt the miners back in the place by proving to be a cruel boss.

Things were in much control as the mine was taken by the government to let things continue and the workers were taken away by the distress that used to be with the place. With regular payments for their work and the effort they made, happiness was certainly back in place with fewer crimes in the area as the police kept a closer watch on all the things that happened and the case had been closed after its legal process simply accomplished.

12
Under the Mask of Power

A car was running down a busy lane as people were trying to chase it. Someone who may not belong to the place has been moving around and the people have not been liking it as they prefer the person to have permission to do so. They tried to capture the man, asked him where he came from and the car had gone away as he kept shouting from inside driving fast to avoid the shouts of the crowd that was still following it from the main lane.

Two men had come in to clear the crowd as it broke through violently with no choice but to hurt the opponents. People had got hold of a banner dedicated to some event and trashed it. They turned to the next round of movement, picked a few chairs and it had become absolute chaos as they all started to fight, thrashing each other and going wild as the people from the other side wished to stop them from doing their best.

Why are they so desperate to hurt the other ones? A child just around 8 years old asked his father as they also had to run to save themselves. It is not for purpose but to entertain. They are paid to do the bidding, the man said with a half smile and a pensive face. The child looked at the people coming and felt strange that they had been fighting so harshly in public. Paid to hurt or to kill? This is an onslaught papa, he said as they all started to run away cowering with the threat of being hurt.

I will explain to you at home dear, for now, run as your mother will beat us if we get caught in the mess, the man said with a smile and they went away. The place was still buzzing with low voices and shouts from the men and it was truly on song. They were looking to do the damage, to catch the man on the loose and a special force had to be called so they could calm down clearing the whole area by their grip.

Haryana has always been like this with so many severe noises coming from it. The place is rich in culture but it has a political vision too. People in the state are more known for their ferocious ways as they can be heard, Re bhai, kas lagri sai' and it was a kind of heavy strength to make things thrashed in pieces simply. Most of the places are known to possess strong culture but outsiders are not able to stick to the song of the people, the police, and those who guard the place in their best interests for the community itself.

I will be taking care of the man if he is out of bounds, a man in his late 30s promised the crowd as it became more wild. What if he tries to catch hold of our money or place, the man raised a hand for pure silence and assured us that he would see to it being an agent for them don't worry, our strength is enough to show him if he cuts lose or we know what to do the best, he smiled as the crowd started to thin and people scattered and started to go back home after the promise.

Ishwaran is a strongly built man in his late 30s, he is well respected in society and has a large business to suffice his actual needs. He is known to call people whenever he needs to and only reveal himself once the crowd is in so no one can suspect him to be the main criminal behind the scenes. He calls them to come to the party, to find out if someone from outside has come and chased the person as a public insult. It is hardly known why he does but most people say that Faridabad has become his playing ground where he likes to satisfy his physical needs and ask people to cover it so nobody can watch him doing so.

Besides he is also responsible for killing people and hiding the crimes as they are mostly done at night in his special quarters and this night is not much different. He could be seen taking someone by the neck as the person requested to leave him alone and asked to follow him. After 15 minutes of quiet, Ishwwaran knocked him onto the ground, raised his pistol from the jacket, and fired him so he fell onto the ground and died. The man slumped down, punched the man, and damaged his face so nobody could recognize it, leaving the body alone in this place.

Tell the guards to clear the dead, he calls to a person who agrees to come there. He turns inside into his quarter, closes the door, and sits down on the floor taking a bottle to drink. He started to feel calm, to be with the night and the man was slowly realising the crime he had done again. The problem with the man is that he starts to count out how has committed the crime and he is never satisfied with it. One less than last year, A shame, he said, putting the bottle down and collapsing totally asleep after it.

His family is never going to know when he is in his quarters as this farm is distant from them and he just plays with the wife telling her he will be back in 3 or 4 days whenever he is off but tips his spies to keep a close watch on them. Your family is safe sir, nobody dares to attack, Munshi the assistant keeps him updated and the man feels peaceful. He has decided to figure out soon what he shall do with this farm and he is playing to separate the will away from his sons who have grown up now may be looking to get their hands into it.

One of his friends suggested that he can arrange events here as we were already used to it. Why not contact local wrestlers, as they can come here and your need for women and the money shall also be totally covered? He told Ishwaran who did have a plan to try it but he was never interested. He didn't dare to face the wrath of the police as he couldn't handle their temperament. A quiet voice inside his head made him think for it but he shall soon try to decide what may be done for the farm as he is still under the effects of the hard drink.

The next morning a cook had come to help him as he was still feeling weak. I am sent by the word to help you with food sir, the man said looking at him as he offered him bread jam and the man felt happier by it. Good men, they do take care of my needs, he whispered as the cook went away closing the door. A call came from his wife and he said everything was quiet as the mob's news had got on the Tv and she had seen him getting worried watching it. You just feel uncomfortable by a lot of men, that's all to say, he said and the phone got disconnected as Ishwran decided to plan to fix the farm as it was the right time to decide its future.

However, the man who had been chased last night has finally found a place to save his skin. A hotel had obliged him with some help, to come in and he had paid money to stay there for 3 nights as he came from a far distance. The man at the reception let him sign to check in and the man felt more comfortable with his nature. This is better, people were chasing me last night like I have done a crime on the scene, he laughed as the man did understand why he was troubled with suspects of who may have made it happen like this.

He gestured to the man to check his room, to have feedback for service and he could have dined out to which he agreed and he had turned away. The hotel didn't know why he was here but the man at the reception felt Ishwaran might have done the trick like he does to everyone to claim money or rewards for his people in the city. However, they didn't know why this man had come and soon it will be revealed that he does have a connection to Ishwaran rather than just being toyed on the celebration night by the public.

I must not tell my identity or they shall be completely after me before I get packing from the hotel, the man said to nobody stopping on the outskirts of a shop asking for some daily items to buy and he obliged. You look like a good man, I will help you sir, the shopkeeper said with a smile and a few ladies went away arguing with him rates of pulses which he waved in a smile as he asked for soap, perfume, and a few refreshing jellies to eat as he saw them being on the counter asking to get the right flavour.

It's not good to be here this late, is it? The shop will be closed soon, one of the ladies could be heard saying openly like she was giving the shopkeeper a threat as he passed the items to the visitor and paid him going away as the same lady saw him with some gesture. It gives the man the impression that such money is rare to pay easily in the local area and he can get an advantage by using it as he wants to settle scores with the old man before he leaves the place.

I am trying to clear the list of names here, Ishwaran said as he called a lawyer at the farm to talk the right over. The park belongs to Simant sir, the parking lot is not under your name and the outer ring must be constructed, the legal person said counting the names and the owner felt bit worried by checking the whole list. He started to talk about the ring with Simant which he had won and mentioned the ring to be cut by his funds and that all shall be under his rights if they go by the plan they discussed last time sitting here.

This takes time sir as the charges are not clear from the court and you await the legal document by their signatures to claim them, the lawyer gave a sharper look on the boundaries marked simply by the legal settlement. I can only hear as much as I pay you or else you do know what we're capable of, Ishwaran raised his voice with his nostrils flared. The lawyer raised his hand in silence showing a document and the man faltered as he knew it may be a list of crimes he had committed which the lawyer knew more than anyone else and can be filed under legal sections against him.

I will stay quiet as you pay me or I can also go to the court, he said with a smile as they got back to the talking point after some sneering. What shall be my job then? I will walk with the owner of the parking lot and settle the matter. Here is your bill to visit me, Ishwaran said, thinking of dismissing the meeting simply. The cook came back as the lawyer went away, handing him his lemon tea and he accepted it. The moment had gone as soon as he had thought with no result and he shall have to wait for a further circle of it so he can fix the actual rights of the farm which he owns partially.

The lawyer knew it was not going to work without threat. He is not in a position to advise or he may have thought to settle it such that the place is huge to cover just by legal means in practical terms. I suppose you can have the right deal sir, he has told the boss many times but he wants to have a clear affair. Although Ishwaran is a man of strikes and fights, he likes to cover the legal process so his status remains clear and he can come out of the accused of mishandling physique and lust for his life so it won't affect his sons and he wants everything to be clean as a track record in public.

The spy had simply come to his room as people could be seen fighting for the place, raising food prices and he couldn't be more than pleased. A few years back when the owner insulted him in public, they were fighting the same way and he is quietly watching it as the voices become deafening in the backdrop. The mob was once more covering someone and it could be worse than this as the man had encountered the one recently in the evening.

He threw a packet with a few chips in it outside from the top so somebody could catch what happened and the man felt amazed. He takes the click of it and sneers in the face as the person goes away rushing from the area of being caught openly. One more throw down this time an empty bag and he laughed watching it all as people tried to grab it tight from his windows with no shame to realise its reality due to lack of the value or actual hunger to have it.

Ishwaran is troubled as he is still on the farm with less noise hoping to get someone who can help him fix the issue easily. Simon had come to talk and he had gestured that he could capture back his land despite the order from the court against him he stepped away with a warning to the boss and more men could be seen as a few gorgeous ladies kept coming for needs to close by shops and the man felt bit hungry for lust as he is not able to control it and a bell rings more close this time.

The calls from home kept coming to Ishwaran as he stayed there, the mind deep in thought with all about the hopes and the way he wished to settle the whole farm out. A woman comes to meet him in the night as she seems to be a general customer and asks to get a room and he obliges. I shall let you stay in the next quarter madam, please agree to it, He asks her to settle in as he calls the cook back to bring food for 2 members and he agrees as he had seen her coming in the outyard with a permit in her gorgeous hands with a shine.

The woman was an old customer who liked to drink with him and they had been closely connected physically for months as she wrapped him in her arms and felt pleasure in staying close with the pure joy of it being so closely entangled with him. Why not ask your wife to give yu divorce? I have enough property that shall be sufficient for both of us if you ask me. This farm is decent enough to fill our desires too, she said, ticking the man and feeling relaxed as they became closer and enjoyed the whole evening being in love together.

As it started to get cold in the evening, Ishwaran asked her to drink some more with her face getting red before she could leave and be happy for the evening spent together.

The woman fell calmly into it as she felt miserable with the thought of leaving him. The man didn't know that someone was watching a lady despite being married and he may soon have to feel regret for this as few people are trying to trick the rich farm owner.

His family may act to be somewhere else in the distant outskirts but one of his sons has started to suspect his movements recently after his friends made a joke on his mother with a man who likes other people's company. He had turned away from his place and canceled school without informing his mother, the son wants to know when his father will go and has located him with the help of his schoolmates who gave him the location after they were confirmed by a local seller who told about Ishwran as he holds a grudge with him and the son had arrived to this farm somehow with help of the local tour guides pushing him forward.

His father kept asking the lady to enjoy the evening and she finally felt it to be enough as she took her purse and left without paying him anything that made him feel empty. However, someone had come before he could speak as his son stood there with a knife in his hand. There was a fight that started to break out and Ishwaran didn't know what he may be doing next as he was a stronger man in bulk and strength. {You tricked my mother, I will tell her or you pay me to be quiet, the younger son said in revolt as the father looked at him with shock and anger on his young troubled face getting white.

I am not tricking her only, you don't know why Simant fought a case against me in the court, the father said with a smile trying to tell a secret as he handed the son some money to claim and start a venture. I know you want to open a business but first know about your mother too, he whispered in a taunt as he shared a few images sent by Munshi the last night, and the son felt easily perturbed watching the movement around him.

The world is not that big to count who is actually right to claim it, the father said and the son was sent off to keep a close eye on both sides as the young lad smirked at the words just told to him and the farm owner felt more calm. The woman may come to meet him the next day again till he says her and he feels happy to have love with her which is now also known to his son. He waits for the night to fall, the cook comes by and he feels perfect to hold on dinner as news of few murders rings the Tv and the farm owner smiles on the reporter who reads by watching it as the news did proceed and he stood there quietly being alone with no hint of a threat coming to him like a secret attack.

It was totally night when the man had come to a strange place without his notice. He opens his eyes and looks for the whole circle around him and Ishwaran feels more than surprised to see who may have brought him here. In response, a man had revealed himself to face him, one who had been insulted by his crowd and it looks a matter of time when he may feel to get a taste of his own medicine by his hands.

I have waited for years to face you being surrounded by your people to do the trick, he said smiling as someone came from the public and the old man saw his own younger son in the scheme of it disgusted he had been leading the charge. He hadn't come to kill him earlier when he had been sent off with some money in return but he wanted to trick him and the son has done his job perfectly as the opponent looks back.

He is paid like you people do to play things your way, the person said as more people started to fill around with the crowd covering the whole area. What do you want? I have enough land and lorries to hand over if you like,' the rich man said, smiling at the crowd who had been gathering around and started to separate with the wind of words of promise. The visitor laughed at him with pure glee as the crowd started to roar on the offers presented by Ishwaran in front of them.

These things can't get me back the years I lost, the torture of my family, my daughter dead and most of all my whole family burnt in this same place, the man said without mercy to the lord in a brave gesture as more people started getting in and there were few raw shouts as gunshots could be heard from the other party to get cover. The visitor didn't have much to say and he kept taking advantage as he came close to Ishwaran and told him to follow the crowd behind him as a tip.

I am not going to kill you sir if you think, the person said, taking him by a tunnel as the crowd roared. He told the farm owner to walk through, turned right and the crowd had thinned as all of them couldn't go in. This way sir, quick before it gets dark, the man said and the farm owner kept following in the wake of his younger son.

A lady could be seen coming with a light and Isharan's fear started to grip him more as she was the same one who he had pleasure last evening as she smiled with joy. I thought to make you captive so you can't stay away, she said with a laugh and they all took the owner inside a place which was strangely lit. I need to find out a few truths if you ask, the man said and it was absolute trickery as farm owners can't do much against them and forget to use force.

It has been three years since I had any confrontation with you, Prakhar said finally as he was called. He has a short figure, keen eyes, and a sharp brain to think and the spy started to look upon him so no one else could be seen. How many ladies have you tricked by now sir? He asked with a straight face but the farm owner didn't oblige. He called someone and told them the plan had worked as they had taken the help of his son to put out a false alarm and had taken the owner in for inquiry.

Ask him the rights of the parking lot, a voice came from the other side to surprise the owner with ropes and the spy did agree to discuss the words. Yes, it has been something we need to know from him as time is not much left, he walked through looking frustrated as there's not much left and police can come here anytime to take things under control and Ishwaran is not aware that it's a deal these people were after rather than taking him simply as a captive to ask questions.

I will take you all to the court, You take my word for it, the owner said with some sort of disgust. The lady came closer and slowly tapped him on the shoulders. I can also go to court dear, we are very much so close, the physical melody we had, she smiled with a kind of mischief as the owner asked what they wanted and they better let him get cleared or else it may be a huge suffering for everyone due to his links in the order.

Prakahr hit him hard on the shoulder as he said this and started to smile. I shall refer you to someone who can treat you for this kind of mess, he waved away as the lady told the informer not to damage him much and he agreed. See, even You can't hit me like you could 3 years back sir, Ishwaran started to smile now and they had released him from the robes that covered his upper body as he simply lunged for the hit onto the man who negotiated it by true force applied for the strike.

There was a sound of something broken, two men were on the floor with the heavier one wrestling the light one and then there was a huge crash as Ishwaran felt worried. Prakhar turns back and starts to kick him and the lady asks him to come back to control as the farm owner was in true pain by it. There was the sound of hand on hand as punches were exchanged and the younger son kept watching it from a distance like he didn't care for it. Keep the morale going mate, Prakhar said and they stood like he wanted this to happen first.

I have been on the search ever since you hurt my family back in that year, Prakhar told the owner like the police may be after him and he should go. The crowd had been watching from the mouth of the tunnel and they separated as the owner came out with not much damage but the informer had not been able to convince him of the parking lot and the owner had somehow survived the fall. Next time, I shall wish to claim for your money and manners, the lady said with a hug to him and Ishwaran had gone broozed and insulted both by body and mind looking at his son with distaste as they both went their ways.

The police had come to the place as they had been summoned by someone. Search it, last time we did get traces of alcohol in large numbers here. They may like to trick us again, one of the inspectors said as the informer was an illegal supplier of drinks. He used to work for Ishwaran in the past but one day when he found out that the agents who he supplies are sending it for scrutiny to trap Ishwaran, he felt more than frightened. The owner kept asking him to carry on the trade and in the process had killed his family members so he couldn't say no.

This led Prakhar to run away, come here after 3 years of being prepared and now he is looking to settle the score but the police are still after him on the loose as they search the inner place and this time they get traces of blood. Presence of a lady has also been recorded sir, the junior said looking at a broken hair as the senior told him to collect the evidence and send it for forensic testing so they can be tested. We may soon find out whether the boss was here or not in the fold, he said, smiling at the past encounters he had with the farm owner.

The police had gone as they got a tip of something else in the other location with more bad news. They had got a call from Hisar where a man had been found badly injured and the release of blood had simply led to death. The chief inspector told the juniors to keep a close watch on this place and he had gone driving his jeep. The Chief arrived at the place with much interest of the place and looked it carefully. He could see the man on the floor as he talked with the person who had called and the villager said that he saw him a few hours later but couldn't help to take him to the hospital as it was costly and very far from here being a rural area.

I shall be asking the forensic team to come here to take the body, the chief said, making a call to the group member as he told them to report at the location as soon as possible. Anyone you had seen who may not be here, a strange bloke, a face not familiar to? The chief asks as the man tries to remember and tels the sighting of a strange lady who had come to offer them sweets but the villagers had denied her and the chief asks the man to come with him so he can be helpful to design a sketch as he took him in his jeep for police support.

The owner also gets a call from someone and he is worried about still being back on his farm. He has not thought of going back home to talk with anyone and has stopped receiving calls from his wife who feels for him to be under threat from outsiders. Sir, I have done what you wanted to do for 1 year, the man is dead, a person speaks and the boss stands up suddenly. What kind of hour is this to call me sir? I am not sure which man you are talking about, the man on the other side told about the person who had tricked Simant into fighting a case against him, to waste his money and now Ishwaran felt it had been too late to do the honours for him as he is worried for the outsiders to attack him anytime.

He shakes off the feeling, tells him to meet him the next day, and has a disconnected call with a smile. The owner felt hungry after so much action and had asked the cook to bring him food even this late at night. I need to fix how to handle Prakhar and Nivedita, they are working together to drop me down, the owner thought, munching his food and he may ask the same person who killed the imposter of the past to fix the whole case

A police inspector has come to the spot, asking a person to find him the owner and he simply refused. Either you take me to the boss or come with me to the station for inquiry, Bhansali said in his official tone he was used to being very strict. He drags the man by the scruff of his neck, lifts him, and with the help of his few other men, the man is taken to custody where he shall be questioned about the death in Hisar.

Leave him now, he is just a small pawn in the whole dice, the chief said as Bhansali gave him a nice treatment. Your boss did plan a murder last year, didn't he? The chief asked, showing him a photograph and the man felt surprised to see it. I am not going to support the panwaris who are the owners of the parking lot, the chief said with a smile asking him to talk further. Finally he revealed that he did kill the man and it was done so simply without much beating or any threat at the station by the head.

Who is prakhar? Why is he back in the city here? The chief asked further to find out details and the man who was a spy for Ishwaran told Prakahr to be a rival of the boss. He used to supply alcohol but he turned against the boss as the owner killed his family members by force, the chief asked Bhansali to write down the statement as a track record and there was a call done to Panaris asking them to come to the station as the chief knew they would deny again.

Yes, they are scared that we work for the land owner after all, Bhansali said to Vidharv who smiled being a junior. Is there any plan to capture them or is it not going to be easy as they are so highly connected sir? The chief shook his head and told them to create a chargesheet for the man they had found. They made calls to the family members of the man killed to come and file for concession as that's the only police could do and they had caught the person who did the damage mostly.

Ishwran had come back home and the first thing he did was to find his younger son and take him inside a room there he did a severe beating asking him why he was involved I didn't do it of my papa, they paid me, and threaten to kill you forcing me to do so, the man stopped beating him and smiled as the son stayed on the floor with fear and worry for it. The father took out his file, checked for a missing document, and felt no strain as all the legal coverage was back in the file and he shall try to connect to a lawyer once more.

A call comes again to the owner and a strange voice speaks from the other side Prakhar wishes to meet you sir in person, no one else is allowed to be there except you, the man said not sounding familiar and the land owner thought this may be the best time to finish the person once and for all. He took out his official gun, checked the bullets, and stepped up before his elder son could see him. The father crept from a secret passage and reached the place where he was told to and he waited for an outsider to come and the secret was hidden into the passage itself as someone came out.

Hello dear, nice to see you here, Nivedita said with a smile, making him frightened from behind. What do you need? I thought Prakahr may be coming to meet, the owner said in shock as she stepped a bit closer to him with purpose. I like to hug, a lot of the time we have done it, aren't you interested? She said, looking into his fearful eyes and smiling. It is your farm that I am after, either you hand me over or else, she said with a playing note as he looked at something gleaming in her hands and she was in the mood to commit something strange.

The man tried to lift the woman off but she had turned onto the other side before he could do so and it was really strange. It was not much action but like a love scene as she didn't punch him but gave him a hug to take things off.

Ishwaran wanted to fulfil his desires, to get involved with lust but this time he had delayed the chance to talk mostly. There was the sound of a few bullets, the noise of a strongly built man, and in a few seconds as nature watched, Nivedita had shot him, becoming the owner of the farm by killing the current owner simply in a passage.

She laughs both with joy and sadness as she already had arranged to get papers as the cook and other people were sent by her and the trick has worked. When he was asleep, they had taken the documents and forged them as Nivedita had clasped him in the evening where she took advantage of her emotional strength. They had done it so smoothly that the owner hardly had any idea of it. Panwaris happily agreed to manage the place which they do as she has no interest in their parking lot and now the farm belongs to her as the main owner of it with no partial settlement.

The only trouble was the sons, one who may come and Prakhar has tricked them into working for him as a supplier which may suit them perfectly. I shall give you the commission to supply my material, he had said as the father was taken to be tricked in the hidden passage. The man had called the younger son to join him and as things folded, he had been tricked into staying and talking about the business and he had agreed to sign a document which meant he wouldn't be coming to the farm either or wish to claim it.

The family is not the only trouble, somebody had come as she stood there with a gun in hand and thinking about the rights of the work. A person in official dress and she has seen her do the crime. You're under arrest, Miss Nivedita, both for promoting physical pleasure and using it to control the rights on property, the female inspector said, taking her by the shoulder and she was totally confused. We already have your men including Prakhar, you come with us if you please, the inspector said with a smile and nobody got a hint of how they had managed to crack it out.

Only one mistake and this is enough for us, a junior inspector said, throwing a cloth piece Nivedita had cut after she had got hold of the documents in the farm. We checked for the false documents tracing your agent. He is in our custody too, the female inspector said, smiling further. They had filled almost 15 men in the jeep and 5 female persons who worked under her all being booked for certain crimes and the mass murder policy had almost come to a close with the last of the men remaining to be caught.

The men started to gather as they came to know that their boss had been shot dead outside. It took local men some time to grab hold of them, to make them quiet by shooting ammonia bombs into the air and the sound started to come down. They were told of the plan. The Police showed them the member who did it and they wanted to let Nivedita out so they could do mass murder but the police denied them to do so as legal punishment rests in the hands of the court.

Your boss was not a pure saint if you ask me, the lady inspector said, talking about his physical assaults and it may be one of those causes that the female member could succeed in it. The farm was a perfect place, we found enough evidence to claim it, Bhansali said as few men tried of charge in and he stopped them being the followers of Ishwaran who used to stay with pride on doing it all of this but his strength had become his weakness as he has been dead.

The wife was heartbroken as she saw the news first on the TV and the elder son felt disgusted. I told Papa not to go searching for more property, he told his mother who shook his head and stood up drinking curd. I hope people won't make much noise or it will be hard to control, the wife said, wiping her tears as she could see the people around the dead body and the phone rang asking someone from the home to come to do the last rights as the elder son obliged.

At the heart of it, a few more fights had been taking place. Police had captured 3 men for illegal drink supplies, traced their connection to Prakhar, and arrested them for such a crime. A lady inspector had caught 3 women who were known to be involved in child trafficking and they were found to be closely linked with Nivedita who may have been a criminal from the beginning but was revealed later. Things had been folding fast but the inspectors had tried their best and the place looks more calm with crimes taking place in low numbers.

The son came to the main station to get the reports of his father and the Police said sorry which he didn't feel much to be of course and they let him take the dead body for last rites as the case has almost closed. They have taken the main evidence from the farm, broken hair, bracelets, garments, and a lot more and their forensic report shows fingerprints of the dead man connecting to the evidence and his crimes as he was involved in it.

Besides they have also got documents the man had signed before committing crimes at his farm and the elder son handed the legal proceedings to the people for scrutiny of them. They have traced the criminals connected from the past, checked how many of them were locked, and the main documents that made police feel calm as the cases were already in the court to be settled by official order and they won't have to work harder to crack the whole case.

The police agreed to submit them and get the final settlement of the person and it had led to close to the case at last as the son went out thanking them. We used to serve your father once, he turned away and see where he has landed in, the junior inspector said as he still had memories of when he was new and had been sent for the security of the events they used to host its fitting that he met the end by hands of a criminal if you ask me, isn't it the same old policy? The lady inspector said and they all smirked at it as tea was handed with jalebis amongst them.

I shall be glad for your service as it's rare to have such a send off sir, the son said as the younger one was followed and he survived the fate of being behind bars as Prakhar had been caught just as he was about to join the false gang. Both brothers hugged each other, and after a few tears about losing their father, they went home as the police felt relief to see how things did have to fold in such a complex and high-profile case simply. The mother greeted them and they were all stunned by the end of it in a somewhat possible way they had been expecting to come.

13
Risking Lives for Riches

It was a strange morning, many of the workers had been feeling sick of doing such tough work and they didn't wish to go to do it at the place. They were asking to get leave of a few days from the boss, to step away from it, or have given excuses but they were ordered to go or may not be paid. It's the money that makes them fear more than anything to be at the site, to do hard work for hours and balance it or it may be cut down.

Work is not the only thing that makes them fear to be at the site, the rich hills have a lot of other things to come as problems and these workers do have to face issues because of it. The concern has become a daily routine as a few of the workers of the site may be seen falling deep in the open places, have a slip or collapse from the stones that take their lives away and the staff would ignore just it as usual news.

How many times, I shall tell you this is not the government who should come to solve the problems actually , a senior reported as two more men had gone missing from the site, probably falling in the valley. You promise to give us some financial aid or to help our families when we are threatened, one of the lower-class workers said and he was slapped hard to ask for such a deal. It was also in the routine to take hard-core hits and stay quiet while at work or you get low wages or hardly any respect.

This doesn't look up to our standards, to be honest. I am sick to face human and natural torture, one of the workers said with a gloomy look. I don't have a plan or I could have revolted in your true support mate, the other said, breaking a stone down as the puff of dust rose, making his pants dirtier. They all had their prayers to the natural Karisma to help them in some certain way but it hasn't been done either as they continue to face troubles and severe problems by the staff.

A gust of wind made them feel strange as the weather was not warm enough to complain even outside in the hills. The sun seems to stay polite here as the workers may be seen outside giving their best to protect and work for the bosses. There was one more cry as a child had fallen below and the mother was in pain. No point, he shall be either dragged or shall be sent into the deep valley lurking on us as monster, one of the workmen said, looking at her to try her best so she can recover the son from its clutches.

After 15 minutes of the effort she managed to push him back but then a slump of stones sounded and they both were falling out of sight as the workers were equally shouting for her. Let them go, few more are easily taken by the strength of these mountains, an official man spoke to them louder than ever and they turned away from pressure and no longer wished to work in the place. No recovery, total damage, absolute onslaught, we still work here, they spoke to each other in the evening and the mood was worse to hear with more losses.

There was the sound of a horn and people started to pack their bags. Close this before they get us or we shall possibly be in huge trouble, The official said looking at the workers who wrapped the whole bundle of stones and had gone before police could reach them to search in. It has been a certain problem they have to face regularly as owners do want to let them work but they do braking and construction beyond the limit which can force police to come to probable sites as surprise visits sometimes to check the work.

An hour later the official finds out it has been a fire van as a few of the woods had caught severe flames which needed to be put down by the brave men and he asks the men to be back. They all felt strained from the effort and tired due to it, and were not willing to come but had to get back. The woman who had fallen off shall not be traced and worse, she shall be removed from the worker's list which makes the work more vulnerable than ever as more names are taken off.

Uttarakhand has a lot of secrets hidden, it is known for the scenic beauty that welcomes everyone but those who work here at risk have no easy job to do as it can make the place never be comfortable for them. Work at the sites is something which is done fiercely and people want to find traces of rich metal but it is also done with severe constraint. People can be seen fighting for the metal, trying to convince their best rights and arguments are more than common with shouts heard from almost every colony about it.

Further, in Garhwal where the migrants come to do work and do stone craft, they have to face a worse mixture of hot and cold weather as things start to get more tricky with heights. They need to be habitual to dip in oxygen, heavy and low waits to lift, and also fight with each other as they grapple to stay and live a tough life in the hills. They can complain to the god that they are put into one of the most risky places but they are also rewarded for their work when it comes to success so there is not much to complain for them.

My brother may be hungry but How can I help him now? A cousin of the son who had fallen with his mother says as they look for more clues or any hope to fix it. The government needs to interfere now, how long should they stop it or let it be left alone? An old age labourer smiled as people kept getting missing and there was a chance of no more hope left. All they could know is that they get a sudden slip, it lets them fall and it has been constant news amongst the press.

What happens with workers in the hills sir? It is somehow strange to feel as few of them could be seen going out of the view. Who may take them? There is surely a way we can help them? A reporter was presenting his report of more workers falling inside the valley and the word had now started to spread like wildfire as police were sent for traces but they were unable to find the men who had fallen and it was becoming a kind of pressure to resolve as more news continued to come about it just being similar to first one.

A noise came from the main area where many people had gathered to demand any action taken by the working staff. The news has started to come out that officials at the sites are not taking care of their workers and they are worried that they can be dismissed if the complaints happen in the right way. Families of the workers who live in different cities have been watching the news and had shared about it on social media where a lot of arguments were happening from all sides. It puts the staff in certain worry they keep doing hard work in the tougher places forcing the workers to come for the job.

They asked to be on target, try to avoid the slippery nature of the stone sites and somehow they were able to bring the top down but the news was still on high about the case with more spice to it. I ask you not to go to the media as they will never pay you money but shall ask to pay them by your pocket instead, Manvendra the official said as he requested workers to complain about the problems and they can't do it either. The mood was getting more than serious and things were on the true toll as more workers came to work. A few of them had simply faltered and some of them had died too in the process of helping their owner get the best cuts by stones as they fell down again.

I will soon be fired if they keep dying, what about you sir? Manvendra asked a supporting person who had been hurt by a working man as he paid them less and he shook his head Nasty job, either to pay them or not. They will argue as their wish to have alcohol become large never shall be over, he said checking for a lump rising close to his forehead and Manvendra looked at it with some smile. He said it was an old trick to face the wrath of more men in numbers, handed him a tube to put and he may feel relaxed somehow.

Manvendra decides to glimpse at the valley stretching below where he had started to peep during the conference last week, Looking down he starts to remember his childhood and how it was an innocent place. He used to be a child of a worker too, one who had to work hard in a lower city factory and he never thought that these people had to face the toughest in life. His childhood became better after his elder brother cracked a government job and from that time he decided to follow in his footsteps rather than his father's. He relishes it as he looks at the valley with the wind blowing at the backdrop to give him great comfort.

The officials were blamed by the media and Manvendra had come to defend them in the conference. We are not planning to fix out any kind of slippery places, We do care for lives, after all, we are humans, He was commenting on a statement by the press where the officials were duped to earn big by exporting the stones and he had to explain to them how choosing the stones is more than required which plays a crucial role to build a settled place in hills which are always tough to construct or create places for them.

It doesn't mean you have to let them drop in the valley just if it is required, one female press member said, commenting back. The official shook his head looking down and felt it had been more critical to adjust the stone sites. You send a few workers to make a place here and I will let them see safely at the end of the task, he smiled painfully as the members shook their heads and the conference was done.

He got a call from his superior to get updates on the process who mentioned not to comment back to the media as they are looking to get loopholes. He thought that it could become an outrage or it could criticise the whole structure as an initial move and he agreed to what his senior had said. Not a word about inner combat sir, Manvendra said dismissing the call and his assistant brought him hot tea with Samosa to cherish upon. He looked at them from behind his goggles and ever since that day he just come this close to see the glow and fading hues of the valley.

Few of the workers had gone away with fear of life upon them and Manvendra had to request local guards to help trace them as they were important. After 3 days of hard work and inquiry from the villagers he was able to find them close to an underground tunnel and he was worried about seeing it. For a moment the official watched closely at the end of the place and the tunnel gave him shivers deep down. It was all just a plan for this one to happen as he could now see it from the past cases.

People who were falling off had been destined to do so as this way it may help the bigger monster to truly leap and the fear was almost upon them as Manvendra tried to shout for help or wishes to close the mouth of the tunnel down by stones. I won't let it happen, it's truly my job to protect them, he could be seen talking as a few villagers had come right to the tip of the tunnel and he saw them being of some help as he went through the ultimate plan to bring them back.

He wanted to save the men, one who belonged to him and hoped that this may lead to stopping the crime connected to the land and its breaking by those who like to earn from it. I won't allow you to break the mould, one of the villagers said as he started to find a way to do it. Manvendra felt the mud slapping his clothes as they had come to him to strike and this day he might have to go from here but He will come back with more men to decide the fate.

A movement took place the next day before the official could go back to the tunnel. There were sounds from people, news flashing, and the tunnel had opened itself getting wide. All the stones Manvendra could see were nowhere to be seen and the mouth of the tunnel had expanded wide, crashing everything as the men who were on top trying to defend had gone slumping deep inside with a crunch they didn't expect but had become part of due to its actual force.

What the hell, help us somebody, the men in front shouted as they were snubbed deep in the dark area. Please, we are small workmen, we have nothing to do with this wholehearted affair of crushing stones, the others who were caught earlier said as they were trusted to withdraw the force of the stones that were tumbling and they were sent leg first inside the depths of the place before anyone could come to help as they stayed in trouble and raw pain due to it.

An idea, we can call it a calamity and shall better stay away from it, one of the officials said as he saw the report and was called by someone to report at the site. Manvendra had asked his corrupt men to stay closer, and not mess with any officials of higher rank and they were called Sir, this has happened due to the force of the tunnel, we are not responsible for it, the same man said as they all came to the site looking to go towards the tunnel but they were stopped by few villagers.

You can't break the tunnel just as you have the right to break the stones away by permits, a few of them said, raising their cutting weapons as they would be prepared to fight with them. Who may stop us? I was thinking the same way, another junior said as Manvendra told him to be quiet and asked the villagers the reasons that they were not allowed to break free of the tunnel directly as he had some suspicion about local beliefs.

One of the villagers who may be looking younger said that there is a temple at the other end of the tunnel, if they break it can cause some effects on their process and the men who had been trapped inside might not come safe. The junior felt irritated to hear these ideas but he couldn't do much as he was tied to the commands of his boss and waited for the orders. Manvendra told him to go and observe the site from the other side, bring him order to control the strategy and the villagers felt better to hear from the main commanding official rather than weak juniors.

Manvendra is also told to adapt to the slope if there is a temple at the other end to check what happens if they bring heavier weapons to protect the men or take them back. For now, they had no idea that this was also plotted by someone to get attention and the real criminal was watching the whole stand out from a distance on the TV. He had a smile rather than pained looks compared to others and he was looking at the visuals carefully checking for results and whether the government may declare it challenging.

A video conference was taking place at the Ministry of Health and Disaster Management Authority. They were talking about the steps that have been taken and what else can be done. You shall keep the media updated as we take the protocol, right? The main boss was informed and they just took it as a crisis that has unfolded in some way or another. After a few minutes, they changed or made a plan B that can come to figure out the first. If we fail to bring them back by our lifters, we will try to adjust it some way sir, the management team said and the person felt a bit dejected.

The juniors of the criminal had been watching the movement closely so they could report it. As soon as the working team went onto the site, they started to shout out some slogans and tried to push them away. You should not try to go inside or take down the tunnel, it's our land of rights, one of them warned the people showing a fist in revolt. The official tried to reason with them but they kept lunging with their words more loudly forcing them to use arms.

There was a sound of metal clanging into each other and the security person knocked down a few men with force as they tried to fight with them. The official knew that somebody may try to trick them and had taken more men down as they tried to fight it out. No, it's our place, you can't knock all of us, the main spy said and the official in the front took him out, striking him with a yellow light that flashed and the man was on the floor dead as his supporter watched with fear.

The official warned them again not to come here or the rest of them will be treated this way too. We have a tip on somebody behind this force, better stay away from the process or you will go to heavens too, the security person warned firing a few bullets into the air and they started to observe the place as the men inside the tunnel felt more than uncomfortable shouting for help, anybody who could come for them and take a step in their recovery.

I shall better be dead as I don't feel anything coming to take us out, the weakest man told the others as they all saw him in pure dismay. It has not been easy to stay the whole night here without anything to get for our stomach, One more person said feeling uneasy and all of them were not thinking to wish except death that may loom soon to clear the whole mess from them and the painful victims of the crash felt desperate than those who usually go down and died as they are still alive struggling to stay here.

News channels were also of no help as they only showed what may be taking place on the floor rather than inside the place with people trapped. They are not able to trace each in the risky terrain below in the beginning. We shall soon bring you fresh reports from the ground 0 places as there is a lot to crack for us once the government starts to take action on request by the people, one of the reporter said with some keen interest that any political person might request her to showcase the news broadly for the party's interest or personal gain by it.

However, the authorities were still not clear whether to take it seriously or remove it from contention and the workers were still inside the place feeling miserable than before for it inside. The CM will know someday, it's better we let him be aware before it gets worse or we may be in huge trouble, one of the assistants in the disaster authority group said and they agreed to bring it into alert finally. The member requested the secretary of the home affairs for the state to take the report and present it to him so the person can feel it to be honest with them about the case.

Are you sure? My state spread rumours more quickly than the accurate details of the action taken, the CM said sitting on the table with calm. He was a man of work, one who likes to only talk about the action and if he finds that it has been a trick, he simply closes it over. Bring the rescue operations to attention if they are not already by the media to cover them, he said in his deep voice and the secretary showed him news which he watched carefully trying to find something unusual in it.

he asks for the foreigner to better not get directly involved by asking to write a letter and had turned back thinking the plan over Manvendra speaking sir, Pleasure to get the orders from CM, a man calls into the secretary and he tells the main plan to bring the machines over to crush down the boulders blocking the tunnel view. The officer agrees and informs that it will be arriving by the next day and should be used but they need portion support for lifting or waiting panels that can help the workers.

Don't worry humble CM has approved to take them into use and the officials can be appointed to do the job, the secretary said and the officer feels glad to disconnect the phone. I will be watching you all, the CM replies from behind like he has not been separated and his assistant smiles as he goes to check and confirm whether they can be taken or not. We are in it together sir, I hope it works well, he says and they have started to take the next step for it.

A person was standing in the outer yard, he was thinking of leaving Haridwar before anyone could guess his presence. I need to be out of here before they catch me, he said trying to turn right a servant arrived looking busy as the man turned trying to catch up with time. A train comes to the front and the man simply takes his seat checking the tickets and he had gone before anyone could enquire about him.

A soft spot, if you ask me, a person speaks to the servant talking on the phone to confirm. I need to keep an eye on him in the train, the servant said in another section of the vehicle while quietly watching. It is not too late before they start to expand the stone thrashing, he said with something to grab onto as he chased the man with desperate hope as a lot of questions remained to be answered.

The train stops at an outer station and the man who had been willing to run off checks for something to throw down. He takes a lid open and forces something to come out and it results in a strange item to fall upon. This shall not be in their hands or I may be not left alone, he tossed a device, throwing the weapon out but someone caught the package to his surprise as the man felt frightened to see the servant standing there with a smile.

You are under arrest for forcing the slip of stones and making the fall happen in the hills, the servant said in his voice, being perfect in civil dress. I am not involved, it was someone who forced me to do the job, the man said looking at the servant who smiled asking him to come with him. He took the man, pushed him towards the area and after 20 minutes of forceful walk, they came in contact with the road to get a vehicle to return.

What's the update on the trap Jagdeesh? Did you have him? A voice asks on the phone as the servant reports that the man has been trapped and caught with the device active to cause mayhem. You sure it's been a weapon that affected the movement? Jagdeesh agrees while talking on the call, told the man shall be brought to the bars soon and they await his confession to find the main concern as they were trying to find actual causes in the lower hills killing the men.

I am not going to tell you the main reason for which we did cause it, the man said as the servant put him into a car, forcefully asked him to sit and they went back. I am bringing him to the station, to provide me cover, the servant called someone and a few working persons came in to try and help things out by covering the servant. They took the chance to get a better move, fixed the process, and safely they took the man back.

Now Mr. Dhanesh, why did you try to run away from us? The senior official said as he was taken to questioning inside a staff office. You are not taking me to jail then? I am more than pleased, he sneered as the officials had a look at him and told him that he must be in conversation first. I will soon be able to take you under my pressure, sir, don't worry about where to question me, the criminal said and things may look tougher than what they see from the open view.

It is not to let you have comforts, here is the document of your current state, The senior said, getting strongly disgusted with it. I only brought you here to show you in CCtv for the records and officials, Dhanesh felt a bit surprised when he saw a camera just moving away taking his photograph. Now we do have a glimpse of your presence, it shall be more than easy to take action as people complain of you out of capture, he smiled as Dhanesh the man felt a bit pain to see things off and his plan had not worked exactly with what he had wanted.

Things were getting easier at the place where workers were inside the downfall as the main villain watched on TV how the officials had traced or been able to use the machines. Can't see this happening to my trusted men, he said in a whisper as more of his fellows were caught and there was more to fear for him as people kept getting traced in the local pub, outside food stalls changed with faces and more troubles came for the people.

Come with me Dhanesh, the man who had brought him said with his signatures to handle him. Now we shall take you to the jail for questioning, Jagdeesh smiled, forcing him to follow him backdoor and the official told him to be on point as he nodded to the senior taking the culprit away with him. Machines had been working better than ever and they had avoided the crash with the temple directly going towards the tunnel to rescue and back at the site manvendra finally had a sigh of relief.

One day sir and that shall be enough to crack the truth out of you, the inspector said, starting to take the order into action as Jagdeesh watched the culprit checking the device. False sites, tricking the people with commission, the servant said and the inspector wanted the culprit to start or he shall be hit badly than before For a few minutes he didn't start to talk at first but then he was hit brutally so he started to talk about the conspiracy that may last for very long.

Come out of it, who may be the main boss and where is he? The inspector enquired and he told the name, his location being not sure the police were shocked to hear it. Vidhyanchal is active in it? The man who was rejected from the official job? Jagadeesh felt more than disgusted and they may have to trace the location for themselves. Our boss has a sharp mind a perfect one that suits the criminal, Dhanesh said and it made the servant smile as things started to go in a positive direction at the tunnel and the CM was happy to do a press conference giving details of the process

All the social media places started to buzz with the effort involved but none of them had considered it to be a criminal effort that has been cracked down by agents. I wonder how the government may be handling this tough aspect of life for them, one of the scholars from the local wrote as people started to see more evidence of all being safe and the media was able to penetrate the inner visuals as they brought updates on the people to be on the right side.

We bring you reports from ground zero where the machines are in the total swing to make it possible, one of the reporters read as Vindhyanchal saw it on the big screen and he frowned. Shall I put the throttle down or It would be too late? He thought, trying to connect to one of his remaining men and he suggested he must wait. How long, the day when they shall have me? He sneered and the call was over as the master sat with no further plot in his hands to recover his strength.

Dhanesh, one last question before we take you for final custody, the inspector had still been on the charge of more criminals being caught with help of the first they had captured simply. Is there any word to convert the tunnel to a secret underpass for travel leisures? It made the man frown but he didn't say much as the police person hit him to respond and he had to accept that Vindhyanchal had been behind the whole plot to create a pass for his royal liking and may have done it.

Ah yes, a direct movement inside the place, any idea you have how badly it can cost? The inspector told beating him as he felt more pain than before the officials had come with documents to shift the criminal caught and the inspector obliged as a few men took Dhanesh away with a smile to fix the course themselves. We will find him anyhow, we don't need you, Jagdeesh said and the captive felt miserable as his boss would soon be under his grip by a plan thought by the senior officials for the criminal.

The secretary reported to the CM on how men shall be brought to the surface by the machines. I need to find by what time they will be out as their families can put things under pressure, the CM asked, looking a bit worried about the long strip of time it had taken to control it. We shall soon be able to adjust the whole course, sir, don't worry, the secretary said with some sort of mischief like he knew the plan and the undercover officers were working hard to find more clues both to get the men and close the secret case.

Dhanesh had been taken to a secret jail so the boss won't know where he has gone underground. The man was a known criminal, one who was an expert in devices and could cause huge trouble if you let him stay loose. You let my master know how I am treated and face the price of it, he said again rasping in his old style but the inspector was not going to hear it. I am honest that your boss shall be under our grip sir, One of them said and his smile turned into sadness because of it.

It was not in clear vision why they wanted the boss but Uttarakhand is known to have crimes of land where people like to catch out the schemes often connected to them. The civil servants were looking to close the case out where Jagdeesh was on the front to trap and catch the persons simply out as they were put under pressure for offering land and it had resulted in helping them to crack the whole case taking the right step.

Things were happening faster at the tunnel site where men were finally seen to get the right help. We are starving sir, for days we had no help to get the actual food sir, one of the people asked to get help on it as the workers were assured to get proper aid. The families were told to have patience as officials were calling them and the foreign people smiled at the effort. Good to see them working for the public now, one of them said as it started to change with the actual location in true control and more criminals behind bars.

Durjayan was finally under the grip as he was one of the right hands of the main boss. Ah yes, we have you now, your illegal property is enough to give evidence instead of making a special sheet for it, this made the villain fear more than before. Already have Dhanesh who has expressed your crimes sir, this made him feel worried and Jagdeesh forced him to come to the prison. It started to become an absolute uproar for the criminals as more of the bhu mafia was truly under the trap now.

Vindhyachal decided to take on the challenge as Durjayan was the last man to all and he may have to do something as he thought using a device to have movement close to Nepal was a perfect option. I am looking to control it with my hands, he whispered as he called to a lady who didn't receive it. It was not under his knowledge that he may soon be falling by the trap set for him where he was going to be in it. There was a certain settled plan discussed by Manvendra as he had gotten wind of a criminal stature and he had talked it quietly to senior officials on how they could solve and fix the whole case.

A phone call arrives and the gang leader answers it. Someone wishes to meet you at the coffee shop sir, the man said and Vindhyanchal obliged by taking his glasses back on his eyes as he stepped away. One more person to get larger money by smaller lands, maybe an outsider he hopes, he thought to himself as the man was waiting in the nearby shop for him with patience. It was a similar trap as the officials had done against Duranjay and the owner was not looking for anything to surprise as he shook hands with the shop owner and paid him some notes.

I need the expansive one sir, the visitor said without an air of being an official in nature. Yes sir, the boss likes to be on the main glass citadel, the waiter said as Vindhyanchal came. He was a dashing man, strongly built and somehow has been known to be a property dealer. In most sense, he may look like a broker but for those who know him, they are aware he can be truly shrewd. He was equipped in battle, knows to use most of the guns and it won't be easy to take him away from here.

The dealer started to open cards offering certain places that are like hidden places but not known to the people. No sir, I already have seen that site, the tunnel crash has made it more vulnerable than before, the official said as the dealer was more impatient to make the deal and he handed him some more designs and maps which the official needed desperately for actual evidence.

Do you smoke sir? The villain asked and the official shook his head in a remarkable smile. You have the chance to do it openly here sir, after all the owner is yours to be honest, he said to Vindhyanchal who baffled to see the comment coming. He didn't mind it as he checked for the gun attached to his belt and he still wanted to convince the man or use force if he did not agree to his plan crossing the true scheme of the offer by his side.

Only one man dared to challenge me and he was finished before he could even think to retort, the villain smartly commented as the official did have a counter to it too. Yes, the man you killed after adding slow poison to his coffee sir, a stalemate but not totally your skill, Vindhyanchal raised his eyebrows as he wanted the official to challenge him for a battle and had taken his knife to fight directly.

Look there sir, your owner is in trouble now with someone taking him, the man said with a broader smile and the boss felt miserable to see a few men taking the coffee shop owner by force as he started to fight with the man sitting in total strength. There was a sound of chairs falling and both of them started to fight. I wish I could have finished you that day when you tricked my relative, Jagdeesh said with a sneer as he threw the villain down and took his gun out, disarming him before he could attack.

I am the best shooter, I always keep one more for the cover, the boss said to the visitor firing from the next one but no bullets came from it. One more false alarm to trick you, sir, it's empty too, Vindhyanchal threw smoke into the air but it was repealed and a few more men came. You are only brave when it's one on one, now let's take you to the station

Jagdeesh said with polite interest and he was forced to stand back as the man punched him to recognize his strength.

I am here to help you with the brutal assault sir, an inspector shouted as more bullets were fired into the sky to counter the threat. There was a voice from behind from the gang as two of the officials were on the floor and the villain had captured them as he struck them with his earlier gun. Jagdesh roars in fury to see them dead as he knocks him down being the only one to resist him and the fight is in total swing as the villain asks to release him from his grip being in a lot of pain after the quarrel.

No sir, definitely not. You would do more murder with them, the official thumps him with a series of punches and he feels bruised and in total pain by it. I shall drag you to the police station so they can enquire about you after being disarmed, Jagdish had broken his knife, emptied the first gun with bullets left and his special wooden weapon blade had been torn with force. All of the problems may come to calm now as the main villain was under the control of the leaders after a severe fight happened in the main area to capture him.

The CM was addressing the public as most of the men had come out one by one in numbers. Their families were watching them with smiles live on the TV and things were under process as the officials took care of the main entry with their skills. I shall not allow anyone to have this land for construction under their control, the chief of the official said, reporting to the secretary and the leader was informing about the weaker portions that may have resulted in the chaos causing such a huge rupture.

Vindhyanchal was however taken to the same place where most of his men were taken for and he could see all of his brave men, either injured or hardly speaking to each other. Our plan failed sir, Not to say what we wanted to do is not going to be true either, they said with a sad face and he didn't say much. All that he cared that they were not dead like the officials had tried to do the honours against him though they failed at the coffee shop.

Jagdeesh took orders from the boss to fix the main case with a tip for the policemen and the chief told him how to handle the criminal at a high-security place. He needs to be handled with care as he can still hurt us, the chief whispered as the servant agreed to do it. I do have a plan, I shall only tell it to the leader of the gang from our side, the servant said, and he went to make it a final act with no loopholes inside to accomplish it.

He told the inspector-in-chief to go through the process and the boss shall be handled separately. I will be cleared soon, the court knows who I am rather than you thinking to be with failed attempts to push me, the villain said with a sneer hoping they could have killed him in a fight as it's no good to bring him being a top property dealer in the city. The official snubbed him and threw his old list of awards from the famous people and it was somewhat a dead end for him from all sides as he was thrown down.

We are not taking you to the jail sir, one of the inspectors said as they drove away with glee. Vindhyanchal thought this may be coming and he wished to fight but they have tied him well in strains with a sub-inspector in charge. I think like nobody knows about the tunnel to be a human mistake, you shall also not be known to the news or media sir, the man said coming out of the vehicle as it stopped in the outskirts of a place visible with rocks.

The person was released from the grip by the help of an employee, he was given his gun and he felt cheated as the policeman surrounded him. With some intent to do the massacre, they have captured him worse than he can think to be. The men in dress said that they were going to kill in the worst state so future villains can learn a lesson by it and the man felt frightened for the first time in life as he was told.

On the count of 3 then, the chief said as they all threw something in the air making the villain have pain in his eyes. 3. 2. 1, go Kill him, there were countless bursts of bullets, and the sound of a bomb and it was like they had been celebrating a festival to crush the main person down. They looked at the rubble, cheered for the task accomplished and the jeep had gone with all men safe except the destroyed body onto the ground demolished by the official act.

14
Tales from Bihar's Heartland

It was a clear night with no clouds in the air as people could be seen sitting outside a balcony for some kind of cultural evening. They were waving their empty hands, smiling at the man who was leading it and it looked like a perfect way to welcome the moment as a crowd started to fill in the area.

It was the birth of a child, one who has just been born in this land and it can't be more than blissful to make the occasion glorious by the party. The family commanded huge respect due to being rich in the area so they wanted to get it settled grandly for themselves. A lot of people had come to see the child and the members had taken it to be a rich procession to form the pact and make it known to everyone who had come to enjoy the party thrown for the infant by the parents.

I may like to find what he may name him, surely a king from the past should be fitting? The older people laughed as they looked closely at the child in the arms of his mother. I am not going to name on our history, but he belongs to the place so he must be name somewhat like it, she said smiling to her husband who was wearing official dress and it was a perfect night for all of them as the DJ kept buzzing in midst of few people willing to make it more spicy.

The visitors felt obliged to find such a great reception held and they wished it could be more than perfect to welcome new life amidst it. All of them wished the family for the moment and they couldn't feel more than blissed to achieve it as the party progressed. However some strange elements had also entered to make it count as all were feeling the moment but these people want to get a tip to it.

Are you mad now? They won't let it happen so they are amongst the top most people who do business, one young man said, mostly around 20 years old looking at a bottle in the hands of an older man who may be 5 or 6 years older than him. Yes our state has a ban on it, so what, I can choose my taste wisely, he said, handing a glass to the young lad who seemed to be searching for the chance. They cheered slowly, lifted the glass, and were hardly affected by the content being banned here.

Bihar is a state of large portions, rich people who are in a high position but it also belongs to those who are struggling to get hold of the movement of the circle. It is somehow true that the government has banned liquor use but in most parties, people can be seen trying to make a drink and force it somehow for their wishes. They had secret bases to get things to their limit and it makes a laugh the way drinking habits are connected, almost going over the law that wishes to stop it from being back with the same rhythm.

I would like a glass too sir if you wish to hand up, a lady had come with a cigarette on her lips and the distributor did not stop as the parents had taken their child and it was almost the last diners show now we trick the people clearly without any intent as they don't know what we want, she says smoking with her pipe and the man handed her a glass as she gulped it down in few seconds but not asking for more from him. The drinking party turned away, silently out of the left side and rattling the entry banner, they had gone as they came from the backdoor.

A horn sounds in the night, the police are on the alert and they wish to catch those who may smuggle the drinks into the main area. The vehicle comes in top speed, turns left and it is out of sight as it ignores this place where the party has come to a close. Those who have been left simply look up at the sky and they are truly fond of the night as they used to drink a lot in the past. Ever since the law came, things have become somewhat calm but only for those who stay in the state.

In the other places outside it is still a routine to go deep and enjoy it as few Biharis could be seen sitting in a ub enjoying the taste. Let it be that our state is not much stronger to digest the actual cusp of it,one of the middle-class men who may be a clerk at the city said, feeling grateful. You better think of going back to Darbhanga, they will tell you manners or how to speak on it, his friends laugh as he raises a glass, takes a sip, and feels simply calm by it as they are talking about the past.

The loss of a man had come into effect in a different place but the police were still tracking the case backwards. I think they may be drunk and might have to fight to finish it, one of the junior sub-inspectors said to his men as they called for clearing the place to see the wounds on the man being beaten. Send the body for detecting the case, we will start to find more evidence related to alcohol, the police staff said as they went away in fury leaving the friend crying with dismay.

Liquor is not just affecting people's hearts and souls, but it has started to spread like a toxin and soon the investigator may find out the raw truth connected to it. People who sell alcohol do have the idea of how it may spread and they are adding a touch of something deadly to life. They whisper not to explain to anyone, make it based on the raw price and more people could be seen affected in physical nature by it as more cases surface in UP rather than Bihar now with the list of them going high due to it.

Get me the case. Why is it so much in the news? A man asks who may be from the revenue department and he checks for rising numbers coming by selling liquor. Why is it so much on the hit list? I didn't know you may get so much profit by it, he smiles and then turns away as a few of them have shrunken profiles with sad faces. The news of people dying from certain chemicals was on the front and the official looked at it with a strange feeling as more people had to face the pain of the way things were circulated.

It was night again, people in Bihar had not been up to look at it as new rules had come to stop the spreading of the liquor and police had been sent to check for the main and exit doors. Show us the pass of anything you have got that is not allowed, one of the inspectors said as he kept a close watch on people who had low profile willing to cash in. We are not much worried about the named item sir, we already had filled the rule, to be honest, one of the middle-aged women said who may be from the organisers and the police had gone after checking the whole scenario.

One man suddenly came like he wanted to gatecrash and he was hit by someone from behind. Sorry, I was waiting for you to come and supply what is not allowed here in the party, the man dressed in civilian clothes said as he took care of the intruder and the people in the backdrop smiled. The dwarf man held 4 bottles that were not labelled correctly and he was hit with some punches to tell the information. The policeman had been waiting to find out why the secret men were involved in it and now they have got the man they had been looking for in the area for days to catch the men out.

Leave it, Thakur, we know they don't open their mouths that easily, the senior said as the man who had brought him started to punish the man. I am not involved, people at the party may have asked to bring it after you were gone, the man said with a baby voice and he was hit harder. It's not what we look for you now, In Bihar it's a habit to take alcohol away under someone's nose and make it effectively served, the senior said and now he forced him to speak the truth he had been hiding from them in reality.

The man told them the false case, a trick to smuggle the beers and sell drinks instead in public, and the leader board agreed to present the case. We know the problem already, It's not a hidden fact on who may be in the course but we have to keep the movement going, the inspector said calling to someone who may be the secret spy and he asked the beer case to settle first as time was not much left for them to crack the case.

In the evening the inspectors had left looking to find more ways as they took the dwarf man to an outer yard where a lot of bottles were cracked open but broken. These are the bottles we had from our raid last night, do you have any idea where they came from? The man shook his head first but then told them that they were smuggled from the UP border with the help of some outsiders. The police asked him to expose the other people but he showed a few fingers like he was depending on them to stay alive with the help of money and they had to keep quiet.

A call comes and Pawar the local inspector tells them of one more site where they need to come fast. The chief told the juniors to visit the place and they found a few bottles left as a trap. They are not used but we are not interested in drinking either, the inspector told Pawar as he checked for no label and threw the bottle into a sik Let's check how strong they are by our current testing mechanism, he said as the content started to boil with it.

In a few moments, it was taken by a storm of fire as the bottles exploded in surprise to see it. Good one, it did catch some fire for us, a lady inspector said as she reported catching two ladies selling mixed drinks in the local area. How many times should they be told not to do this in public? Pawar said as he checked the report and smiled like he had got a trace as he saw the names being on the hit list. He tips the lady inspector to talk with the captives and enquire about a murder last week.

After five hours of hard-core detention by the lady inspector, both of them did open up and the wires were linked with the dwarf man as they confessed to be working for someone. Are you the only one employed or there are broader links to find more on the subject? The inspector asked and the ladies tipped her on the ways when they were first brought to Bihar through the border and now the actual case had started to come forward with time moving in the right direction for it.

Thakur was in the act again as he caught more people in the same way he did the dwarf a few days ago at a specific party. He would go dressed as a civil man in public parties, may find persons who may be trying to add alcohol, and would put them behind the bars with strict orders. Only the one who is not left is the boss and will grab him soon, he said as more cases started to come in Up and people were found dead including the clerk who had cheered well in the drinking party with nobody noticing the cause for the death.

It was somehow linked with the tragedies in Bihar but the police are still on the loose for the smaller targets and they may have to work faster if they wish to catch the whole racket. Sir, we have news of people going to Up for some drinks to get, Thakur calls the chief with total energy and he orders the police to go undercover for the search mission to find the whole mess. They did connect to UP police to be together and they agreed as people were dying from hard drinks that were getting more popular again in the news but the cause is not sure to them as they try to go deeper.

Milind speaking sir, I have found two men selling liquor who come from Bihar, Shall I follow them? Thakur tells the police officer to keep an eye on both of them as he starts to find the connection from the past. He checks for the list handed to him by the dwarf man after a lot of beating in the past and he smiles looking closely. Ah yes, a secret trap to connect the false trail as usual, he says to nobody and turns his jeep away in the centre of Uttar Pradesh with a lot of noise and hustling voices.

Kritagya speaking sir, I have got the man who is responsible for sending the murder plot to the dwarf, the junior said and Thakur felt more than joyous for it. Keep an eye on the people connected to him basically, the process is simple but comes with heavy prices, The junior agreed and caught hold of more men who were trying to run off as the Up police tried to take them off with more voices of the vehicle coming. Kritagya reached a bridge, tricked someone by stealing the liquor at a low price and he finally got the reward by catching the main person.

Come with me sir for inquiry at the station, you are also important to us, Thakur said to a man selling bhatura and using a soda bottle to make it tastier by mixing the soups. You are the people who make locals habitual as you set the trap for them, he said lifting the inner case where 2 liquor bottles were hidden for his taste and the man had been taken to create false liquor and sell it in low prices to customers in advance to get more money and Thakur felt disgusted to see it being done in open.

It's not my fault sir, I got this from an agent, please listen to me, he shouted but Thakur as usual had no feelings and took him to custody showing the orders from the UP police. I may like to ask only one question. Who is harsh Thapa? I am sure you people know him well sir, the man shook his head in refusal but the usual beating up had started as the man asked to leave him and the police station was filled with shouts again with Up Police joining the course of it as they knew Thapa may be involved with it.

Kritagya calls the policeman from Bihar informing him that he has caught the agent who directly deals with that in Nepal and Thakur felt more than elated. Now you shall speak if you like to, let him bring the man, he said, clapping with rest in pure smiles. They have been tracing the men but the fact was the police was still far from even solving it as more cases of people dying by liquor were coming and it has gone out of a concern now as those who trick the drinkers are in total swing as they are working in the open too.

I can't be sure that thapa visited India, sir, in recent time, the man who had been taken by the bridge told Kritagya as he took him for further inquiry. My senior may be able to tell better or not how you deal with the illegal supplies, the inspector said and they arrived at the place for questioning. Thakur waited with other men as the street seller was locked behind bars for good by them as it was crucial and they started to test the credibility.

No information on the inner men involved sir, Milind calls back as he traces past the main market where people can be seen eating food. He goes close to the cafeteria, checks for a man with a bottle in hand mixing the treat and he closes on asking him to come with him. What's the problem? I don't look like a criminal, do I? He said as Milind asked not to talk and just followed him, taking the man out from the crowded area for his liking as it could be tough to get hands-on with him there with a lot of people having a close eye on them.

You are under arrest Mr. Tanwar for supplying drinks both in Bihar and Haryana with no one questioning you, Milind says to the surprise of the man or the fact that the policeman knew him very well. You didn't take me last time when you visited the tea shop, I was standing there all the time, the victim said surprised and the policeman said it was a trap to see him with his eyes that he had been mixing something in the liquor for his liking so no one could doubt him and now is the time to take him for custody.

It's a good ploy to trap us and be taken for more scrutiny, well I don't have any choice now, the man said walking with him to go back and be taken into custody in the station. Thakur was already arguing with the man they had caught at the bridge and he felt a bit calm as he saw Tanwar being captured. Well done Milind, we are on a better road now, the Bihari said and they all smiled as Tanwar didn't take much effort to snuggle out the truth in his mouth who accepted the crime.

Five of us used to have dhabas in UP. We thought it may be more useful to invest some hardcore tips in it, he started looking at them as he spoke with no shame. He pointed to the person to be his partner in Farrukhabad 3 years back but had left for Kanpur to do the trick for himself. We kept it quiet as more drinks came to us and we added a special coupon system for those who want to mix it in their dinner, he said with a smile and Thakur thought he did well to take the Bhatura seller for the right means in the market.

Why kill your customers then? Let them have a breathing space after all for themselves? Kritagya asked Tanwar who looked a bit concerned but had his word for it. They were trying to expose us, we started to get some threats from outsiders especially those who come from Bihar that we either accept them as workers or face the price for it, he couldn't be sadder as he spoke this and Thakur felt that they were all connected as a trap for the large bidding in the market happening from long.

The good thing that happened was that deaths had started to go down after they had caught Tanwar. They were still happening but not in that large numbers and it made them feel happier. There was no sign of Thapa however Thakur has been tipped to keep a close watch at the UP border if he arrives. Poisoned drinks were still circulated by hand and there is no link possible connected to Tanwar as he is not allowed to meet any visitor directly at the prison.

We have got someone by the name of Vanshika sir. She is connected to the case where two ladies were involved in illegal supplies and murders, Kritagya said on a cold evening as Thakur looked to come to the case. Bring her in, we can see what she may be able to help, or tip us, he said as the UP inspectors said it may not be easy to grab her and asked the Bihari Lady inspector for help. He wants to set the score around her but is not able to due to the strength and sharpness of the criminal with a Bihari background attached to her.

They go to the main quarters where Vanshika can be seen dressed in rich clothing, she welcomes them and the lady inspector simply asks her to come with them. Why take us now? It is not the evening before the rehearsals, she gestures to the banner in the backdrop but the lady officials are not in the mood to talk. One of them slaps her which she feels is not being right, and gets offended with abuse as the other 2 ladies take her dragging the resident fiercely in the jeep for illegal beer supplies in Bihar and Nepal.

Tell me, Miss, where is thapa ji? Your ex-boyfriend as they call him? Vanshika felt angry as they pronounced his surname and told them they could be in huge trouble as her papa is an official who looks at the revenue of the state in person. I guess we were coming to the point, I shall think of it late, the lady inspector said hitting her as she was forced to tell her that Thapa did come to Bihar last month in a false promise to trick people and he was the one who planned the whole murder plot rather than Tanwar's boss and the other that made the police get shocked.

I wanted to export drinks outside so we wanted Thapa to send us at a cheap price, she concluded as the police finally got to know how the supply of weaker liquor started. You may have helped the dealers to send the drink that made them have stomach pain resulting in deaths, the lady constable said with a clear look of disgust and Vanshika felt worried to find that the whole trap had been broken as she was taken to be behind bars.

Keep drinking the dirt of your crimes now as you wait the trial, it's good for people like you to be punished, Thakur said as she sobbed with no choice and they wanted to get more updates on Thapa by her but she refused to have any further leads and they were fine with it as a pretence.

One thing they know firmly is that the supplier did visit India and they were going to make a plan to work for them soon.

The chief of the Bihar police had thought it for himself as he decided to send more people to Nepal under his orders and settle the case. Thakur reports to him that Thapa had come to Bihar and he must get help from Pawar to find the local men who can tell the truth. In a few days, Pawar was able to identify the men who helped Thapa to stay for a few days and they were treated badly in the station. He asked for their loyalty, put them in detention and they agreed that Thapa visited Bihar and showed his pass he had given before going which proved to be the final verdict of his stay here as evidence to attach the testimony.

A noise was coming from a room where few children were kept with doors closed. A man came from behind looking at the windows and then he turned with a smile. Come on now, I need to taste your favourite drink the man said and this may be the way Thapa may taste whether his drink is somehow decent or it is venomous to kill humans. He forced a few young ones to have a drink who had vomited and it smiled at him to see them struggle as he likes people to be in true pain somehow.

A perfect way to find how Nepal has got corrupted, he says, throwing the bottle down and it broke into pieces which he didn't care to clean himself. It may hurt the children's feet who were asked to walk without slippers and the poverty with corrupt souls could be seen very clearly here. Thapa called someone to bring more drinks, and asked them to be sent to the border where he may deport them to Bihar and his mind was clear.

I am not getting calls from Vanshika, where is she? Thapa asks a man who may be one of his informers in UP. He tells him that the police had taken her for inquiry and have not returned her makes him fume but Thapa is known for his word as he calls directly to the police persons in

Nepal and tells them to connect to UP so they can send a threat message. I am warning that she must be released or you shall not see the next morning, He says with a smile as Thakur hears the voice he had wanted from yrs and the plan was settled to cover the marked man.

Tell him by your call that we are coming with Vanshika to Nepal, the Policeman said with a smile as the Nepali inspector supported him. Oh shab, I will give you one hundred percent support sir, the man said and the phone got disconnected as Thapa ran to find the man who may get involved to help the Indian police and he wanted him dead. It didn't work however as he felt trapped and the Nepal police were on high alert which made things work this time.

Come with us mate, we knew it would let you fall for the plan, the senior inspector said, shooting a few bullets as the men supporting Thapa fell on the ground with no mercy. I will kill them to you if you like, the inspector said and it was a total blast of song as Thapa was covered by fires from all sides like he may need protection but his men were falling on the heap one after another in it as the guns were sounding clear to everyone simply.

A few men started to argue that this had been a total cheat as Nepal police started to gather the men in connection to the leader. They told Thakur that the main culprit had been caught and they could come to take the man in. For a moment the Bihari inspector felt this to be a trick as it was not so easy for Thapa to come and surrender against the police. He took his main police stick, changed the main crossroad, and went on to the border with his men covering him in the official jeep.

Come with us sir, I have got him after so many wounds as you may feel better, a Nepali sub inspector welcomed Thakur with something to offer and as he looked it was a drink they had caught in India. Thakur threw it in the air in disgust and felt that they may be cheated here. Nepali police had played a double game as they released Thapa just when Indian people had thought he was caught and Thakur fumed more than ever going after him.

This is my land, sir, the men will be like vultures on the dead flesh, Thapa said as he ran away with a smile. Thakur had been to Nepal before and he started to chase him with his trick to bring secret men working the best. I haven't been just here before to waste my time in casinos, the inspector retorted with more bullets in the air. A few men had died who belonged to the local Nepali tribe and the local police converged too hoping to get some personal favour.

There was a sound of something falling, Thakur was on the floor and a man had come with a smile. He looks to be an Indian, his eyes looking dark but tough to weather the winds and he smiled in the position. My men were defeated in the past, not this time, Thakur saw the agent and he bent down in salute as the man looked more than delighted to see him again. never die attitude, that's what I like the best the man said and he launched a bomb into the air killing all the local men approaching with sticks and stones to throw things down.

The man pushes Thakur in front to put a false trail as few men come. He tips the inspector to shoot them and he obliges Thanks sir we thought you were out of sight for years but now you're here to help me, the junior says with a smile as he raises his hand and launches more bombs towards the sky. There they are, trying to pretend they sell Goats but what they sell liquor, the bomb falls on a huge tanker and it explodes with the close by farm catching fire due to the blast

The men who had owned it started to shout about it as more gun fires took place and Thapa was nowhere to be seen amidst it. It may be possible that he had managed to escape but then Thakur hears a voice in pain. I am not coming to do your bidding, leave me, the voice said and it belonged to the person who had been the main criminal. I will not be hurt this way as I rule here, thapa said as he may be under somebody's grig becoming tighter with time and he was struck well by the Indian forces.

The boss had tricked the liquor seller into going towards the farm and he was soon going to be in their hands as his men had almost been dead. I ask you to come back to India Thakur, it's an order of an official, a call came and it was Vanshika's papa who had made it. The inspector was on duty and he dismissed it as he was in an outside place with the order given by his command. He keeps striking as Thapa's voice becomes a sound of no interest and he shall be dead here at his land before anyone stops them from killing the idiot down.

Kritagya came to the main office and after he had located the person, he simply took him away at gunpoint. You made a call to our senior at Nepal this hour, it's our duty to let him do his main work, he says as the official was taken and father has also been sent behind as he threatens to lodge a case and book them under legal sections nothing is more painful than people dying by false drinks and that is most alarming, the leader in Nepal said and Thakur has finally head in closing the job as Thapa was dead by their hands and Nepal has been turned bloody with many people dying with him.

The police had not been totally at bay after the death of Thapa as more cases were coming, they didn't have much idea of what had been happening but the process hadn't worked for them. How did it come to surface again? Milind asked and he was sent to the main market to collect more criminals who may be out plotting the crime. Keep it to yourself, folks, we are on the mission, Thakur said to them as he had begun to find illegal liquid with people directly involved.

There was a fight in a food stall, a man was taken again and he asked to leave him also as Milind forced him to come with him. One more from the Tanwar gang, come with us, sir. Your boss is waiting for you, the inspector said as he slapped him. No I am not involved, tell the man that I lost the bait, he said as the inspector took him away for inquiry as Kritagya had come to action after they found more news of the wrong liquor.

He starts to ask his spies to active the channel and they help him catch a few men who had been seen at the border Kritagya catches a truck driver on the loose from months in hit and run case, he brings him to the station and they ask him about the missing deal as he was also connected with Thapa from the past. I used to smuggle the beers to Bihar sir, he says as the police start to treat him and things are still folding fast as they catch more people on the loose selling wrong chemicals in the market.

The women police were also in action, especially at the UP border where they caught three ladies trying to send their boxes and they found them to contain liquor. Let's take you to the special ward then, It will be good for all of us, the lady inspector said, hitting a woman brutally and they revealed the grand plan of selling the rum in Bihar as elections were close and it may be brought into use. Political ploys may be suited but your lies are harder than them to call upon, the inspector said and all of the three women were charged as they were detained in prison for their crimes.

I have made the note of when they sold it last and I am not sure whether it may work or maybe helpful, Kritagya said to women police and they asked to keep an eye on the border with more crimes coming soon. We can't rest now as more cases are coming and they will be sold out she said with an eye on the women just caught. The sides were on the roll and the police may somehow reach the criminals left to clear it soon who work as undercover agents and have been on the loose.

Tiwari speaking sir, I have got news of a few men trying to send false liquor in the market today, a spy calls Milind and he trudges off in search as Thapa's men in Indian wear are not stopping. ah yes, the main gang, I am looking for you, the inspector says coming to a decorated stall and he had asked the man to come with him. Why sir? Who shall after my shop then? I am a popular seller, the man said and Milind told him to do it quicker or his shop will be broken.

The police gave him a decent treat at the station as he accepted the plan to sell infected drinks to make people ill by selling them at low prices. I only intended to let them feel for the illness and I don't wish them to die, the man says as Thakur treats him well they ask the last time he got the order to which he says it had been the day when Thapa was died which made Thakur felt bit worried as the main policy works from here rather than being in Nepal itself.

More people were rounded up either at the main market or in hidden places and the operation was on high alert as Milind had brought 10 more men all involved to sell liquor that makes people get ill or force them to die with pain by drinking it instantly. How come you people are seeing it so easily when it's not allowed to do so, Thakur says as more people are filled in the cell and few are shifted to the other location. The police had a decent hand and they were somehow coming to wrap up as the politician who they had captured would be facing a court trial soon and shall be punished.

A man had come to visit him 3 days before and Thakur had a suspicion that he had only come to tell him about the progress of the deaths. I am not going to tell who came to visit me, the politician had denied and they couldn't use force to put pressure on him. You have orders to take care of me so I shall see how you do as I am taken to the court, he says with a smile talking to his daughter behind bars. Vanshika did have a peaceful glow as her papa was not in actual trouble and they had no plan to expose those who had been involved in the case, killing a lot of men with false drinks recently.

If we tell them why it was settled, we may all be behind the jail, the father had said to her and she did incline her head towards him. We may have not got enough money or revenue by it, but your position counts, she replied as the spy said that the politician did have a plan from some sources and Thakur asked them to find out. They went to Pilibhit and traced a van driver who was sending liquor to the western frontier and he was taken by police for questioning so they could find more.

I was not sending it to Bihar sir. My job is to transfer the bottles to Pooranchal and inside Rishikesh if you ask me, he spoke more clearly and the police didn't wish to go beyond. By further inquiry, he tells about a man, someone who is popular for selling drinks and he may be involved. It was time to drop the curtains down on the real criminal now, one who had been taking advantage of this chaos and Thakur was ready to do it. He calls some officials from a department and tells them to plan a raid that can prove worthwhile for them and find the truth.

The income tax department was strict about the way things work and they had started to attack a few shops. Give me the idea of hiding money inside the jars and I will crack it, one of the officials said as he was tipped by Thakur to raid central Up shops and the plan had started. The men who wore local dress in a car went to investigate as they tricked the opponents. I am looking for some bottles to send to Bihar Illegally, Can I check in? One of them said and the shopkeeper obliged as they struck the place, and more money was taken away from the cells inside.

The men started to trick most of the shops as they collected a huge amount of cash and the boss wondered where it may have come from. This is the cause of people dying in Thakur, one of them made a video call showing the bundles and heaps of them. This is so much to count, where did it come from? In response the man sent him a photograph and the image was more clear than before as the links had been connected by help of the Income tax department and they were going for it.

You attack from the main area, I will go left and it shall be a community drive for us, they all planned and the next day people started to run in a rush as vehicles started to come in and the main liquor seller was going to be in their claws. I wish they wouldn't have used Thapa, it made their life worse once he was dead, the income tax officer said and they had finally reached the place. It's been a few years that the politician was not seen doing any such crime and now he shall be apprehended for illegal liquor sales and deaths happening due to it.

It took them just a few hours to reach Orissa for their search, to track the man and they had forced him to reveal the whole problem created for money. The Income tax officers cracked main places, found money installed in main stores and the machines were ordered to accomplish the raids. The money was getting larger than before and it kept coming for them as special devices and machines were used to count it whole.

The income tax people may not be shocked as they knew what to do as they sent the police to catch the politician from the main place. He was simply taken for his deeds and must face the charges for it. You shall also be considered after the revenue one, come with us sir, the policeman from Up said and they had finally rattled the jars that had been hiding the money and the politics of it as more crimes folded in vision. They were able to clear the money mongering by alcohol, a lot of cash has been found and the case may close out finally with some positive hopes in it for the bright future.

15
Jannat's Veil of Secrets

It was a strange evening, few people could be seen outside a village ceremony and they couldn't judge what may be happening in the backdrop. The only thing they could find was that someone had been dead and it was a last right ceremony that had been arranged to pay respects to the dead as family members were only talking to explain and the people present had tears in their eyes as the parents cried remembering the son.

I watched him grow and look at what had become of a man dead during the mission, the father said as a few members looked closely. It had been nothing worse to see the man being shot, three bullets opening a wound, and the dead body on the floor. Our government has done a lot for us but it's not that big a price to pay back with our soldiers dying in numbers, the father said, crying harder than ever.

They got the chance to lift the cloth covering the man and now the people who had gathered understood that the man had sacrificed him to protect the nation. Being a proud member of the core command, he was known to be a great fighter so they are not sure. Been a trick, somebody may have cheated him from inside, one of the visitors said as people had tears and they were shocked to see him being dead.

The parents express gratitude to those who have come and offered them food to have in final memories of their son. He was fond of all this taste. The sweets you know dear, the mother said with tears in her eyes as the younger brother watched with dismay. They can't expect much from those who have come as they have lost the only man who was earning in the home and the choices may get limited from here onwards for them.

The younger son may have his business but he is not earning much like the official and it may put a burden on them. I have a brother to look after me and my key needs, I should be happy to do what I do, the younger son used to say but now he has been heartbroken. Ever since the news came out, they have not talked much and it's been just a strange mood as they have lost something precious by it.

Kashmir gives you something to linger upon, a place to hold but it also has threats too. The biggest problem is the border line where multiple factions run the power. Once it used to be just a fight between the tribes, it changed to military action when freedom came to reality and now China like powerhouses has also come to associate the plot with their needs. all of them look to resources rather than capturing the borderland and it's one of those pinching realities that people miss out on when they argue about their rights.

The place holds infinite scenes, those who come here call it a jannat and it can't be more blissful than before as people like to visit tourist attractions. The military person felt it to be closest before joining the ranks while he was in training. He got the great virtue of sitting in shikaris, going through famous Pakoras, and being a part of the culture with a lot of Muslims as friends. He never thought that he may be trapped in a certain scheme as he was proud to hold a great position in the ranks after he was appointed.

He proved his might from the start and had used the strength in countless operations here both in the woods and across the borderline being a potent member. I think he may get a high promotion soon, what do you say? The army friends used to talk about it but Prashant was never exposed to strength and power as he was a calm man who only belonged to his duties rather than riches. Coming from a strong business family, he never wished to go into money and it stayed at a backside for him as he served his country.

Encounters were mainly a daily routine for the army men as they took their jeeps or were ambushed from behind. The same old trick, I shall get you folks, Prashant used to say as he would trace the location of the men who had taken the arms after destroying the Indian working force. How does he get us, I never thought he may be of this calibre, one of the local Muslims said being the informer and they were all never one step ahead of him at the battleground.

Nevertheless, he was dead and nobody is not clear why it happened without a hint or trace in the wind. People in Kashmir are in true joy as their level of information was only decoded by Prashant and his death is a kind of relief to them. Now we can go to trace our business with higher intent sir, Basheer the local milkman said with a laugh as they distributed sweets. The senior said it was not the time to celebrate as the army could send stronger men and they had better stay vigilant for the mood.

We need an inquiry to find who killed him, you get it? The father had said as he visited the local police station and they did smile painfully. It's a higher level of assault sir, tell the officials to get involved in it, the policeman at the main gate said with some hope. The father looked at him with pity and told him to get him documents and he shall do the process to file an investigation with the help of the Indian army as he has no trust in the local men.

I wish they could see him fighting one last time with his true bravery on the show, the younger brother said in his room, being quiet and being painful to feel it. I can't take revenge for my brother but I do want someone to take the lead forward, he thinks it is alone as he has not taken orders, refused to get payment for the last 3 days and his business was booming all of the sudden which he hates to see as he knows his brother is not coming back.

However Basheer is not in his home, he had been missing for 2 hours and his family had filed a complaint to trace him as he had not gone for his duties somehow. It looks like the lower-level informer is in some kind of threat and they may hurry or he may lose his life. The police check his traces and find some blood at the main borderline and after 10 minutes of searching, they are able to identify his body on the floor but absolutely dead.

We are sorry, we arrived late, this is the last note we have found, the policeman said reading it through that state of Basher willing to leave for Afghanistan where he wants to do investment. He used to be the core informer helping the outsiders which the Police didn't know and now Prashant has died so his role is almost over. They may have got him, If you ask me, the cousin said looking at the dead body in front and the basher's signature in the letter.

As police requested to take it for evidence or scrutiny, they agreed to do the process after which the body should be handed back. However, the police got a tip as they took the body for testing. Sir, the dead man had been playing with us. He is giving facts to illegal suppliers on how to smuggle minerals and also confidential information on a regular basis,' the spy said and the phone got disconnected, forcing the inspector to read the actual letter more closely as he was involved in tricking the country and sending it outside after all.

Mahesh, are you there? I need the file created by Command of Staff Prashant sir, is it possible? The inspector calls to a junior who appears from the backdoor with a file. Sir list of all criminals charged by the commanding officer in his career, he says with a pride and sadness that he is not to do further honours. We need to see Basher in the list, the inspectors whisper as the man has gone and he has found the name connected to the sheet finally.

Charged for torturing local families into subduction for 2 days, The inspector reads more closely connecting it to the words in the letter. Going to Afghanistan for trade, If we see to the past he has been already there before, the inspector tries to further open the list of charges and the milkman was a secret spy who used to follow Prashant sir but failed and had to pay the price by him occasionally and he was commonly seen trying to trick the senior in public.

A report has come on the desk of a policeman who was asleep and his assistant woke him up as he was very deep in slumber. Sir, the urgent call, you can't miss it, the person had asked for the tea and after drinking it the man fell asleep. He looks at the report on the desk, scolds the junior why he didn't wake him earlier, and tries to read it through as it talks about something that is getting common in the hills.

Deaths of officials in Kerala, I didn't know they could reach here, the inspector read through and his mind started to act. Murderer at the border of Jharkhand and even reports of people missing so fast, He thought about what this all could lead to and tried to call someone who may be a spy in the area. He tells the person to meet him urgently as he pay him something to start the trace as it was needed helping to settle the main officer case in Kashmir and find the murderer.

I am not that brave to go across the border sir, the spy said as they met and the policeman handed him some money. You have to cross the border but not in Kashmir, you shall do it In Kerala, now tell me how it fits? The official said with a gleam in the eyes of the spy. He told him that the case had begun from the other state and they can only reach a solution if they are able to figure out the limit of it as there are a lot of folds in it.

I will enter from the other side, the plateau gives me the choice, Mahesh said, reading the case file and willing to join the action. We must be ready as the enemy is terrible and can cause deception in nature, the other inspector said as they received the official letter from Prashant's father and they had begun their search. The inspectors wanted to find the trick and they felt Basher to be linked with it so they had started the call.

The border area has witnessed a few more deaths during one more operation where a man with his two soldiers had died in it. The opponents have also been knocked down in the process but Mahesh feels more disturbed as he reads it in the papers. He belongs to a police family who used to work in Jammu and was tipped off in the same way as Basheer had been before the murder. The family was taken to the cleaners and Mahesh wants to find out how it can be more prudent to fix the old records if he is able to crack the case by his own skill.

Avdesh speaking sir, I have got the trace of Basheer as far as I can be sure from the recent facts decoded, a spy told Mahesh who took his cap, started the jeep, and left. To his bit of amusement, the location was not directly at the mainstay and he turned away to find the road going towards Kabul instead in search. Is it the same way where he was last seen before the murder? The policeman asks and the spy agrees coming to guide him as he reaches the main pass to fight things out in total mood with few people in the backdrop.

A clan could be seen talking who hold a package of dates and have been closely talking. They were speaking in Pashto, the border lingua and Mahesh smiled as he knew some portion of it. The men were talking about the loss they had in recent times and suddenly the inspector stopped as they mentioned Basheer. I am happy he is dead, pak was not giving us enough to chew by his aids either, one of the men with a beard said and Mahesh thought to talk with him as they all stood up taking the orders to be final.

A man with a knife rose from the hidden place as they stood up and he was more fierce than to be considered at first glance by the visitors. He raised himself, saw the chance, and had a target on those who had more date packages to capture by force from the travelling people. I need to sell them or you shall be dead, he thought but Mahesh lunged on him, throwing the man down. The Afghans were surprised to see an Indian this far to whom they thanked as his wish to talk with them finally became real; as he asked about Basher and who may have killed him.

The man you have just knocked on is the main traitor, the clan leader spoke looking at him with disgust. He mostly takes our date packages away so we can't sell them, and also ask for bargains from those which we sell, the other men joined and Mahesh walked towards the man again. He lifted him by the scruff of the neck, forced to kneel and he was recognized. The person was Khursheed, a person who was known to be a trader but had been accused of murder and now the policeman had finally got it. He was on the run for months and the trap had finally worked with the help of Avdesh.

You did kill Basheer then? Not to mention the assault on women last year and the murder of the local trader to gain his business? Mahesh said, punching him as the policeman expressed gratitude and the Afghan had gone, expressing the same to help them in their trade. I swear I didn't want to kill Basheer, I was asked to do in heavy pay if you let me explain, Mahesh said all the explanation shall take place in the jail and he lifted him to come with him side the jeep as he handed a tip to the spy for cracking the case for him and he waved thanks.

The other inspector had been on the outskirts to find out about the Kerala gang. He had traced some of the Muslims to be in the locality and he had gone to enquire about anything they might know about it. He was first greeted with abuses but he had got habitual to it as he stood firm to collect the facts to cover the case. He was told by a friend from the community that the people of Kerala were looking for a pass to travel outside India and they must be taken care of. The inspector thought of the plan, he called a spy after coming to the station and the plan was set to become effective.

Dhanvant, you will go to the greater area of Kerala to get me details, agreed on it? The spy responds that he has already started to trace and he sends him two photos of the people missing from the region. These are the high-ranked criminals sent by the Middle East to do most of the damage sir, the policeman points them down and matches the past record where he was able to find them being connected.

They had been active in Kashmir valley in the past with activities such as pelting and had gone to Kerala recently the criminals were high profile so they wanted them now in custody before they went away to another place absent or hidden in a new state. The inspector sent word to a secret agency that may be able to look into the matter and has decided to get help from his superiors in Delhi. However, he may have to prove the man was present first and it is one more challenge that lies in front of him in the process to captivate the criminals and let them surrender.

On Thursday evening Dhanvant calls the inspector to reach Jammu for an urgent meeting. The official agrees to go and decides it may be the best time. I will arrive in the next 3 hours, wait for me, he said as the spy tipped him off to something unusual and the cop arrived to investigate. Show me the main gate of the place, he says, watching someone on the floor and it was one of the men missing from the main gang. The inspector feels it may be a trap and he simply lets the man get wounded so he may not be able to run away from him despite his best efforts to do so.

You have used my spy so your friend can kill me, hasn't it? You have fallen for the trap mate, the inspector said, making a strong blow, and as he received the man, gunfire happened from behind which the inspector canceled smartly. He turns and simply throws the other man on the floor wounded by the fall. The spy who had been tricked starts to act and it becomes an equal fight. They were ready to converge on each other and after 30 minutes of harsh fighting the inspector stood up bleeding but both of the men had died in the fight.

The secret agency has started to track the killers and they have reached the Khaibar pass to find actual details about it by informers. I am looking to get more info on the last month's raids here if you can provide me, a man dressed in business robes asked, showing some money as he was a secret agent and they had found some movement in the zone. This is the last month's final report, sir, you have it, a Muslim said handing a document he had gone to after receiving it

Three passes are closed and only one is open for trade; then how can Syrian men come in to take their revenge? The certain official said as he glanced for details from the informers. Mahesh had sent them a photograph that looked to be familiar to the man who had tricked Prashant and it is somehow possible that outer forces were involved. We need to have updates from the outer border to go deep into the case, the agent said and they have started to crack the whole case.

We have caught the Kerala gang, sir, most of them have been detained this morning, the inspector from the Local wing said as he called the agency to confirm they were the intruders. A few of them been missing for 3 years now, It's good you caught them, ask if they know the commanding officer after treating them well one of the agents responded and the inspector was on the top trying to figure out the actual influence of the trickster upon them if the gang may know him somehow from the past.

This man has not been in touch for the last 4 years and we are not in touch, I know your boss by the name of Prashant, one of them said as the police cop started to ask them about the death and they were not sure who may be involved. It's time before I start to go more harshly to treat your physical stature or you better tell who may have done it, the police cop asked, most of them started to go harsh and they had to reveal the person who was the leader.

One of us used to be his spy who would tell him when to take the business to the next level, a man of around 30 confessed as the police decided to go harsh on all of them. We do our trade via the tariff system of the mountain passes and he is the boss as you know, it gave a hint as to who may be involved but the policeman asked them to speak of his name. We can't be safe neither here nor there, so he can be exposed. The younger lads spoke and they said that Haidar was involved in the whole mystery himself.

I see this is why sir was dead before we reached him, top planned murder with the role of the outer border men, the inspector said retreating to a corner to tip the agency about the main criminal and they agreed Haidar is not in India, we may have to trace him either in Pakistani or Afghan territory which is out of bounds, the agent responded to the police with some sadness as they planned to fix the tariffs and also cover the dangers it contains while they make a raid in the boundary.

A bomb had echoed in the local area and a few people shouted as they were dead before anyone could move to see what had happened. Haidar has gone back to Karachi and his presence makes things very clear. He kills 2 men without any mercy, takes their licence and hotel pass to enter, and follows their identity to capture the place by force. More men were shouting as a few of them were taken by force to work for him. The boss took the pressure to be on his side and it struck him with more pride as he had got hold of his scheme.

He has been the leader of the area and he doesn't dare to see any complaints by anyone. Not a word or I will kill you too, he forces a lady to come with him and might spend the night as a criminal with her. My husband is out of the city, you better tell him first, she squeaks and Hidar had gone followed by his men to cherish his possible life as the lady feels insecure in knight and his man may also be dead if he protests from the other side against Haidar who is a political person.

Why don't we complain about him to Indian forces, they will soon catch him surely, a shopkeeper says as the man approaches to ask for a chicken and he has to sell him at half rates. The man felt disgusted and Haidar smiled like he knew how to play. Keep the shops open or else you know, he smiles while taking a brandy in advance without paying and he is gone making the man feel miserable due to it.

More blasts take place in a secret cellar which was known to contain an expansive metal collection as few men had been chasing it to claim in the past. Haidar had already nicked the metals to offer them to the lady he had taken upon being his ex-girlfriend and he wanted her to accept him with the riches he owned. Your husband shall be blasted the same way in the night as these men were guarding the place, he sneers, making her stay captive as he eats and drinks in the night with true joy of the fact that he commands the place being the actual owner.

All the time people had known how Haidar worked for the public or how he planned the blast but with the Kerala gang active, he had the advantage and had been accessing the move in Kashmir without fear so the agency had stepped on the gas. People knew him to be a mask in the city as he would distribute food, help the weak, and let them thrive with his money spreading the word of true courage and glory but they don't claim of the crimes he committed openly.

However, he uses them to his advantage as he tells them to do crime for him and get rich and they were somehow under his grip from the start. No loss and no pain, all is yours to gain, he can be heard talking to ladies of the weaker section who bow to him as a great messenger who works for them you do a lot for us bhai jaan I am sure we will help you negotiate the plan soon, a young lad told and he smiled asking him not expose as people can catch secrets from thin air and he had gone.

He has also forced them to shoot themselves if they are caught by the police and most of them have done so being loyal. For your noble cause bhai jaan they would be heard speaking and it has made the villain stronger in the past. The agency had taken him 2 times but in both cases, he had come out clean with a trick to force the local inspector to do his bidding, and his mind -works sharper than ever to be a professional of the crimes but his sins are getting higher and soon one of his men might trick him.

The agency is somehow behind the track as they can feel him leave Karachi, enter the local port and he had gone around Iraq for some personal needs too. He knows how to gain weapons and where to use them as the local agents reported his presence in the Middle East for some time and then he had been back. The capture of the Kerala gang has helped to bring things under control and a few tariffs have been imposed as Haidar feels frustrated to find how things are not going according to him or the way he likes the best to clear the dues.

He can smell something fishy in it as he kills a few local tariff collectors and asks their ladies to come to his place if they want the rest of their families to stay alive. One of you must have tipped the Indian informers or they can smell the boot of my rafters, he scolded as the ladies said no to come and he went away not interested in the lust for now or the gains to offer. I shall see what I can do against Indians as I have succeeded to finish Prashant with my old revenge completed, he smiled and the don had gone out again.

A voice call comes and Haidar receives it as he expected the delivery. I need the pack of explosives by tonight, come to the port, he said to a man who may be the agent and the person on the other side agreed. Bring the cash, I am not interested in checks, the person spoke back and the leader agreed and they were those who he can't cross despite being on such high standards and the boss feels uncomfortable as he decides to go home again with the deal to be final.

He does not know about the trick, I have always been his trusted agent, Mursheed the man said as he keenly looked into the port with some gleeds. This will be the best order I shall make handing the bombs of high calibre and the mann to an agency called RAW who will pay me higher, he smiles as the lights start to dim and the night may be coming fast to fix the whole course of it by his hands.

Back in Kashmir, one more murder has taken place as one who was closest to Basher as an informer had been shot down by the murderer. The police had been called to find the men and they had somehow been able to catch the person responsible this time without much concern for it. Mahesh took him in his jeep without the fear of it exploding as the man had warned him and given him proper treatment at the station as he asked to leave him or they would get the curse of it.

Come to think of it, I am not killing you as it is in the orders for us. Your boss will be in our grip tonight, he says in a strange voice taking the phone from the person and he has got all the details he wanted safe in it. Proof of what I am saying to you, the port shall be the end of him if you ask me, the inspector smiles as the man repeats that he does not know past crimes and the juniors put him under pressure to speak about last month's murder at Jammu road hallway which he accepted.

Haidar said to do it or he would kill my wife in his grip, the man spoke finally and the other inspector felt calm to hear it. What power he has, controlling you from the other nation and you doing his bidding, the man slapped him and he felt more than frustrated as the messages were coming. The RAW was almost at the final act and things started to get dark as they were preparing to do the assault. The murder of the couple on the honeymoon, spreading drugs for a 12-year-old, and all other crimes were accepted by the man and most of the open case files were closed after the final settlement.

Last question, how much did Haidar earn by all these crimes, to be honest? The man was in detention again and he was told that an American paid him huge dollars that could make him rich and be openly involved in crimes. A smile came to the man who had been esquiring after Mahesh had been sent to the fieldwork and the inspector felt miserable to see that developed nations trap the whole case to set others under their puppet used for personal gains and fix the course of it.

A flash takes place at the port and Haidar reveals himself being directly into the area. He had come into the boat and he stepped out as Mursheed received him. The boss gestures to a coffee shop close by and they go before anyone can see him coming inside. Mursheed had planned not to expose him during the weapon deal as Raw wanted to show him exporting the weapons as they had seen him coming and wished to get attentive to the plan they had made for him.

Haider expresses thanks as he tells about the death of Basher by an Afghan militant and Mursheed promises to take revenge like he was going to do it. He hands the heavy box and the boss starts to check it being his style to find the quality. Absolute choice, one that I like the most, the client felt strained like he wanted to say about the threat, but the time was not in his control so Raw decided to act with its men circling from all sides with no hint of their presence to the visitor.

There was smoke that furled from the box and Haidar looked at it with surprise. With a flash of light, the box had been opened wide exposing the other protected weapons. Trickery or the pure joy of joining me for the battle? The visitor said as more raw members started to arrive at the port, allowing their boss to feel it through and ready to strike the main villain with their weapons completely loaded to open the true game.

One for my master you killed, a man said being a junior of the Kashmir police and a glass exploded. Mursheed tried to retaliate but Raw had got what they had wanted as the policeman shot him dead as he turned to strike back. Haidar had taken his gun out and he started to fire as few of the police personnel were also on the floor being wounded badly by the gun. They stood up and counted for a few numbers as an explosion happened and the whole box that contained the true weapons had been unleashed in the night.

Strike after strike came out that struck the whole place destroying it and the villain watched it with dismay shouting the men out. I knew you would trick me so I planned it too, he shouted as another bomb was launched but the opponents were too much in numbers and too many to fight. A physical tangle broke out where an official hit the man with his forceful fists and the punches were shared as the victim felt in pain due to them. The fight started to make noise and now it would take an actual stance as Haidar has called to his supporters to match the night in Karachi visible by true force of it.

I call them men and they will prove to you why so, he said as stones and rods were exchanged but the men from Raw smiled as one of them gestured to the package he had just demolished. Let us show you the power of the actual blasting capacity of them, he said, sending a light to the last remaining parcel of the box and he lit it brightly beyond the noise and howls of people fighting. For a moment it turned into a true red light and it transferred into a blue one. It merged with the weapon inside the box and a sound of blast took place taking all the men of the opposite section, making the boss fear for the first time in his life.

Do you want to come with us or fight here for your life? The senior official asked and the villain shook his head, firing more from the gun to retaliate against them. It won't last too sir, let me show you, one more light passes, and the barrel of the gun turns empty and burnt Now tell me, are you interested in fighting more with us or let us take you to India? The senior said, taking him by the scruff and they punched each other as the force members dragged him to the boat to come with them and surrender after such long years of struggle.

They took him in a secret boat away and unknown to anyone as they knew it could become a mess if they exposed him as Dubai police had also been looking for the person on the loose. However, people were going to know about the death of Murshid and they could either call him a coward or a perfect man to fix the ends nicely. The member of Raw told the senior government members and none of the politicians thought to defend the villain as they had also lost a lot of money and family members due to him so he was taken for direct inquiry and was forced to express his crimes.

I was appointed to lead the terrorists but I failed, he begins as the members ask him queries about the bomb blast in Karachi a few years ago They told me to do it in India or other nations but I wanted to test them first and they had dismissed me, he smiles by telling how he came in contact of the Kerala gang who were thinking to join ISIs but they also flopped. None of them could qualify for the global ascendancy of the group and we also felt the terror policy may be falling against masses within the internal force in the ground, he speaks about how things started to fold and congratulates Raw on its work to stop the threat before it could expand in the nation like India.

Why did you turn against Kashmir then if you were not willing to? A senior member asks and Haidar looks at his watch on his wrist. A date was written on the back cover of it and the members understood Alright, you thought the local men were involved in the bomb blast that happened in the school, is it? The man nodded and he had a kind of strange glow that made him look like a ghost but he was still alive in front of them. He told how it became a hatred for him ever since and he started to believe in the pak thought process to make things count for his nation after it happened.

The chief said that he was not going to hold him back as they had got the orders. They are not going to toy with him like Kasab in the area, nor are they going to send any reports to Pakistan as they may deny or refuse to recognize and the agency wishes to finish the man finally as a punishment. It's very simple you know, there is an end written in the name and it's goodbye haidar, the man in the front said and he raised his gun to fire him as he welcomed the death, dying like a man who had lived for ages and had accomplished his will.

The members started to celebrate as they had closed the case and all the areas were covered. People in Jharkhand were left due to lower levels of crimes and they got imprisonment of 2 or 3 years due to their policy not being in the actual swing. As for the people who were active in converting others, they were imprisoned for longer years. The main leader was taken by the specific forces and it came to an end as people who did well wished each other for success. They got a call from the President for the wishes and they expressed gratitude with a permit to shoot the member dead. It helped save the nation from ideological lashes it could create and everything was under control finally by the end of Haidar the true mastermind.

- The End -